HARBOR

The Traveler Series Book 8

Tom Abrahams

A PITON PRESS BOOK

HARBOR

A Traveler Series Story
© 2019 by Tom Abrahams
All Rights Reserved

Cover Design by Hristo Kovatliev
Edited by Felicia A. Sullivan
Proofread by Pauline Nolet
Interior design by Stef McDaid at WriteIntoPrint.com

tomabrahamsbooks.com

FREE PREFERRED READERS CLUB: Sign up
for information on discounts, events, and release dates:

eepurl.com/bWCRQ5

PITON PRESS

For Courtney, Luke, and Sam
Without whom I am nothing.

And for the fans
Without whom Marcus Battle is nothing.

*"Solitude, isolation, are painful things
and beyond human endurance."*

—Jules Verne

WORKS BY TOM ABRAHAMS

THE TRAVELER
POST-APOCALYPTIC/DYSTOPIAN SERIES
HOME
CANYON
WALL
RISING
BATTLE
LEGACY
HARBOR

A DARK WORLD:
THE COMPLETE SPACEMAN CHRONICLES
SPACEMAN
DESCENT
RETROGRADE

THE ALT APOCALYPSE SERIES
ASH
LIT
TORRENT
AFFLICTION

PILGRIMAGE: A POST-APOCALYPTIC ADVENTURE

EXTINCTION RED LINE
(COAUTHORED WITH NICHOLAS SANSBURY SMITH)

POLITICAL CONSPIRACIES
SEDITION
INTENTION

JACKSON QUICK ADVENTURES
ALLEGIANCE
ALLEGIANCE BURNED
HIDDEN ALLEGIANCE

CHAPTER 1

APRIL 20, 2054, 3:15 PM
SCOURGE +21 YEARS, 7 MONTHS
ATLANTA, GEORGIA

Population Guard Captain Greg Rickshaw cracked the knuckles on his fingers, popping them one at a time. He did this as much to relieve the pressure and stiffness in his joints as he did to intimidate the man in front of him.

Each pop echoed in the concrete cell. Each one made the other man blink like a frightened puppy. Sweat beaded above his upper lip.

Rickshaw watched him intently. His expression was flat, devoid of any emotion. He breathed slowly through his abnormally large nostrils and they flared.

Those nostrils and his large knotty hands were the dominant physical features that defined Rickshaw. He used both for effect, and his reputation preceded him.

He was powerfully built and looked much younger than his sixty-five years. He'd survived better than most post-Scourge, and much as he manipulated the joints in his fingers, he'd done so with the power structures that collapsed and reformed in the ensuing years. Rickshaw was good at forming alliances with the right people before he flipped on them, selling them out for the next best thing and promises of more power.

As the captain of the government's Population Guard, he was admired for his tenacity and quick decision making, and feared for his ruthless application of the law.

Across from him, chained to the stainless-steel table separating the two, his quarry was on the verge of whimpering when Rickshaw finally spoke. The captain had been in the cell for a good ten minutes without saying a word or making a sound other than his breathing and the crack of his knuckles.

"Before the Scourge," Rickshaw said, "when you weren't even a dirty thought in your daddy's head, I knew this dog breeder. You know what a dog breeder is?"

The man blinked twice, perhaps considering if this was a trick question. He shook his head.

Rickshaw folded his hands on the table, his fingers laced together. "It's someone who makes a living by forcing dogs to get pregnant. Then, when the dogs are ready, they sell them."

Although the air in the cell was cool and dry, it was fetid with the nutty odor of dried urine. Rickshaw flared his nostrils again and crinkled his nose against the smell. "What's your name?" he asked. "Where are you from?"

"Call me...Booth," he said. "Warner Robins."

Rickshaw raised an eyebrow. "Warner Robins?" he asked. "Nice place. I was there before the Scourge. Did some contract work at the base. Rented a place off Huber Road."

Booth didn't respond. He shifted in his seat, and the cuffs strained against his wrists, the chains screeching against the stainless tabletop.

Rickshaw smiled. He unlaced his fingers and placed his palms flat on the table. "That's neither here nor there. Right, Booth? I was talking about dog breeding."

Booth's shoulders slumped and he leaned forward. His eyes darted around the cell, checking the two armed guards positioned on both sides of the solid metal door. They were statues, unmoving and seemingly disinterested in the conversation.

"It always struck me as an odd thing," said Rickshaw. "Dogs would have litters of puppies, one after the other. The little mommas would give birth, lick the babies to get 'em breathing and moving, then nurse them for weeks. Then somebody comes and takes the babies. One at a time they get bought, adopted, whatever."

Rickshaw lifted one of his hands and waved it like he was shooing away a fly. He watched Booth's confused reaction, the uncertainty as to where this was leading.

"We were populating the world with all these designer puppies," said Rickshaw. "Way too many of them, given that there were plenty of dog pounds full of homeless dogs."

The light in the room was bright and sterile. The overhead LED lights were designed to mimic a hospital room, pre-Scourge fluorescents that washed the color from their reach.

Booth was pale, his skin sallow. It might have been from the lights. It might have been the fear racking his body, which now shuddered. His teeth chattered.

Rickshaw was using both hands as he spoke. Wide, sweeping gestures accentuated his message. "But it was fine for people to take these dogs the world didn't really need and put them to good use. Train them. Make them whatever each buyer wanted them to be. That was acceptable."

Outside the room, a door clanged shut, and someone shouted, pleaded for help. There was banging, heels of fists pounding on metal. Booth's eyes flitted past Rickshaw. His nose twitched.

"I even knew this breeder once who would do these temperament tests on the puppies before selling them," said Rickshaw. "They'd put the puppy in a stressful situation and test it. How would it react to an open umbrella or a loud noise? What would it do if you pinned it on its back or held it in the air with its legs dangling? Can you believe that, Booth?"

Booth's attention was on the banging beyond his cell. His eyes were fixed on the door pinned between the two armed guards.

Rickshaw reached out toward Booth's face, at his distant gaze, and snapped his fingers. "Booth? You hear me? I was talking about temperament."

Booth blinked back into focus. He nodded loosely, his jaw slack.

Rickshaw put a hand on his own chest, tapping his shirt. He wore a high-collared tunic underneath a black leather duster that draped along either side of his chair. The color of the long coat matched the black leather Spanish bolero on his head.

"This is next level to me," said Rickshaw. "Temperament testing? Not only are we taking a newborn baby from a mother, but we're testing it to make sure it's the right fit for the strangers to whom we're selling it. Don't you think that's next level?"

The muscles in Booth's jaw flexed, as if he was trying to still the chatter of his teeth. He shrugged and held his shoulders up toward his ears for an exaggerated minute before he lowered them.

Rickshaw smiled again. His dimples deepened on his thin cheeks. "I'll take that as a yes. Next level. The systematic buying and selling of babies. The careful placement of them in an environment where they're most likely to thrive. It was a system that worked. The economics of it worked. It worked, that is, until it didn't. Until the Scourge and the drought meant dogs didn't have much of a place anymore other than on spits and in pots."

Booth's eyes were glassy now, his chin trembling, and he was shivering. Rickshaw caught a whiff of something distinctly reminiscent of excrement.

"Do you understand my point here, Booth?" he asked rhetorically. "My point is that what we do as the Pop Guard is a necessary function. And it's no different from what was once a perfectly acceptable system of birth, sale, and employment."

Booth's face flushed pink, even in the harsh overhead light, and tears silently rolled down both cheeks. They dripped from his chin and hit the table.

"Am I comparing humans to dogs?" asked Rickshaw. "Yes and no. Take it however you want. I'm merely explaining to you how there is precedent within Western society."

Rickshaw knew how crazy he sounded. That was the point. He didn't actually believe humans were like dogs. He liked dogs more. He wished he still had the mutt he'd found on a roadside as a kid.

His point was to send Booth's mind reeling, to put him off-balance, to make the poor rube believe that he didn't value human life. That would be useful in the coming minutes as he worked to extract information from Booth.

If he wanted to be a martyr like the nom de guerre he'd employed, let him. But Rickshaw doubted he'd stay silent. Whatever Booth knew, he would reveal it. However little he kept secret, he'd release into the ether. It had worked before; it would work now.

Rickshaw folded his hands and placed them on the table in front of him. He rested his forearms there and twisted his neck from side to side. A series of short cracks rippled through the solid room. "I say all of that to say this," Rickshaw droned. "Have you ever seen a beaten dog, one that didn't end up in the right situation?"

Booth furrowed his brow. That pressed the tears down his face faster. He shook his head.

Rickshaw grinned broadly and slapped the table with both hands. Booth jumped in his seat. Another putrid waft filtered into Rickshaw's nose, but he swallowed past it. "Of course not. Given your age, you might never have even seen a dog at all. Doesn't matter though. The point remains the same. You catch my drift."

The banging in the hall stopped. It was quiet now except for the slide of Booth's chains across the hard surface of the stainless table.

"A beaten dog eventually bites," said Rickshaw. "It tries to get even. But not before it relents. Not before it cowers and licks its wounds. Not before it quits the behavior that got it cornered and in trouble in the first place."

Rickshaw stood and used a boot to push back his chair. The feet scraped across the concrete floor. He dragged his fingers along the stainless steel and walked slowly around the edge of the table toward Booth. "I need answers. I need you to be a good boy. Do you understand?"

Booth swallowed hard and shrank away from Rickshaw. The binds dug into his wrists, the chains drawing taut.

Rickshaw flipped back the heavy leather edge of the duster and revealed a matching holster. He slid his hand onto the worn wooden grip of a revolver and flipped the holster's latch.

Booth's eyes fixed on the hand, the gun. He squeaked a protest, a plea.

Rickshaw withdrew the gun and spun it in his hand. Back and forth it spun on his trigger finger. The smile evaporated from Rickshaw's face. His dimples disappeared. His gray eyes darkened and his expression hardened.

"You gonna be a good boy?" he asked and pressed the revolver's muzzle against the meat at the back of Booth's right hand.

CHAPTER 2

APRIL 20, 2054, 3:30 PM
SCOURGE +21 YEARS, 7 MONTHS
GUN BARREL CITY, TEXAS

It was best Marcus keep his distance. He leaned against a VW bug. It was the old original VW with a simple air cooled engine. Like a lawnmower, easy to fix and easy on fuel post Scourge. He was standing with his ankles crossed and his arms folded across his chest. The woman next to him was slender, petite really, wearing denim overalls, a soiled gray T-shirt, and leather Converse high-top basketball shoes. There was no trace of the shoes' original color. They were coated in the reddish brown dirt that seemed to find its way onto everything in Gun Barrel City.

Several feet away and out of earshot, Lou and Dallas held each other. He had his hands on her belly, his lips pressed to her forehead. She leaned into him, her chin down and eyes closed. She had one hand on Dallas's side and the other draped across David's shoulder. The boy was clinging to their legs.

It was difficult to watch and yet not watch. Such a private moment out in the middle of a cracked lake bed scattered with dead bodies and expectant mothers.

The woman shifted uncomfortably and averted her gaze. She alternately ran her hands through her shoulder-length black hair and chewed on her cuticles. The skin around the beds of her nails was inflamed and swollen.

The VW was hers. She called herself the conductor and wouldn't give a name. When the Stoudemire family was finished with its emotional reunion, they would pile into the toy car and drive back to the funeral home.

Not far from them, still at the water's edge and wary of the strangers, was the gang of pregnant women and their children. They stayed put, awaiting instructions about what to do next.

Neither the conductor nor Marcus wanted to listen to the Stoudemires as the initial relief dissolved into emotional second-guessing. Dallas was both angry and relieved. Lou was defensive and thankful. David appeared to be bewildered.

"You left him," Dallas said for the third time. "They could have killed him."

"But they didn't," said Lou. "He's fine. That's what matters."

"He's not fine," Dallas snapped. "He killed a man. With a knife. He can't even ride a bike and he's a killer."

Lou seethed now. Her face reddened and she tensed. The muscles in her neck were visible as she jabbed a finger at her husband. "Don't you ever say that. Don't you ever call him that. He defended himself. He did what I taught him to do. Am I a killer? Is that how you see me?"

Marcus sympathized with Dallas. He understood his point. Lou had made a choice to save a bunch of strangers at the possible expense of her son. It was both selfish and selfless, a paradox of a choice.

He also understood why Lou had done it. It was honorable. It was human. And in this world there were so many inhumane choices, decisions one had to make to stay alive, to maintain some semblance of sanity, that doing the unthinkable in the pre-Scourge world was unquestionably right.

Most of all, though, Marcus was glad not to be the object of Lou's ire. He'd been at the pointed edge of her sharp tongue too many times to count. She was passionate and uncompromising. He watched her flip the switch on her husband, from being defensive to attacking in the blink of an eye. There was still something feral in her, and he wondered how much of it was her father's doing and how much of it he should take credit for.

Lou jabbed the air with her finger. It might as well have been poking a hole in Dallas's chest. "We're alive," she said and nodded toward the water. "They're alive. Their kids are alive. Our kid is alive."

Dallas raised his hands in surrender. The tension on his face, his narrowed eyes, did not relax. "Fine. I'm not doing this. Not here, not now. We have more important things to do than argue about what might have happened."

Smart man, thought Marcus. *Live to fight another day.*

Dallas and Lou stepped closer to the VW. Both of them eyed Marcus, then the conductor.

"What's next?" asked Lou. "Where do we go?"

"I'm going to take you back across the street," she said. "When I picked up David and Dallas, they said you had some gear strapped to the horses."

"We do," said Lou. "Then what? And what about all these women? Their kids? We can't leave them here."

The conductor chewed on her nail for a moment. She was surveying the refugees. That's what they were. "I'll take care of them. I'll make sure they find good places. But I can't move them all at once. The largest group we can handle is six. Anything bigger than that gets too complicated, too tough to move."

Marcus uncrossed his legs and stood up straight. He aimed a thumb at the VW behind him. "You can fit six in this car? I doubt that. And our truck's no good. No spare tire and there's an issue with the front axle anyhow.""

The conductor's expression shifted. She chewed on something in her mouth, her lips pursed. It was if this hadn't occurred to her until now. "I'm not the only conductor," she said. "We've got others. They've got other forms of transport."

"How many others?" asked Marcus.

The conductor picked at her index finger with her thumb. "Other what?" she asked. "Conductors or forms of transport?"

Marcus scratched an itch on his chin. "Both, I guess."

"I couldn't tell you."

Marcus looked west toward the horizon. The sun was hanging lower in the sky now. It cast longer shadows. The sky was cloudless, though the blue was pale, muted. Exhaustion crept into his joints as he stood there. The adrenaline that had powered him across the dirt, from truck to horseback, and had given him enough strength to end the fight, had long since dissipated.

He uncrossed his arms and flexed his fingers. They were stiff at the knuckles. He rolled his wrists to loosen them. "Let me ask you this," he said. "Where exactly are we headed?"

"I can only tell you the first stop," the conductor said. "Then I hand you over to someone else. C'mon, enough talk. We need to get you back to the funeral home."

"I'll walk," said Marcus. "I've got stuff to check. You go ahead."

The others shot odd looks at him, though none of them argued.

Lou stepped closer to the conductor. "Since he's walking, can we take Andrea and her boy?"

"Who?" asked the conductor.

Lou stepped closer still. "Don't look at her now, but she's the dark-haired one sitting by the dead horse. She's got a little boy. She helped me."

Dallas stepped into the huddle. "Why would we do that? Take her, I mean."

"We have room," said Lou. "The conductor said we could have

six people. You, me, David, Marcus, Andrea, and her son. That's six."

"Not if you give birth," said Marcus. "It looked to me like you were in labor when I got here."

Dallas's eyes widened. "You're in labor?"

Lou put her hands on her belly and shook her head. "No. I keep having false contractions. I've had three of them the last couple of days. I'm close but not there. When my water breaks we'll both know."

"What about her?" asked the conductor, jutting her chin toward Andrea. "Is she close? She looks like she's about to pop."

Lou frowned. "Nice," she said sarcastically. "And I don't know. But we can take her."

The conductor shrugged. "Fine with me. But somebody will have to sit on a lap. I only have four seats."

"David can sit on Dallas's lap," said Lou. "Andrea can hold her boy."

"I'll tell her," said Marcus. "You all hop in. I'll meet you at the funeral home."

"Better yet," said the conductor, "I'll drop them off and let them in the building. Then I'll come back and get you. That'll give you time to do whatever you have to do."

Marcus nodded his thanks. He leaned onto his right leg and stuffed his hands into his pockets. Andrea eyed him suspiciously when he approached, tightening her hold on her boy. Marcus squatted like a baseball catcher in front of her and kept his voice low.

"My name's Marcus," he said. "I hear you're Andrea. What's your boy's name?"

Andrea's eyes flitted toward the VW then shifted back to Marcus. She studied him without answering.

"Look," he said, talking with his hands, "Lou over there has taken a liking to you. She says you helped her. She wants to help you and…" Marcus settled his gaze on the boy, letting his sentence hang in the air between them.

"Javi," Andrea said. "His name is Javier. We call him Javi."

Marcus tipped his hat to the boy. "Nice to meet you, Javi." He turned his attention back to Andrea. "We're headed to safety. My guess is it's a tough journey. Won't be easy. Maybe more Pop Guard, coyotes, who knows? But you're welcome to come with us. It'll be Lou, her son David, her husband Dallas, and me. We also have a guide. Someone on the railroad."

Andrea's expression wrinkled with confusion. "Railroad?"

"Underground railroad," Marcus said. "It's a secret path to freedom from the government, like before the American Civil War in the nineteenth century."

"Civil War?"

Marcus pressed his lips into a flat line and shook his head. "Never mind about that," he said. "Point is, you have help if you want it."

Andrea rubbed her nose with the back of her hand and turned to look at the water. The other women were preoccupied. None of them seemed to notice the conversation between the two of them.

Marcus pressed. "*Do* you want it?"

She nodded. "Okay, but what about the others? I'm not any better than any of them. There's a newborn too."

"They'll get help," said Marcus, "but they won't be going with us. The railroad will take care of them. They'll go in smaller groups. Five or six people at a time, at most. They'll get their help. Okay?"

"Okay."

Marcus stood, helped Andrea to her feet, and guided her to the VW. The others were already stuffed inside. Andrea lowered herself into the front passenger's seat and then waved Javi into the space between her belly and the dash.

The others greeted her and she thanked them. Marcus shut the door and knocked on the roof. The conductor started the engine and puttered back across the lake bed, pushing dirt into the air.

Marcus pulled his hat from his head and fanned the dirt from his face. He coughed and started walking toward the truck. From the back of it, he pulled out his pack. He picked up the gas containers one at a time, testing their weight. One of them was full. Another had plenty left. Awkwardly, and without using his legs, he pulled the cans from the bed and set them on the dirt. No doubt the VW could use the fuel.

He crossed the expanse toward the water, his shadow cast to his left, and walked south. He adjusted the pack on his back and pulled from it two jars of honey. He called for the women to move toward him. There were four women, five children, and an infant. All but one, the one holding the infant, moved closer to him. She hung back, standing ankle deep in the water, not far from the boots of a dead man lying facedown, blood staining his back.

Marcus cleared his throat. "All right, you're all going to be fine. The woman in the car who just left is coming back for you. She and her friends are going to find a way to get you and your kids somewhere safe."

He scanned their faces. They reminded him of the women he'd seen in Syria, the ones whose husbands had died, whose homes were obliterated in war. Their faces were gaunt, their clothes hanging on them as if made for someone two or three sizes larger. Their children clung to their sides, with knobby knees and distended bellies only somewhat smaller than the pregnant ones their mothers carried with arched backs and measured hobbles. None of them reacted to what he'd told them, and he wondered if they spoke English or could hear.

The one in the water, swaying with the infant at her chest, finally spoke. She lifted her chin and looked down her nose with distrust. "Why should we believe you? How do we know you're not like them?"

She lowered her chin and jutted it toward the body in front of her, then the one with a hole in its neck, lying closer to Marcus. She sneered. Actually, Marcus realized it wasn't a sneer. She was one of those people whose mouth never fully closed. The teeth were always visible.

Marcus shrugged. "You don't. And nothing I do or say is going to prove to you I don't have bad intentions. But what choice do you have?"

"What's that in your hands?" the woman asked, not really answering the question but hinting that she might give him the benefit of the doubt.

Marcus tested the weight in his hands and looked down, running his thumbs across the embossed glass design on the faces of the mason jars. "It's honey. Pretty fresh. It's got some sugar in it, which could give all of you a little boost. It's also got some other health—"

"We know what honey is," said the infant-holding woman. "Are you giving it to us?"

Marcus ignored the snark. He couldn't know what hell the women had been through. And given that the one holding an infant was also pregnant, he imagined there was a story there he didn't want to know. So he smiled.

"I am," he said. "I'll leave it here for you. Divvy it up however you want. The woman with the VW will be back for you. Before dark. Promise."

He squatted enough to set the two jars on the dirt. He spun them so that what he considered the front of the jar, the embossed side, was facing the water. His knees protested as he stood, and his back seized for an instant, but he tipped his hat and started scouring the beach for leftover ammo and weapons.

He shouldered four rifles and stuffed another six magazines into his pack. His body didn't like the extra weight as he began his march back to the truck. It felt as if the top half of his body was pressing down onto the lower half, like a telescoping cup or rod.

Before Marcus reached the truck, the VW was speeding back toward him. Its engine whined and the tires whooshed along the dirt until she stopped next to him. He motioned to the gasoline containers. "Think you can use those?" he asked, unhooking a bungee cord hooked to the handle opening the trunk.

He dumped the rifles and his pack into the otherwise empty space. They mostly fit, re-snapping the bungee into place with the lid half open but secured.

"Sure," said the conductor through the open driver's side door. "I'll get them on my final pass. I figure I'll take you first. We've already got your next conductor waiting for you. He's going to take you to Tyler."

Marcus walked around to the passenger's side and climbed in. His knees hit the dash, and though he tried sliding the seat back, there wasn't enough room.

"Tyler?" he asked. "Texas?"

The conductor put the idling bug into gear and pushed the gas. The car zipped in a semicircle as she turned around. "Yes. Tyler, Texas."

"Why?"

"That's where you'll meet up with the conductor who'll get you close to the wall," she said, shifting the manual transmission into second and then third gear. "I don't know what happens after that. I'm surprised they told me as much as they did."

The car bounced and whined up an incline toward the highway. The guns rattled in the trunk.

"So you're taking us to Tyler?"

The conductor shook her head. Her hair whipped into her face and she brushed the bangs aside. "No, I'm getting you loaded up. You're taking the horses."

"All of them?"

"All but the one you left with the women at the lake," she said. "There are four horses at the funeral home. You'll take one. So will Dallas. Lou will share with David, as she's been doing. Andrea will share with Javier."

She downshifted to second and then skipped first, slipping the car into neutral as she coasted into the parking lot. The horses were still tied at the telephone pole. The front door to the building was open.

"Where are we going?" Marcus asked.

"To Tyler," she said. "Then to—"

"No, on the horses. You said it's a short trip to meet the next conductor."

"Purtis Creek State Park," she said, slowing to a stop. She applied the emergency brake, which ratcheted into position. "It's not far from here."

She opened the driver's side door with a metallic pop that sounded like the door didn't quite sit properly on the hinge. The conductor slid out of the VW and marched toward the entrance to the funeral home. Marcus sat in the low seat, his knees against the hard dashboard, taking an extra moment. He puffed his cheeks and gathered the strength to get up.

Like someone climbing through a hatch, he spun to his side and, with his door open, used the frame to pull himself from the low seat. It was approaching the golden hour. The sun was high enough to provide plenty of light but low enough not to dampen the colors of the landscape. Everything seemed to glow. The air had cooled but was still warm. He walked around the front of the VW and checked the rifle supply, then stepped to the covered entry to the funeral home.

It was darker inside the building. The air was thicker, stale, and musty. Dust floated in the space, suspended and heavy.

Marcus coughed against it as his eyes adjusted to the dim illumination in what he saw was a welcome area. The burgundy carpet was worn in a path that forked from the door to a pair of archways opposite it. Intricate moldings of dark stained wood framed both arches. To Marcus's left was a sitting area with two large wingback chairs and a round table. Atop the table was a single yellow rose in a vase. There wasn't any water in the vase. The rose was fake.

To the right was a hallway. Marcus couldn't see more than a

couple of feet down the corridor. It was too dark.

He took another couple of steps inside the building, leaving the door open behind him, and moved toward the arch to the right. Muted conversation and flickering candlelight came from that space. Its twin to the left was dark and silent.

Before he reached the arch, the conductor appeared from beyond it. Eyebrows arched, she had a quizzical look on her narrow face.

"You coming?" she asked. "We don't have a lot of time."

Marcus moved stiffly into the room. It was larger than he'd expected. At the far end of it there was a rectangular platform, like a permanent catafalque.

On the walls were framed oil paintings of waterfalls and leaf-strewn wooden paths. They reminded him of the cheap artwork hung above the sagging beds in cheap motels. He remembered them from his childhood, the long road trips with his parents that doubled as vacations and treks to see extended family.

He hadn't thought about those trips in forever. The only things missing were the laminate wood-paneled walls made to look like oak or mahogany and the cheap televisions that promised HBO but rarely delivered. All of that was before the Scourge. Before he'd met Sylvia. Before he'd signed on the dotted line and served his country. Before he'd killed people. Before everything that now defined him in a way he didn't much like.

He was thinking about a particularly cheap motel in Hardee, South Carolina, near the state line, his mother complaining about the lack of hot water in the shower, when the conductor interrupted his ill-timed reverie.

She put a hand on his shoulder. "Hey, old-timer," she said, "you with us?"

Marcus blinked himself back to the present. "Yeah," he said, ignoring the ageist nickname. "I'm here. What's next?"

The conductor motioned over her shoulder with a thumb, drawing Marcus's attention toward his companions. They were sitting in chairs, stuffing their faces and their packs with rations.

Lou was digging into a jar of peanut butter with two fingers, scooping it out, and shoving it into her mouth. David was munching on cookies or crackers, while Dallas kept taking long pulls from a bottle of water, a jagged piece of jerky in his other hand. Andrea held a canteen in her lap. It was next to her son's head. He was asleep, his legs curled into the adjacent chair. It didn't look remotely comfortable. The kid had to be as exhausted as Marcus, if not more. Who knew what he'd suffered at the hands of the smugglers?

"Grab something to eat," said the conductor. "Take what you can't. You'll need it on the road. We've got about fifteen minutes; then we need to get you on the move. I've got to get back to the women at the reservoir."

"Hey," said Marcus, "why is the town abandoned? I would have thought somewhere with readily available water would be a draw. You'd think it would be overcrowded here."

"It is on the other side of the reservoir," said the conductor. "The north side is pretty packed and so is the west side, closer to Dallas."

Marcus watched Lou slather her fingers with another blob of peanut butter like a child raiding the pantry while her parents were away.

"Why not here?" Marcus asked.

"It was crowded, relatively speaking. But there were a couple of incidents in Gun Barrel. It got a reputation as unsafe and people left. That was a couple of years ago. Nobody's come back. They will. Eventually."

"Incidents?"

"Unprovoked violence," she said. "Families attacked. Tribal caravans."

"No gangs have set up here?"

"They stick to the cities," she said. "There's the occasional nomad who wanders through. At worst there's a tribal caravan moving between cities, but that's it. It's kind of a good secret right now. The railroad will use it as long as we can."

Marcus thanked her for the explanation and walked to Lou. He picked up an overturned plastic chair and set it next to her. He sat on it backwards and leaned on the back with his forearms.

She licked her teeth, sucking the peanut butter from them, and worked the insides of her cheeks. Aware Marcus was judging her, she stared at him with half-lidded eyes and a flat expression. "What?"

"Peanut butter?"

"I haven't had it in years," she said. "It's heaven."

Marcus rubbed his chin with his thumb. "You've got some heaven right there. Or maybe you're saving it for later?"

"I'm not apologizing for enjoying peanut butter. Not even a little bit."

His eyes darted to her fingers, the ones that had served as a spoon. Then he smirked. "When's the last time you washed your hands?" he asked. "I mean, it's not like I'm Mr. Manners, but sheesh, Lou. That's gross."

She stared at him blankly for a moment. Then she lifted her peanut-butter-coated fingers, the index and middle on her right hand, and lowered the index. A smile spread across her face before she took the middle finger and sucked the remnant peanut butter from it.

"That's twice now," said Marcus.

"Twice what?"

"The finger. That's twice. I take it your passive-aggressive nature has remained intact?"

"Is that a question?"

"An observation," Marcus said.

"Nothing passive about it," she said and offered Marcus the jar.

Dallas piped in. "I don't miss this."

Marcus took the jar and tipped it to look at the contents. It was raked with finger drags. He considered passing, but he was hungry. "Don't miss what, Dallas?"

"The banter," said Dallas. "The back-and-forth. It gets old."

"Not as old as Marcus," said Lou.

Marcus snorted, stuck a finger into the jar, and slathered it with the smooth, sweet and salty paste. How long had it been since he'd eaten peanut butter? He couldn't remember. He wasn't even sure if he could recall the taste of it.

"Where did you get the peanut butter?" Lou asked the conductor.

The conductor sat on the edge of the catafalque platform. She finished a swig of water from a canteen and wiped her mouth with the back of her hand. Marcus noticed, for the first time, the radio on her hip.

"Atlanta," said the conductor. "Peanut farming is still a thing near the city. That and corn."

"Even with the drought?" asked Dallas.

"It's modified," the conductor explained. "They take a lot less water."

Marcus sucked the peanut butter from his finger and relished the taste. Memories flooded back to him. His childhood, eating peanut butter and honey sandwiches on the front porch of his friend's house, swatting the interested bees that buzzed around them as they ate. He remembered Wes eating sandwiches cut into four corners, raspberry jelly leaking from the edges of the sopping white bread.

He finished the mouthful and joined the conversation. "Same in Virginia," he said to the conductor. "There are crops. Tobacco mostly. And all of it is genetically altered to withstand dry conditions. I'd worry about the long-term health effects of all of these modified foods, except that I don't worry about it."

Dallas shook his head and chuckled. "That makes no sense."

"The genetics?" asked Marcus. "It makes sense."

"No," said Dallas. "You make no sense."

Dallas cleared his throat. Doing his best Marcus impersonation, he lowered his voice, pulled his chin into his neck, and affected an air of self-importance with a stiff neck and squared shoulders. "I worry about things," he aped, "except I don't worry about things. I say things. But I don't say them. I don't eat with my fingers except when I eat with my fingers."

"Jumping on Lou's bandwagon?" asked Marcus.

"Always been on it," Dallas shot back. "I started it."

Marcus smiled. He took another finger pull of peanut butter. Before he ate it, he motioned at Dallas. "My reasoning makes sense even if you don't get it."

"It's old-man reasoning," said Lou. "He's got three brain cells left, and two of them are packing up. The third one doesn't blame them."

The radio on the conductor's hip chirped, drawing everyone's attention. Even Javier opened his eyes and sat up. The radio chirped again. Static filled the room.

The conductor plucked the radio loose and lifted it to her face. She glanced at the display and twisted a control at the top of the device. With her thumb, she punched a series of buttons on the face of it. Then she lifted the radio to her mouth and pressed a transmission key on its side. "This is conductor 416. Status, please."

She let go of the key. Looking at the display again, she narrowed her focus. She was reading something on the display. The radio chirped. Her face twitched, her eyes reacting to whatever she saw.

"What is it?" asked Marcus. "Everything good?"

Looking up, a serious expression on her face, the conductor shook her head. "We need to go. There's a tribal caravan on its way here."

"Why?" asked Lou.

Dallas stood and helped David with his things. Lou took his cue and stood too, putting her hand at the small of her back. She winced as she got up.

The conductor clipped the radio to her belt.

"How could they know we're here?" asked Andrea. It was the first time she'd said anything since Marcus had entered the room.

She had one hand on Javier's back, rubbing it up and down, the other resting atop her belly. Her small features were tight with concern.

The conductor sidestepped a couple of the chairs and moved toward the door. She glanced through the archway and then at her charges. "They're not here for us," she said. "They don't know we're here. They're here for the water. But if I don't get you on the road and get those women to safety…"

It wasn't necessary for her to finish her thought. Marcus understood the sudden gravity of their situation.

"We've got another conductor coming this way," she said. "They should make it in time. But I've got to start moving the women now just in case."

"How long do you have?" asked Marcus.

"An hour. Maybe less. They're coming from the west. You should be okay, but you've got to go. You've got enough on your plate as it is."

Truer words have never been spoken, thought Marcus.

CHAPTER 3

APRIL 20, 2054, 3:50 PM
SCOURGE +21 YEARS, 7 MONTHS
BAIRD, TEXAS

Norma stepped from the barn into the warm, cloudless afternoon. The door creaked on its hinges and rattled shut. She'd been meaning to grease it, silence the noise, but hadn't gotten around to it.

Exhaustion seeped into her bones as she crossed the property toward her front porch. It was the kind of tired she felt in the backs of her eyes, her shoulders, her feet. She was certain that if she laid down on the dirt and rested her head on an outcropping of weeds, she'd be asleep within a minute.

When was the last time she'd gotten good sleep? Her mind, foggy from the lack of rest, couldn't remember. Then she kept thinking about how she wasn't able to think clearly.

She rested a hand on the short wooden railing that ran alongside the steps to the porch and used it to guide her toward the front door, which she'd left open. She kicked away a rock from the bottom edge of the screen door and let it slap shut behind her as she entered the house.

Norma's vision darkened until her eyes adjusted to the interior light, or lack of it, and she turned to close the heavy door. With it shut and locked, and the space darker still, she blindly walked the hallway from memory. Her feet trod the familiar seams and boards in the floor, and she edged toward the kitchen and the stairs.

Her hand on the round finial at the base of the balustrade, she hesitated, considering whether or not she was hungry. Deciding she wasn't, she gripped the finial and spun herself onto the stairs.

The quiet unnerved her, and the steps creaked under her weight as she ascended.

There was no Lou and her strongly held opinions. No Dallas and his affable acquiescence to everything Lou. No David and his smile-inducing giggles or balance-threatening leg hugs.

She missed them already. The ache was in her gut. It churned there, drowning out the other sensations.

Norma reached the landing on the second floor and trudged to her bedroom. She pressed one hand against the door and slowly turned the knob with the other one. As quietly as she could, she pushed it open.

"I'm awake," said Rudy.

He was sitting up in bed, having scooted his back against the headboard. His color was better, though not good. A smile twitched at the corners of his mouth. Then he smirked.

"Where've you been?" he asked. "I was calling you, but it wore me out. Your boyfriend got you too busy?"

Norma chuckled and dropped onto the edge of the bed. The mattress gave and bounced. Rudy winced and gritted his teeth.

Her eyes widened and she put a hand on his leg. "Oh! I'm sorry. You okay? Did I hurt you?"

Rudy opened his eyes. "I'm good," he said. "Just sore. I'll be good as new in a couple of days."

She rolled her eyes. Rudy was always the optimist. "My boyfriend will be so disappointed."

"I bet," he said. "Especially when I get out of this bed and pummel him eight ways to Sunday. Nobody touches my Norma but me."

Her face flushed and she pursed her lips into a flattered smile. "You're getting possessive in your old age, Rudolfo Gallardo. I think I like it."

They sat there staring into each other's eyes for what might have been a full minute. Or three. This was a silence Norma didn't mind, welcomed in fact. It distracted her from what the two of them had lost. Rudy opened his mouth to speak when a noise outside interrupted him. They exchanged a quick, concerned glance before snapping their attention to the front of the house.

Norma stood from the bed and moved to the window. She shielded her eyes and pressed her nose to the glass, scanning the property for the source of the noise. She saw nothing, but the noise repeated itself. It sounded like wood banging against metal.

"Is it the barn door?" asked Rudy.

Norma stepped back from the window and shook her head. Her eyebrows were drawn with concern. Her expression tightened. "I don't know. I closed it."

"That's where you were?"

She nodded.

"Radio?"

Another bang. And the distant sound of voices.

She looked toward the bedroom door. Her pulse quickened. "Did you hear that?" she asked in a hushed tone.

Rudy lowered his volume too. "Voices?"

She nodded and moved to the bed. "I don't like this," she said. "Could be Pop Guard."

"Already? That's awfully fast."

"Who else would it be?"

"If you were just outside," he said, his eyes shifting between the window and his wife's worried gaze, "how come you didn't hear them? Would you hear them?"

"I don't know. I guess. Maybe. Could be they came from the back side, by the highway."

"From the north?"

"Yeah," she said. "I'm gonna go look."

Rudy frowned. "No, stay here. You locked the door. We'll have time to figure something out if they break in."

Norma steeled herself. Her jaw tightened and the muscles in her neck flexed. She shook her head. "No, Rudy. I'm not waiting this time."

She moved to the nightstand next to Rudy. There was a loaded handgun there and a spare mag. She stopped short and reconsidered. Her rifle was next to the front door. She'd left it there before going out to the barn. "Stay here."

His expression soured. "Where else am I going to go? C'mon, don't do this, Norma."

She winked at him and blew him a kiss. "Stop me."

CHAPTER 4

APRIL 20, 2054, 3:55 PM
SCOURGE +21 YEARS, 7 MONTHS
ATLANTA, GEORGIA

Sally ran her shaky fingers along the dark semicircles that punctuated the exhaustion on her face. They were a lighter shade than before, more lavender than deep purple. The lines that defined her forehead and radiated from the outside corners of her eyes towards her temples weren't as pronounced as she remembered them. Her reflection was as repulsive as she'd found it two days before. That was all good.

What wasn't good was the withdrawal. Despite Gladys's insistence that she was ready for the trek, Sally wasn't so sure.

This wasn't her first detox. She'd tried, and failed, to stop cold turkey before. She could get the shakes up to ten days after going clean. Her memory might lapse. Things that weren't there would cloud her vision, disorient her.

Her stomach pressed against the sink, she leaned into the mirror in the powder room. She stretched back her lips and studied her teeth, her tongue, her uvula.

For the first time she noticed thin wrinkles in her earlobes, like someone had folded them and left a crease right down the middle.

Had they been there before?

She was running a fingernail along one of them, her thumb on the back of the lobe, when Gladys knocked at the door.

"You okay? Need anything?"

Rather than carry on a conversation through the door, Sally unlocked the knob and opened it. Gladys stood there with a thin smile, her plucked brows arched high.

"I'm fine," Sally replied. "Where were you? You disappeared."

"Business," said Gladys. "Making sure the logistics of your upcoming trip are taken care of and that everything is—"

Sally waved Gladys to the side with her hand. She tugged at her shirt and walked past her host. "About that…" she said, making her way toward the kitchen. "I'm not clean."

Her bare feet were sticky with perspiration and made peeling noises on the tile with every step.

"It's been less than three days since I got here. Less than three."

She held up three fingers to illustrate. The kitchen was warmer than the bathroom or the hallway. The oven was on and the dry heat hit her as if she'd stuck her face into it. She stopped and turned to face Gladys. "Could you turn on the air? I'm burning up in here."

Gladys eased past her around the kitchen island and over to the double ovens on the far wall. With a flick of her wrist, she wiggled her fingers in the air dismissively. Sally was certain the woman was mocking her. "It's you that's hot, not the air."

Gladys opened the refrigerator and pulled from it a large pitcher of water and got a glass from the cabinet, filled it with the water, and set it on the counter. She motioned at the glass with her eyes. "That's for you. Nice and cold."

Sally plucked at the front of her shirt and fanned herself. "Thanks," she said and moved to take the glass.

Gladys reached into the top of her dress and pulled out a small folding knife. She used the knife to slice a lemon on the counter next to the sink and offered a piece to Sally, who declined.

"What's with the knife?" she asked.

"You can never be too careful," Gladys replied. "And nobody would ever think to check an old woman's breasts."

Sally almost laughed. It sounded more like a grunt.

The glass was cold in her hands and Sally thought about pressing the side of it to her cheeks but gulped half of it before taking a breath like a four-year-old drinking juice from a sippy cup. Another couple of healthy swigs and she'd finished it.

The cold water helped. Her gums, teeth, and throat were cooler, her throat soothed. Still, she sweated. In her gut, she felt a constant unease. It was as if she knew something was off, but she couldn't put her finger on it. Like she'd entered a room to do something but couldn't remember why she was there.

Her heart thumped unevenly. At least that was how Sally perceived it. It fluttered, skipped, and her balance was off. She was not ready to lead anybody into the fire, let alone along an increasingly challenging underground railroad.

Sally leaned against the kitchen counter, the glass still in her hand. She focused her gaze on Gladys, who, as always, appeared unaffected by everything around her but the wrinkles in her skirt or tuck of her blouse.

"I'm not ready," said Sally. "If it's today, tomorrow, or three days from now."

Gladys was unmoved. She wiped the knife on a towel, folded it, and stuffed it back into her bra. "And you know this because...?" she asked, straightening the collar of her dress.

"I've done this before. I've gone cold turkey. It's not pretty. And if you've done this before, you know, helped addicts like me, then you'd know too."

"You'll be fine," said Gladys. She tugged at the cuff on one sleeve and then the other. "I have no doubt."

"I don't get what we're doing here," Sally said. "Why not put me out to pasture without this one last mission? Get somebody better?"

Gladys pursed her lips and lifted her chin. "There…is nobody better," she said in a halted cadence that sounded like it was painful for her to admit.

Sally laughed. It was a sudden burst that surprised both of them. Gladys's eyes widened; then she frowned disapprovingly.

"Sorry," said Sally, "but I find that hard to believe. You've got a gazillion people who are better than me for this job. And truthfully, I still don't know exactly what the job is."

Gladys shook her head. "I don't have a gazillion people. Not by a long shot."

She lifted a hand and motioned toward the kitchen table. She crossed the room and pulled back a chair for Sally. The feet squeaked across the floor and echoed. It amplified the quiet in the house to which Sally had become so accustomed she wasn't aware of it. Gladys sat next to her and put her hands on the table.

"We're struggling," she said. "And I don't know how much longer we can keep the train running."

Sally's expression hardened with concern, though she remained silent.

"The Pop Guard has gotten serious about stopping us," Gladys said. "That's why they've sent more exploratory teams to Texas. It's why they are in Arizona and Illinois and Nebraska. They want to put an end to us." Gladys scratched her forehead. "And they know about the Harbor. They know we've established our own colony of sorts, free from their control. We have information that tells us they've renewed their efforts to find it."

"I didn't even know the Harbor was a real thing until a couple of days ago," said Sally. "I always thought it was a rumor."

"We wanted it that way," said Gladys. "It had to sound too good to be true. It had to be something the Pop Guard dismissed as fantasy."

"What changed?"

"We don't know for sure, but in the last few months, several of our conductors have gone missing. We've had seasoned people disappear. We've had new people work with us for a few weeks and then they're gone."

"I still don't get why this means you need me for some special mission," Sally said. "I'm not the best choice. There has to be *somebody*."

"The passengers on this trip are special," Gladys said. "They're connected to a close friend. I needed somebody I can trust. I trust you."

Sally's brow furrowed. "You don't know me."

"I know more about you than you think," said Gladys. "And I know enough about what you've sacrificed. I also know how skilled you are."

Sally leaned back in her chair. She swiped her fingers across her forehead and rubbed the sheen of sweat on the thigh of her pants. "Skilled?"

Gladys pressed her palms flat against the table. Her expression flattened. "Here's my dilemma. Our conductors are either too inexperienced to do the job or they're like you. The inexperienced ones, I can't even trust half of them. And there's no middle ground. There are those infant conductors and there are the older ones. The ones like you. They've seen too much. They've done too much. And those experienced conductors are worse off than you. Or they're…"

Sally raised her eyebrows. "They're what?"

"We don't have a lot of conductors willing to kill," Gladys said. "You won't hesitate to do what's needed."

The words slapped Sally across the face. Her face flushed and twitched. Her shoulders hunched and she shifted her body away from her host. All of it was subtle and simultaneous gut reactions to the assertion that Sally was a killer who put mission above self, who saw gradations of morality.

Gladys must have noticed the change in Sally's demeanor. She forced a smile. "I didn't mean that to sound the way—"

"Yes, you did," said Sally. "And you're not wrong. If it's me or my passenger versus a Pop Guard soldier, I'm taking out the soldier."

The women sat silently for a moment. Both of them exchanged glances, held them, averted them.

"I'll be honest," said Gladys. "You're not my first choice for this. Well, you weren't. I had someone else in mind. It fell through. And after what happened the other night with the chopper…"

"The guards I killed."

Gladys nodded. "That told me all I needed to know."

"Who was the other choice?"

Gladys sighed. "His name was Booth. At least, that was his working name. He disappeared. We're pretty sure the Pop Guard has him."

Sally nodded. "I'm sorry."

"Don't be. Just do your job when the time comes. I'm convinced that, even in the throes of withdrawal, you're better than anyone else I've got."

"That's not encouraging," said Sally.

Gladys forced a weak smile. "No. It's not."

CHAPTER 5

APRIL 20, 2054, 4:00 PM
SCOURGE +21 YEARS, 7 MONTHS
ATLANTA, GEORGIA

Rickshaw pulled the trigger again and Booth gasped. It was a ragged breath born of mental exhaustion and unadulterated terror. Rickshaw had heard it before.

"Every time I spin it," said the captain, "you've got a one in six chance of losing that hand. One in six is less than seventeen percent."

"I don't know anything more," said Booth. "I told you what I know."

Rickshaw lifted the weapon and spun the cylinder. It ratcheted to a stop and he lowered it again, pressing the muzzle against the back of Booth's hand. Booth held his breath. His face reddened. Rickshaw smirked as he pulled back the revolver hammer. He pulled the trigger.

Click.

Booth exhaled and slumped. He shook his head again. "I don't know," he said. "I swear. I—"

Rickshaw lifted the gun. "Blah, blah, blah," he mocked in a whiny voice. "I don't know. I don't know." He spun the cylinder. His face hardened. His eyes bored into Booth's. "You do know. You've already told me about two of the conductors. You already gave me an address. You know more."

Booth shook his head. Sweat flung from his face, snot stuck to his nostrils, and thick spittle clung to his chin.

Rickshaw pressed the gun down. Hard.

"Please," Booth begged breathlessly.

Rickshaw pulled the trigger.

Click.

"I'm new!" Booth sobbed. "I'm new. I told you what I know. They don't tell us much. Only what we need to know for our job. We—"

Rickshaw pulled the trigger again without spinning the cylinder. *Click.* He grimaced and pulled the trigger again. *Click. Click.*

"It's fifty-fifty now," said Rickshaw. "And you're not new. You've been doing this a long time. You've killed my men. Ten of them in the last year."

He lifted the weapon and opened the cylinder without spinning it. A broad grin formed on his face. His gray eyes darkened. He started to lower the weapon when he looked at the floor. His expression soured. He stepped back and shook his leg.

With his chin still lowered, he raised his gaze and glared at Booth from beneath his heavy lids. The corner of his mouth lifted when he spoke. "Again?" Derision more than pity dripped from his words. "I didn't think you had any more piss left in you, *Booth.*"

"Okay," said the captive. "Okay. I do know one thing."

Booth's head hung low against his sweat-drenched collar. He squirmed in his seat. His hands were balled into tight fists now, like that would protect him from a point-blank gunshot. A glossy sheen of sweat, tears, snot, and spit coated his face and neck.

Rickshaw took a step around the spreading bright yellow puddle on the floor and moved to Booth's side. He bent at his waist and spoke softly into the trembling man's right ear. "Good for you," he said, the words like venom. "I knew you'd come around."

"T-t-t-hey have a p-p-place," said Booth, "where they take all of the passengers."

"I'm listening," Rickshaw slithered.

"It's c-c-called the H-H-Harbor."

"Where is it?' asked Rickshaw. "I already know what they call it. I don't know where it is. They move it around."

"W-W-West V-V-Virginia," said Booth. "Th-th-the G-G-Greenbrier."

"The resort?"

Booth nodded. A string of drool stretched from his lower lip to the edge of the stainless-steel table. "Yes," said Booth. "It—"

The percussive blast of the single gunshot shook the air in the room. A resonant ringing pierced Rickshaw's ears. The guards by the door jerked from their positions, startled by the unexpected shot.

Booth's head, what was left of it, was limp. It was forward and to the left, hanging on his stretched neck, chin on chest. His eyes were open. He'd never seen Rickshaw lift the weapon and pull the trigger with the muzzle at the back of his head. The Pop Guard captain did it too quickly, too quietly for anyone in the room to notice.

Blood and gore mixed with the rest of the slimy mess on the floor, chair, table, and wall. Rickshaw licked the front of his teeth and flipped open the cylinder. From his pocket he pulled a handful of rounds and slowly pinched them into the cylinder until he'd filled it.

He spun the weapon twice and dropped it into his holster. He edged his hands along the side of his duster and straightened the heavy fabric. He jutted his chin toward Booth and eyed the guards. "Clean this up. It's disgusting."

Rickshaw exited the room and marched along the brightly lit hallway. They were two stories underground, and the sound of his boots clacking on the solid floor was thick. The walls and ceiling absorbed what might have otherwise echoed along the corridor.

His duster rippled at his sides and billowed behind him like a heavy cape. His broad shoulders, carried with immaculate posture, and confident swagger told anyone who passed him in the hall to make way. He wasn't shifting course. If they didn't give him a wide berth, he'd bowl them over.

One guard, not paying attention, traded shoulder blows with Rickshaw as the captain neared the end of the hall and a bank of twin elevators. The collision knocked the guard off to one side. Rickshaw was unmoved. His body, like the walls and ceiling, was good at absorption.

He punched the elevator call button and waited. At his sides his fingers flexed in and out and the knuckles cracked. Soft pops of air relieved the building pressure in his joints.

The elevator doors hissed open and Rickshaw stepped into the empty car. He leaned into the bioscanner and stared into the pulsing red light. The doors hissed closed and the system's androgynous voice addressed him.

"Captain Greg Rickshaw," it said, "to which level are you traveling?"

"Four."

"Please stay clear of the door and hold onto the provided handrails. We are ascending to level four."

Rickshaw felt the push of the floor under his feet, his stomach lurched, and the elevator accelerated skyward. He gathered himself and stumbled back a step to grab a handrail opposite the car's door.

The interior of the elevator car was as cold as the cell from which he'd come. It was bathed in the same bright white LED light the government engineers seemed to prefer. Rickshaw would have preferred something more antique, the soft yellow glow of a filament lightbulb.

The elevator slowed to a stop.

"Approaching level four, Captain Greg Rickshaw," the computer voice said. "Please watch your step and have a pleasant day."

Rickshaw thanked the computer. The door hissed open and he exited. He acknowledged a man and a woman waiting to step aboard the elevator with a tip of his bolero. They pressed tight smiles onto their wary faces and hurried into the car behind him.

The buzz of the bioscanner preceded the door hiss, and Rickshaw moved with purpose toward an office midway down the hall on the right. He thought about how he'd thanked the computer for doing its job. A smirk twitched at the corner of his mouth. It struck him as odd, but funny, that he'd ignore people for their niceties but thank a computer. He wondered, for a brief moment, what that said about his psyche. Then he pushed it from his mind and leaned into another biometric device that scanned the particulars of his eye, pressing his right thumb to a pad underneath the pulsing red screen.

"Thank you, Captain Greg Rickshaw," said the voice. It was the same one from the elevator. "Welcome back."

With a metallic click and hum, the door was unlocked. He pulled the handle and pushed. The door swung into his office, and the overhead lights immediately flicked on. These lights were canned and recessed into the high ceiling of his unremarkable office space. The door clicked shut behind him, locking him inside and everybody else out.

It was sparse, with white walls, a solid gray floor that matched the rest of the fourth floor and his eyes, and a clear Lexan desk built into one of the walls. From one spot in the office the desk and its contents appeared to be floating. From another spot, the desk disappeared altogether.

He flipped back the tail of his duster and dropped into the ultramodern ergonomic chair at the desk. His weight sank onto the hydraulics, and air puffed from the chair's mechanics.

It was remarkable to Rickshaw that as bad as things had gotten in the world, he still had a comfortable chair in a climate-controlled office run by a centralized computer system, which ran the entirety of the government headquarters.

As much of North America lived in what was best described as the Wild West, and most of it was without reliable power, the central government had revived much of the technology lost in the years after the Scourge.

The Centers for Disease Control was a big part of that. As it worked to find a cure for the disease and then replicate it so that Texas might again fall into the fold, its scientists and researchers had reverse engineered surviving tech. Then they'd made it better.

While there wasn't the infrastructure, or the governmental desire, to make the tech available to the masses, it served those in power nicely. Never before in modern history had the divide between the haves and have-nots been so wide. It was good to be one of the haves.

Rickshaw tapped his desk, and a virtual keyboard glowed in its surface. He tapped a few keys in memorized succession, and the wall in front of the desk produced a large projection of a topographical map. He swiped his fingers on the wall to zoom in on the map. Red dots appeared in clusters along the map. There were dozens of them stretching from Arizona to Nebraska and Florida. There were dots sprinkled through Texas, though the concentration was sparser there, and in Georgia the dots merged together into larger red markings.

Rickshaw leaned back in his chair as far as the ergonomics would allow, and scratched his chin. He studied the spots where he had Pop Guard teams deployed. There were two thousand stationed all over the place.

His job was twofold. It was to run the Population Guard program and, at the same time, snuff out any rebellions against it. Neither of the tasks were easy. Both made it difficult to sleep. Both made him anxious, ornery, and quick triggered.

Despite record numbers of captures and reassignments for the families who had thumbed their noses at the government mandate of only one child per couple, Rickshaw's superiors put increasing pressure on him to stop the railroad.

The tribes in Texas cities were a threat too. The larger they grew, the more zealous their indoctrinated members became; the central government understood what they might attempt, the power they might seek to grab. It was no secret. But those tribes were easily a generation away from wreaking havoc beyond the wall. The railroad, however, was now. It was happening. It was giving lawbreakers an out, a sense of control, a way to free themselves of the constrictions to which they should relent.

Rickshaw was getting close. With each capture of a conductor, a porter, or a would-be passenger, he was piecing together how the celled structure of the railroad functioned. He believed he was at the precipice of a real breakthrough, a significant gain in intelligence. This could be the thing that relieved the constant pressure.

He leaned forward, the chair creaking its disapproval as the hydraulics pushed out air, and slid his fingers along the wall-projected display. The image zoomed in and Rickshaw touched one of the red dots.

The display changed and gave him detailed information about a team he had on the move from Charlottesville to Lynchburg, Virginia. They were the closest to The Greenbrier, an old resort and spa built in 1778.

They were motorized, which was better than the horseback teams in Texas, and patrolling the edge of the wall, so they could be there in hours. Rickshaw typed in another set of commands, and the display on the wall changed again. From this screen, he could access the government's radio network. They had enough transceivers and working towers that he could either directly or indirectly communicate with many of his teams in the field.

He could dictate his orders to the central computer. The computer would find the latest route to the end user. It wasn't perfect, but it did the trick most of the time. Though the farther the communication was intended to travel from the headquarters in Atlanta, the less likely it was to be virtually instantaneous. That was one drawback of the government's insistence on keeping all of its tech consolidated in Atlanta.

"Computer," said Rickshaw, "send a message to Population Guard team 304-681. This communication is classified."

"Hello, Captain Greg Rickshaw," said the computer. "I am standing by to receive and forward a classified message to Population Guard team 304-681."

"Have the team go to The Greenbrier Resort in White Sulphur Springs, West Virginia," he said. "I want recon. They are to observe, and if the specified area is occupied they are to question anyone there to determine there numbers and status."

He waited for the computer to respond. It took a couple of seconds before it repeated his message verbatim.

"Is there anything else?" it asked.

"Yes," said Rickshaw. "Alert the team to check the bunker."

The computer acknowledged his request. It alerted him that the message was sent.

"I'll notify you when the message is delivered, Captain Greg Rickshaw."

Rickshaw exited the messenger application and entered the government search engine. He typed in his keywords, and the wall populated with detailed information about Greenbrier's history.

In the late 1950s a one-hundred-twelve-thousand-square-foot bunker was built underneath part of the resort. It was maintained for thirty years as an emergency bunker with its own power plant, diesel fuel storage, and water supply. A call team of undercover workers employed by Forsythe Associates managed the facility in the event of a large-scale disaster. It was a secret until the news media revealed it in the last decade of the twentieth century. It became the stuff of legend and a popular tourist activity. The resort gave tours of the bunker until it shuttered a year after the Scourge. Rickshaw had once stayed there with his family. It was 2018 maybe. He couldn't remember the exact year. He'd taken the tour and remembered joking about how, when the world ended, it would be the perfect place to hide. Apparently others agreed with him.

CHAPTER 6

APRIL 20, 2054, 4:05 PM
SCOURGE +21 YEARS, 7 MONTHS
BAIRD, TEXAS

Norma stepped onto the porch and carefully shut the screen door. She clung close to the front of the house, inching along its facade with her back to the wall. The shotgun was in both hands. Her right was underneath the butt, her left under the barrel.

Norma had picked the shotgun instead of a rifle for two reasons. One, the rack of a shotgun was as big a deterrent as a gun to the head. She liked the sound of it, the fear it instilled in would-be targets on the other end of it. And two, she imagined that any confrontation would be at close range. She didn't have to be as accurate. And while she didn't have as many rounds in the shotgun as she could carry in the rifle mag, the handgun tucked into her jeans would provide secondary defense if needed. Norma hoped she wouldn't need it.

Her heart pounded so loudly in her ears she worried the intruders might hear it. She worked to keep her shallow, rapid breathing under control. Around the side of the house, men chattered. They spoke in low tones, almost whispers.

One careful step at a time, Norma inched her way toward the corner. Her feet slid along the pine slats of the porch so as not to induce a creak or groan from the aging boards.

A horse nickered. The barn door creaked. She drew the shotgun closer to her.

"Easy there," said one voice. "It's all good."

The horse nickered again. The voice, a man's, reassured the horse with shushing noises.

A second voice, deeper than the first. "Ain't nothing of value in that building. Maybe a little bit of food. Nothing else worth taking."

A third voice. "There's some electronics in the barn. Radios and such. We could sell it. Maybe trade for something."

Norma crouched and peered around the corner of the house toward the direction of the voices. The men were facing her, but none appeared to notice her. Their attention was focused on one another.

There were three men and four horses. The men were standing near the horses. All of them were armed. They wore jeans and boots. One had on a barn jacket that looked too big for him. Another had a long-sleeved T-shirt bunched up at the elbows. The third had his button-down untucked, the cuffs rolled at his forearms.

All of them were unkempt, their faces streaked with grime and dirt. Their weapons were older. The horses were malnourished. None of them were Appaloosas.

These weren't Pop Guard. They were poachers.

Norma hid again, her back to the front exterior wall of the house. She puffed her cheeks and exhaled. They'd dealt with poachers before. It never ended well. As relieved as she was the Pop Guard hadn't returned, this was a mixed bag.

Sometimes poachers were nothing more than good people who'd become desperate. Other times they were bad people taking advantage of the region's relative lawlessness. Both could be equally as dangerous, equally as unpredictable.

Norma had no way of knowing with whom she was dealing. She couldn't take the chance of confronting them, but couldn't let them steal. She gnashed her teeth and cursed under her breath, tightening her grip on the shotgun.

She leaned over to take another peek at the men when a loud pop startled her. She nearly lost her balance, but recovered as a second and third pop, in quick succession, cracked the relative silence.

It took her a moment to realize the pops were gunshots. And they were coming from inside the house.

Her stomach churned. A knot swelled in her throat. She stood and ran toward the front door. With one hand she flung open the door and bolted into the house. Behind her the screen frame snapped against the house.

She stumbled as she rounded the corner to climb the stairs. Her heart raced. Blood pumped in her ears, at her temples. Waves of nausea coursed through her body as she stomped up the steps two at a time. Breathlessly, she gripped the shotgun with both hands. At the landing on the second floor, she pumped the weapon and leveled it.

Marching fast, her eyes wide, a sudden rain of sweat rolling down her face, she kicked open her bedroom door and put her finger on the trigger. Ready to apply pressure, she scanned the room. A man was facedown on the floor next to the bed. Blood pooled around him.

Norma gasped until her eyes met Rudy's. He held the handgun Norma kept in the bedside table. It rattled in his hand, still aimed at the dead man on the floor.

Norma lowered the weapon and rushed to her husband. "What happened?"

He shook his head and swallowed. The gun waved in his hand. "Are there others?"

Norma was still trying to process the scene in front of her. Adrenaline surged through her, her lungs and legs burning from the sudden exertion into the house and up the stairs. The stress of the approach had her confused now. She stepped next to the dead man. His head was turned to the side, one eye staring blankly underneath the bed as if searching for a missing sock.

"What?" she asked, unsure of the question. She hadn't really heard him.

"Are there others?" Rudy said; then his eyes jerked past Norma to the door. He lifted the weapon.

Norma swung around. The sounds of feet pounding up the stairs answered the question. She silently moved across the room toward the closet. From that position, whoever entered the room couldn't see her until he stepped farther into the space.

She lifted the shotgun to her shoulder. Finger on the trigger, she nodded at Rudy and then focused on the door. Her husband had the pistol leveled already. He held it with two hands, trying to steady it. She was his only protection. He was a sitting duck.

Norma exhaled, trying to calm herself as she recognized the sound of steps in the hallway outside the room. They slowed now. There was whispering. Norma sensed hesitation. Her trigger finger was flush against the curve, ready to push. She took a step closer to the door and set her feet shoulder width apart.

The door pushed wider, creaking on its ungreased hinges. "Marlon?"

Rudy took his first shot. The man who'd spoken stumbled forward, and Norma fired. A wide blast of shot pounded the target to the floor.

Norma took another step forward and pumped the shotgun again. The profile of a man moved into her view and she took aim. She and Rudy fired simultaneously. The poacher must have fired too. The bedroom erupted in a hail of gunfire. The smell of gunpowder and the drift of smoke filled the room.

It felt as if it went on for an hour, but it was seconds. Then it was over.

Three men lay dead on the floor of their bedroom. The fourth was hurt but alive. Norma heard him grunting his way back down the stairs. She locked eyes with Rudy through the haze.

"You okay?"

Rudy nodded. There were three bullet holes drilled into the headboard. He was unscathed. "You?"

She nodded and then jerked her head toward the hallway. "I got this."

Norma stepped over two bodies and the spreading pools of blood to maneuver her way into the hallway, and stopped at the top of the stairs. The injured man was halfway down the staircase, bloody hands on the balustrade to keep him upright. He was unarmed. His balance was uneasy, his breath rasping between grunts.

Norma racked the gun and leveled the weapon at him.

He halfway turned and raised one of his hands. "Please! I don't–"

The shotgun blast ended his sentence for him. He tumbled backward, headfirst, down the remainder of the stairs, his body crumpling awkwardly at the landing on the first floor. His expression was fixed in a contortion of pain and fear. The jagged edges of a broken bone punctured his forearm beneath the folds of his untucked button-down shirt.

Norma stared at him, the shotgun still aimed downward, smoke drifting and dissipating in the air in front of her. The adrenaline ebbed and her stomach tightened. Her ears rang from the blast. Tears welled in her eyes.

She lowered the weapon and walked back to her bedroom, avoiding the pair of bodies at the entrance, and moved to the bed. Rudy was sitting up, the gun on his lap.

Sinking onto the edge of the bed, she tossed the shotgun onto the other side of it and put her hand on her husband's leg. Her vision blurred from welling tears and she clenched her jaw to keep from sobbing.

Rudy grunted and pushed himself forward, leaning toward her. He spoke softly, reassuringly. "It's okay. We're okay."

Norma turned to him, her eyes searching his. She shook her head. A realization washed over her. "It's not okay," she said, her voice thick and nasal from the tears. "I shot a man in cold blood. He wasn't armed. He was leaving, trying to get away. I looked him in the eyes, ignored his cry for mercy, and shot him."

Rudy put his hand on hers. "You did what you had to do."

The words stuck in her throat. She swallowed and forced them from her lips. "I did what Marcus would have done," she said. "I did exactly what he would have done, what he's done countless times."

"And we're alive because of it," said Rudy.

He kept talking, uttering reassurances and soothing sentiments intended to make her feel better, to justify what she'd done. Norma didn't hear him. Her mind drifted to all of the times she'd judged Marcus for his actions, for his brutality and his wanton disregard for the sanctity of life.

But there, in that moment when she'd had a choice, when she was the one tasked with protecting her home, her belongings, her husband, herself, she'd opted for the one with the absolute solution.

Had she been too hard on Marcus? Had she failed to see what it was of himself he'd sacrificed for the benefit of those around him? She'd judged him so harshly. Norma sniffed back her tears and used the back of her hand to wipe her cheeks dry. When Rudy was finished consoling her, she thanked him. Then she steeled herself and locked eyes with him. She'd made a decision.

"We can't stay here," she said. "We need to leave."

CHAPTER 7

APRIL 20, 2054, 8:30 PM
SCOURGE +21 YEARS, 7 MONTHS
PURTIS CREEK STATE PARK, TEXAS

Lou doubled over in pain. Through clenched teeth and between hissing breaths, she confirmed what everyone else suspected.

"This is it," she said. "I'm sure of it."

"Eight minutes," said Dallas. "Eight minutes apart."

"We've got time, then," said Marcus.

Lou shot him a glare that, even in the darkness, drilled a hole through him. She leaned against a tree, her fingers tearing at the thin bark. Sweat gleamed in the dim bars of moonlight that shone through the thin canopy of branches and dying foliage.

They'd stopped and dismounted eight minutes earlier, after Lou had almost lost her balance atop her horse. Dallas insisted they stop at the edge of the park. Lou argued at first, and they'd traveled another half mile before she couldn't take it anymore.

"I don't think we have time," said Dallas. He was next to his wife, his hand on her belly. "We're going to do this here."

Marcus scanned the woods surrounding them. There was no hint of anyone, not even their next conductor, who was supposed to meet them in a half hour in a parking lot somewhere along the western edge of a dried lake bed.

The woods were eerie in the muted white moonlight. In the relative dark it resembled a forest in the aftermath of a fire. The trunks were barren. They stretched like arms, reaching for the sky, their brittle fingers spread wide and grasping for something ethereal. This was as good a place as any. They were south and west of the meeting place, having left the road miles back. Marcus closed his eyes and listened to his surroundings. Other than Lou's intense respiration, there was nothing: no breeze, no chirping insects, no croaking reptiles.

"What can I do?" Marcus asked.

Dallas had a hand on Lou's elbow and was lowering her to the ground, inching her down the trunk of the tree. "Get me a saddle blanket," he said.

David was standing off to one side, his hands balled into fists and covering the lower half of his face. "Is Momma okay?" he asked. "What's wrong?"

Marcus took a step toward the boy, his boots crunching on dead leaves and needles. He held out an arm to David. "Come here," he said. "Help me get the blanket."

David checked with his father. Dallas nodded and smiled weakly at Marcus. The shadow across his face hid some of Dallas's concern, but not all of it.

David walked to Marcus, and the two of them walked the short distance to the horses corralled at a cluster of trees twenty yards away.

Andrea was still on her horse. Javier was leaning against her in the saddle, asleep and snoring loudly for a child his size.

Marcus moved past her to his horse. He put his hands on the horse and bent down to unlatch the saddle. It would take him a minute to untack the horse so he could reach the heavy wool blanket on the horse's back.

He was nearly finished with the task when Andrea cursed under her breath. Then she cursed again in Spanish. The saddle in his hands, Marcus eyed her. She was staring at him, a pained expression on her face.

"What?" Marcus asked.

"You're not going to believe this..."

"Try me."

"My water broke."

Marcus didn't follow at first. He was preoccupied with Lou, and he wasn't thinking about the fact that their newest companion was also pregnant. "You need another canteen?" he asked. "I've got another—"

"No," she said, exasperation seeping into her voice. "My. Water. Broke. I'm in labor."

Marcus cursed in Spanish. He didn't even know the word was in his vocabulary. It surprised him as the word escaped his lips. It seemed to surprise Andrea too. Her eyes widened.

She started speaking in Spanish to him. The words were cascading from her, too fast for Marcus to understand. He might not even have understood her had she been speaking English, her cadence was so rushed.

Marcus dropped the saddle at his feet and held up his hands to stop her. Then he grabbed the blanket from his Appaloosa and handed it to David. "Take this to your dad," he said. "Your mom will need it. Then tell your dad I'm going to be busy for a moment, but if he needs anything, you're the one to come tell me. Okay?"

David clutched the blanket against his chest and nodded earnestly. The boy spun and ran back the short distance to his parents. Lou's breathing had subsided. Marcus couldn't hear it anymore. The contraction had passed.

He turned his attention to Andrea. He approached her horse as her boy stirred. Javier sat up straight, his eyes still closed, yawned, and stretched.

"Need help getting down?" asked Marcus. "I can set you up like we've got Lou over there. Try to make you as comfortable as possible."

She answered him in Spanish.

Marcus waved his hands. "*No hablo Español,*" he said. "Only a few words."

She frowned. "Oh, okay. So you just cuss in Spanish?"

Marcus reached up to take Javier, and she helped guide the boy to him. He shifted his weight and gripped the sleepy kid under his arms. Javier was surprisingly dense. Marcus grunted and stepped back from the horse to lower the boy to the ground.

"I don't know where that came from," he said to her. "Didn't mean to offend."

"None taken," she said and held out her hand for him to help her.

Javier knuckled his eyes and yawned again. He wobbled in place but kept his balance. "Where are we, Mama?"

"In a safe place, *mijo.* We're okay," she said, and her hand slid into Marcus's.

Andrea gripped his hand tightly and he helped her to the ground. The moment she planted both feet on the thin layer of dead leaves, she let out something between a wheeze and a groan. Letting go of Marcus, she drew her hands to the underside of her belly. Her knees bent as if she was ready to squat.

Marcus put an arm around her to steady her. She grabbed for his shirt, taking a fistful of fabric into her hand. Shafts of moonlight cut across her face as she bent over, weathering the contraction.

Behind him, Marcus heard a suppressed wail and a guttural moan. Had it been eight minutes already?

"Let's get you comfortable," Marcus said, trying to focus on Andrea. He lowered her to the ground next to an adjacent tree. Then he waved to Javier. The boy ambled toward him, still hampered by grogginess.

"I need you to hold your momma's hand," he said. "You're about to be a big brother, and we need you to be a big boy. Okay?"

Javier glanced at him warily, but checked with his mother. She tried smiling at him through her clenched jaw. She reassured him, sounding like someone counting in the middle of a bench press.

"It's okay, *mijo*. I'm okay. He's right. You're going to be *un hermano. Sí?*"

Javier took his mother's outstretched hand. She squeezed it.

Marcus went to the nearest horse and fumbled with the saddle buckle. His hands were trembling as he worked the strap free. He told himself to calm down. "Of all the things to freak out about," he muttered. "Childbirth? It's not even your kid, Marcus. Get it together."

He pulled off the saddle and tossed it aside. Then he yanked the wool blanket from the horse and swept it like a cape to open it. It billowed and he laid it on the ground next to Andrea and Javier. "See if you can get onto this. It'll help."

Andrea lifted her hips from the ground and slid onto the blanket. Javier helped her as much as he could and then sat on his heels next to her.

Andrea was breathing through pursed lips. She glanced up at Marcus, a thin line of light washed across her face. "It passed. Can you count for me? Let me know how long until the next one?"

"Sure," said Marcus. He crossed his arms, uncrossed them, planted his hands on his hips, then slid them into his pockets before crossing his arms again. "What else do you need? Water?"

Lou groaned loudly behind him, cursing Dallas.

"I'm okay," Andrea said. "Just count."

Marcus was counting roughly in his head. He was at twenty. He took a couple of steps toward Lou and called out to Dallas, "Was that eight minutes?"

"Six," said Dallas. "Give or take."

Marcus was at thirty-four or thirty-five. "Six?"

Lou lifted her head. Light hit her face. A sheen of sweat glistened on her brow and her cheeks. Her olive skin was a shade paler in the moonlight. "Six," she snarled. "After five. Before—"

She tossed her head back and spittle sprayed from between her clenched teeth. Dallas held her hand with both of his. He spoke softly to her. Marcus couldn't hear him above her grunting.

Marcus counted sixty. One minute. Then seven seconds. Ninety. One hundred twenty.

Lou's heavy breathing subsided again. She lifted her head. "Water," she rasped.

"Got it," said Marcus. "David, come here."

David jumped up, seemingly happy to leave his mother's side. He hopped, almost skipped, toward Marcus and the horses. Marcus reached into a pack alongside one of the horses still tacked up and withdrew a large, full canteen. He handed it to David. "Take this to your mom."

David did as he was told and Marcus moved to the adjacent horse. As he pulled another canteen from a pack, Lou groaned again. It was so loud he thought it was Andrea. But that couldn't be. He hadn't reached three hundred yet.

The counting stopped when he turned around, the canteen in hand. It was Andrea. She was leaning on her elbows, a pained expression on her face. Then, as if on cue, Lou moaned again.

Stunned, Marcus limped to Andrea and lowered himself to one knee. He uncapped the canteen and offered her some water. She shook her head and squeezed her eyes closed. Tears, sweat, or both rolled down her cheeks.

He looked across her to Javier. The boy appeared as lost as Marcus felt.

His mind drifted again, only for a moment, to Wesson's birth. It was easy. At least that was what the doctors and nurses had told him. Sylvia was a pro. The labor lasted six hours. The birth itself was textbook.

He remembered how much of a mess he'd been. War? No problem. A complicated sales deal with high financial stakes? No biggie. Negotiating with a huge energy company for the rights to use the natural gas on his own land? Piece of cake. But watching a baby being born? It made him weak in the knees.

"I think it's happening," said Andrea. "I need your help."

Marcus nodded blankly.

"My pants," she said. "Can you…?"

Her eyes widened and she cried out. Her head was back, her chin toward the sky. Sweat glistened on her neck. Her chest heaved.

Marcus moved along her side and tugged at her pants. He slid them down, trying to avert his eyes while doing the job. Then he had her exposed and ready to birth the child.

Andrea lifted her knees and grabbed them with her hands. In the distance, Lou cried out. The two women were like wolves howling at each other, speaking some tribal language only they understood.

Marcus understood what was happening. He was delivering a baby. In the woods. At night. And he had the easy part. Swallowing against the lump in his throat, he moved into position.

"Okay," he said. "I'm here. You're okay. You're doing great. Just push."

He didn't know what else to tell her to do. There was nothing else he *could* do except catch the kid as it came out. His stomach lurched and bile crept up toward the lump.

"Push," he said. It was hard to see anything. He thought he could see the head. Maybe. Maybe not. "Push."

Andrea grunted at him and spat an angry retort. "I *am* pushing."

"You're doing a great job," said Javier. Then he spoke Spanish to her. She replied through short puffs of air. The muscles in her neck tensed, drawing taut. A blood vessel strained against her skin.

Several agonizing minutes later, the baby was in Marcus's hands. But it was blue. Even in the dim light, he could see it. It didn't appear to be breathing, at least not that he could tell.

The look on his face must have given away his concern.

"What's wrong?" Andrea asked anxiously. "Is something wrong?

Is the baby okay?"

Marcus pulled on the child and its heels slipped free. He flipped the child over, revealing its pinched face. Marcus ignored Andrea's urgent questions and studied the baby, looking for the problem. What was keeping the child from—then he saw it.

He quickly slid his fingers between the child's neck and the fleshy rope still attached to the mother and turned the child at the same time, maneuvering both in his hands. The umbilical cord came free, untangling from the child. Marcus lifted the baby and slapped a palm against its back. He slapped again, ignoring Andrea's pleas, tuning out Javier's shrieks.

On the third smack the child coughed and opened its mouth. A soft wail swelled from the baby's chest. A deep breath and another cry, louder than the one before, warbled and filled the space around them.

Marcus sighed. "It's okay. It's okay. The baby's okay."

He handed Andrea her child. Javier beamed. Andrea was exhausted, but held the naked child tight against her chest. She shushed the crying newborn, her hands rubbing its pink, slimy back. A swirl of dark hair was matted and shiny.

"It's a girl," said Andrea, through tears. "A baby sister, Javi. *Una hermanita.*"

Marcus fell back onto his backside, relieving the pressure on his lower back and the fronts of his calves. He wanted to vomit. The whole adventure had him light-headed. He avoided looking straight ahead. Andrea, oblivious and immodest, was still undressed from the waist down.

He reached toward her, leaning on an elbow, and folded one corner of the blanket over the lower half of her body.

She thanked him. "You're my hero," she said, a tired laugh accompanying her admission. "Really. I couldn't have done it without you and Javier."

Javier's grin broadened, if that was possible. His face was as close to the baby as he could get. He was making clucking sounds and cooing. It was adorable and reminded Marcus of and older Sawyer with Penny. Sawyer, Lola's son, had been the perfect big brother to his adopted sister.

Marcus sat back again and braced himself with locked elbows, digging his palms into piles of leaves. "I have a feeling you'd have managed without us. You're the hero here. I just played catcher."

Andrea shook her head. Then her face brightened. "I have an idea," she said. "I'd like to name her after you."

"Me?" he said. "She's a girl."

"You're Marcus?"

"Yes."

"What's your last name?"

He hesitated, then answered, "Battle."

She giggled. "That's a silly last name. I can't name my baby after that."

"I don't blame you."

"What's your favorite woman's name?" she asked. "A woman important to you?"

Marcus looked past Andrea to the Stoudemire family. Dallas was holding their newborn. A boy, born a minute or two before Andrea's girl. Lou ran her hand along Dallas's head, fingering his bangs from his face. David, like Javier, hovered next to the child.

The growing crescendo of groans and wails and cries had given way to sighs and exhausted laughter. Marcus wiped his eyes with the back of his hand. "Louise."

"Louise?"

"Yeah," said Marcus. "If you want to name your girl after a woman important to me, name her Louise."

Andrea appeared to consider the name, mull it over, and test it in her mind. Then she nodded and smiled. "Louisa. Yes, it's perfect."

"You okay here for a minute?"

"Yes," she said. "I have Javi. I'm good."

Marcus stood and limped toward the Stoudemires. His knees and ankles loosened more with each step. He was nearly to Lou when Andrea called out, panic in her voice. It was almost a shriek that made the hairs on his neck stand on end. His skin tensed with goose bumps.

"Battle?"

He swung around, his hand reaching for the pistol at his waist. As he pivoted, he leveled the gun at his hip. It was a move he'd perfected during his time as the sheriff in Baird so many years ago.

Standing in the dark next to the horses was a tall, broad-shouldered shadow of a man. His presence was palpable.

The adrenaline surged and Marcus took two deliberate steps. He kept the gun pointed at him. His finger was on the trigger, ready to apply pressure.

"Whoa!" The man lifted his hands above his head, his fingers spread. "Hold on, partner. No need for that."

His voice was resonant, with a pleasant gravel to it. It reassured even as his presence alarmed.

Marcus kept his finger ready to fire. "Who are you?"

"I heard the commotion. Coulda woke up a bear on Christmas. I mean to tell you, if y'all were trying to be surreptitious and all, you get a big fat fail."

Marcus moved closer, keeping his gun leveled, and repeated his question. "Who. Are. You?"

"I'm guessing y'all came from Gun Barrel City?" the stranger asked, sounding like he knew the answer. "And you're headed east. That a fair assumption?"

Marcus didn't say anything. None of them did. Andrea's baby, Louisa, was crying. It was a soft, agitated whimper.

"I'm fixin' to head that way myself," said the stranger. "Maybe catch a ride on the railroad?"

The tall man stepped forward now, finding the light. His face was round. It matched his broad bulbous nose and small wide-set eyes.

He was bald with a white, bushy mustache that hid his mouth. A deep line creased the middle of his protruding chin.

None of that was as distinguishing as his height. He must have stood six feet five or taller. His girth matched it. He wasn't fat, but wasn't trim either. Everything about him was big, including his meaty hands, which he still held up at his shoulders.

"How did you find us?" asked Marcus.

He jerked a thumb over his shoulder, pointing north. His mustache shifted on his face as he spoke. "I was at the parking lot. Got there early and waited. Then it got late. Y'all weren't there. Air's real still tonight. Sound carries. I heard the unmistakable sounds of a woman in labor."

He chuckled. His eyes flitted past Marcus and then back to him. "I say it's unmistakable," he said, "but truth be told, it could just as well be cats fighting in a paper bag. No disrespect intended."

Marcus lowered his weapon but kept it in his hand and glanced back at the others. They were paying rapt attention. Dallas was now standing a couple of feet behind him, a rifle leveled.

"It's okay," Marcus told Dallas. "You can put it down. This is our conductor."

Marcus shifted the gun from his right hand to his left and stepped forward, offering his hand. "I'm Marc—"

"No names," the tall stranger cut in, taking Marcus's hand with a tight grip. "That's part of the deal. Keeps things copacetic. I think they call it plausible deniability. Any of us fall into the wrong crowd, nobody knows anything."

"Fair enough," said Marcus.

"I mean"—he released his grip and ran his thumb and index finger along the edges of his mustache—"I already know your name. That pretty little lady over there called it out when she saw me. Sorry about that. I shoulda been less surreptitious."

That was the second time the new conductor used the word *surreptitious*. Marcus wondered if he'd looked it up in a dictionary and was using it as many times as he could to reinforce its meaning.

"No problem," said Marcus. "I'm sure you can forget it."

The man smiled. His mustache stretched up and out, revealing his lower lip. His white eyebrows arched high on his head. "Forget what?"

Dallas joined Marcus at his side. He'd lowered the rifle, but held it in both hands with the barrel aimed at the ground.

"What now?" Dallas asked. "Both women just gave birth."

"That doesn't change anything," said the conductor. "We've got to get a move on. It ain't ideal, but that's the truth of it. I can't get the van any closer than it is. So we're gonna have to walk to it."

"How far?" asked Dallas.

The conductor shrugged. He ran a hand across the top of his head and then rubbed the back of his neck. "Maybe a quarter mile. Not far. Like I said at the top, I could hear the women rattlin' on."

"All right," said Marcus. "Give us a minute. We'll get everybody together. We'll make it happen."

"Yeah, you will," said the conductor, all hints of humor gone. "You got no choice in the matter. With them babies, we'd best get a move on. Otherwise you might as well hand them over to the Pop Guard with a bow and bottle."

CHAPTER 8

APRIL 20, 2054, 10:00 PM
SCOURGE +21 YEARS, 7 MONTHS
ATLANTA, GEORGIA

The chime from the computer woke Rickshaw from his uneasy sleep. He was leaning back in his chair, his feet propped up on his desk, ankles crossed.

"Captain Greg Rickshaw," said the digital voice, "I have a message from your team at The Greenbrier Resort. Would you like me to play it?"

Rickshaw cleared his throat and sat up in his chair. He knuckled the sleep from his eyes and pinched the bridge of his nose. Sometimes he couldn't stand the formality of the central computer and its directives.

"Yes," he said, his voice thick with phlegm, "play the message."

"Of course, Captain Greg Rickshaw, I—"

"For the love of all that is good and holy," he snapped, "would you please refer to me as Rickshaw? Save it in your protocol."

"Saving your request, Rickshaw," said the unfazed androgynous voice.

Rickshaw tried putting a face to the voice and couldn't do it. The images flipped between a feminine-looking man and a masculine-looking woman.

"May I proceed with the message?" asked the computer.

"Proceed," Rickshaw said dismissively, his voice sounding closer to normal.

"The message was transmitted from the team, via a series of radio connections, to governmental headquarters here in Atlanta," said the computer. "Given the series of relays, the estimated transmission lag is approximately nine minutes. The message is verbatim."

Rickshaw spun in his chair and opened a cube-shaped refrigerator under the desk. He plucked a bottle of black-market spirits from the icebox and set it on the desk. With a twist of the cap, the bottle opened, and Rickshaw drew it to his lips. He took two healthy swigs, relishing the burn in his cheeks, on his tongue, down his throat.

His head buzzed from the bite of it. He touched his fingers to his numb lips and thumbed away excess drink.

"We arrived at The Greenbrier on schedule," said the computer, reading aloud the message transmitted from the mountains of West Virginia to the Appalachian Plateau in northwest Georgia. "A survey found evidence of residency on the grounds and in the main building. We made contact with seven people: four men and three women. Our teams discovered no children on the grounds or in the aboveground portions of the main building. The women did not have subdural evidence of motherhood. Nor did our scanners detect any devices implanted in the men."

Rickshaw took another pull from the bottle and spun the cap tight onto its top. The second mouthful tasted warmer than the first, his mouth having cooled from the initial guzzle. Condensation clouded the bottle, and drips of perspiration rolled down its side, pooling on the desk.

The computer droned descriptions of the men and women, their living conditions, the lack of children. The men and women denied any knowledge of underground railroad activity.

"We had one of the men lead us to the entrance to the bunker complex," relayed the computer. "We entered the complex and performed a thorough sweep of the rooms, tunnels, and storage facilities. We found evidence that untold numbers of people, including children, lived in the underground facility."

Rickshaw sat up. The recording now had his full attention. "Computer," he said, "stop. Replay last fifteen seconds."

"Okay, Rickshaw," said the computer. "…entered the complex and performed a thorough sweep of the rooms, tunnels, and storage facilities. We found evidence that untold numbers of people, including children, lived in the underground facility."

Untold numbers.

"Mother—" Rickshaw eyed the bottle, but his head was already swimming.

"Yes," said the computer, "it's reasonable to draw the conclusion that the untold numbers of people included both mothers and fathers given the presence of children. Shall I proceed with the remainder of the message?"

"Yes," Rickshaw said through gritted teeth. It sounded more like a growl than a command.

"There is evidence the men, women, and children were here for an extended period of time," said the computer. "It could be as much as several months. They are gone, though. Our subsequent interrogations of the remaining men and women procured intelligence that puts their departure somewhere between two and three weeks ago."

Rickshaw balled his fingers, the knuckles popping as he did. He raised his arm to pound the heel of his fist onto the glass desk but stopped himself. Nothing good could come from the short-lived relief of a violent outburst. Instead he flexed his fingers in and out and used his hands to push himself to his feet.

They'd come so close to finding the Harbor. Rickshaw had to look at the bright side. They'd identified the existence of the fabled sanctuary and rooted it out. The families were on the run. They were looking for a new harbor. If he'd successfully found the Harbor once, he could find it again. The tension in his hands, in his neck, eased. He exhaled audibly.

He would finish this. He would find the new harbor. He would annihilate it. Then he would tear up the virtual tracks of the railroad spike by spike.

"Is there any more to the message?" he asked the computer. "You stopped talking."

"That is the end of the message, Rickshaw," said the computer. "However, there is an addendum."

"An addendum?"

"Yes. It's sent as a separate message. Would you—"

"Play it."

"We have one surviving man from among the men and women who lived aboveground in The Greenbrier. The others would not cooperate. We believe this man may have information as to where the others have traveled. We are bringing him back to headquarters and delivering him to you."

Rickshaw grinned. He wasn't sure if it was the message or the alcohol. It didn't matter. This was ultimately good news. They were getting closer to finding the Harbor and to undoing the railroad.

CHAPTER 9

APRIL 21, 2054, 3:15 AM
SCOURGE +21 YEARS, 7 MONTHS
BAIRD, TEXAS

Norma keyed the radio. It was a long shot. She hadn't slept, couldn't sleep, and wasn't about to risk keeping Rudy awake. Once the sun came up, they'd have their work cut out for them.

"Hello, this is NGBTX1," she said, identifying herself with the nonregulation call sign. "CQ, CQ, CQ. Is the frequency busy? Anyone there?"

She'd created the call sign using her initials, the first letter of her hometown, the postal abbreviation for Texas, and the number one. It was easy to remember.

"NGBTX1 calling," she repeated. "Is this frequency busy? Anyone?"

"GA NGBTX1," the respondent said. *"I hear you. This is GFAGA5. I hear you. Very strong signal, perfectly clear copy, five plus nine."*

She was there. Gladys was awake and near her radio. Their communication wasn't planned. This was luck. Or maybe it was something bigger than that, like destiny or kismet.

"Good to hear you, GFAGA5," said Norma. "I've got an update."

Norma had never learned the correct way to communicate on the radio. Hers was a hybrid, nonofficial lingo. It was as close to real amateur operator language as Creole was to French, but it did the trick.

The response was laced with static but intelligible. *"GA,"* said Gladys.

GA was shorthand for "Go ahead." Norma held her fingers above the transmit key and waited a beat. When Gladys didn't add anything, she pressed down.

"We're leaving," she said. "It's not safe here."

Saying it aloud made it real. Telling someone beyond the porous confines of her property made it real. Having the plan formulated in her head made it real.

The sudden tightness in her chest surprised her. She was light-headed. The time between her transmission and Gladys's response was excruciatingly long. Finally the silence gave way to static.

"I hear you," said Gladys. *"Is that your only option?"*

Norma pressed the key without hesitation. "Yes. Another attack today. Can't stay. Will head to that place you mentioned."

Norma wondered, even as she said it, if she was being rash. They'd survived in Baird for more than a decade. Much of it, they'd managed on this property south of the highway and outside town. This was a good home. At least it was as good as any place in Texas. From what Norma had learned of life north of the wall, it wasn't much better. There were haves and have-nots and nothing in between. You were predator or prey, pro-government or anti-establishment. Everything north of the wall was black and white. At least in Texas, inside the wall, there were shades of gray. She stared at the handgun on the desk. She'd set it next to the transceiver when she'd sat down in front of the equipment.

It was loaded, a fresh magazine in its grip. She'd chambered a round on her way from the house to the barn. Norma reconciled she couldn't be too careful now. Not with two attacks so close together, not with her husband nearly dying twice.

The radio crackled. The voice on the other end was more tremulous than before.

"Are you sure?" asked Gladys.

Norma steeled herself. "Yes. Can you repeat the code? I have a pencil."

"Okay, NGBTX1. I have the code."

Norma picked up a broken pencil from the desk. The ferrule on its back end was bent, creased together. The eraser was gone. Its tip was oddly shaped and whittled to reveal what was left of the graphite. The yellow coating on the pencil was pocked with divots, teeth marks or digs from sharp fingernails. She held it above a piece of torn cardboard she'd ripped from an old cereal box, poised and ready to write.

"Thirty-six, zero, three, zero, seven, seventy-five, six, seventy-six, zero."

Norma repeated the numbers back to Gladys and thanked her.

"Don't thank me," said Gladys. *"I can't ever repay you for what you did for me. Just do me a favor, NGBTX1."*

"What's that, GFAGA5?" asked Norma. Her eyes welled. A knot swelled in her throat, making it difficult to swallow. She noticed her hand was trembling when she lifted it from the transmit key.

The transceiver hummed. There was a squeal, and the beginning of the incoming transmission warbled until the sound flattened and was intelligible again.

"Be careful. It's not an easy road."

Norma promised her she would be careful. She ended the transmission, and the door to the barn creaked behind her. Somebody was there.

A wave of energy surged through Norma's body. She grabbed the gun and swung around while at the same time trying to stand to face the intruder. From the edges of her vision in the low glow of the barn light, a dark image loomed inside the entrance.

As she moved, trying to raise the gun and take aim, she lost her grip on it, accidentally flinging it to the floor like a Frisbee. It skidded across the grit-covered concrete and spun in a circle near the feet of the intruder. The intruder, still in shadows, bent over awkwardly and picked up the weapon. Norma was frozen.

"Didn't mean to scare you," said Rudy. He was leaning on a crutch fashioned from a broom handle.

Norma let go of the breath she was holding and cursed. "You scared the living daylights out of me. What are you doing down here?"

Rudy inched his way toward her. He was using both legs, and she realized the crutch was more a cane.

Chuckling, Rudy stopped a couple of feet from her and handed her the gun. "What am *I* doing?" he asked. "What are *you* doing?"

Norma set the gun on the desk and leaned back. She rested her hands on the top of the desk and locked her elbows. "Finalizing plans."

His eyes shifted to the radio and back. "Gladys?"

Norma nodded. "I'm surprised I reached her, given how late it is."

Rudy took another step toward her. He favored one leg and winced. He reached out and pulled himself into the chair. Norma helped him ease into it. He smiled his thanks.

"Or how early it is," he said. "Depends on how you look at it."

"I thought you were asleep, Rudy. You *should* be asleep. We've got a long day ahead of us tomorrow."

"Every day is long," said Rudy. "Tomorrow isn't going to be any different. It'll just take a little more pain medicine than usual to get through it."

Norma turned to face her husband and faked a smile.

Rudy's face soured. He frowned and his eyes narrowed with worry. He reached out and gently stroked her cheek with his thumb. "Hey, were you crying?"

Norma's lips quivered. Her chin trembled. She shook her head, but that made the tears come. Holding back the emotion only forced it out with a blubbering wail that she didn't recognize as her own.

Rudy leaned forward, both hands cupping her face now, and tried soothing her. Norma's body shook from the release of raw emotion. Everything she'd held back was loose now.

He stood, balancing himself gingerly against the chair, and wrapped his arms around her, drawing her body against his. His hands, still strong despite his injuries, held her. His fingers laced through her hair and he lowered his lips to her ear. "Let it out. It's okay."

For what might have been five minutes or thirty, Norma stayed close to her husband. Worries, pains, memories coursed through her as she stood there in his embrace, letting his weight hold hers.

When she finally caught her breath, she pulled away from him. Her bloodshot, puffy eyes locked onto his and she smiled. "I'm sorry. I don't know—"

"Don't worry about it," Rudy said. "I'm just so surprised you're that upset over having almost shot me."

That elicited a genuine laugh. Norma put her hand on his chest and then ran it across the rough stubble that traced his jawline. "I needed to get it out, I guess," she said. "A lot's happened in the last few days. I've been holding it in." She exhaled and sucked in a ragged breath. She hitched as the air caught in her throat.

"I get it," he said. "It's good to cry."

Norma realized then his eyes were bloodshot. His face was wet with tears. He'd been crying right along with her.

"I love you," she said.

"I love you," said Rudy.

"Are we doing the right thing?" she asked. "Leaving this place?"

He sighed, and his eyes drifted. "I don't know," he said. "I don't think there's a good option here."

"How so?"

"If we stay, we're sitting ducks. It's only a matter of time before the Pop Guard comes back."

"We already knew that," said Norma, leaning back against the desk again.

"Yeah," said Rudy. "But this poacher thing puts it in perspective. We can't keep fighting off everyone who comes here. And more will come."

Her gaze drifted away from his. Images of Lou, David, and Dallas flickered in her mind. "I think about how alone we are now," she said, her voice wavering.

"So I'm chopped liver?" said Rudy.

She blinked back to focus, meeting her husband's playful stare. One eyebrow was arched higher than the other. She noticed his color wasn't good. Even with the warm light above the desk, he looked pale. Dark circles framed the undersides of his eyes. He looked older somehow.

"No," she said. "Not today anyhow. What I mean is, we're alone out here with no backup."

"I know what you meant," said Rudy. "I was kidding. I don't disagree with you. Better to take our chances out there than to stay put."

"Can you make it?" she asked. "You're still in bad shape. You don't look good."

He held out his hand and wiggled it from side to side. "*Mas o menos*," he said. "I'm okay. Not great, not awful. But I don't think we can wait here until I'm fully healed."

"It's settled, then," she said. "We leave at dawn."

"That doesn't leave us a lot of time. And you haven't gotten any sleep."

"I'll sleep when I'm dead," Norma said.

Rudy frowned. "Not funny."

"Wasn't meant to be. C'mon, I'll make you some coffee."

CHAPTER 10

APRIL 21, 2054, 3:30 AM
SCOURGE +21 YEARS, 7 MONTHS
TYLER, TEXAS

"This is where we say goodbye," said the conductor. "You wait here until the next conductor comes along."

He was in the driver's seat of the van, turned, with his hand on the back of the passenger's seat so he could see his cargo. His fingers drummed on the ripped vinyl that only partially covered the seat.

Marcus was sitting in the front passenger's seat. He unbuckled his seatbelt and inched forward, turning to face the conductor, and rested an elbow on the dash. "How long do you think that'll be?"

The conductor shrugged. He frowned and his mustache drooped. "No tellin'. Plausible deniability, remember? We try to keep things compartmentalized."

"I get that. Are we talking a day? Two?"

The conductor shook his head. The hand on the back of Marcus's seat stopped tapping. "No, not that long. A few hours at most."

"What's the procedure?" asked Dallas.

"He or she will find you," said the conductor. "They'll come knocking. They'll have a vehicle. It'll accommodate all of you. You'll head east."

"Past the wall?" asked Andrea. She was sitting on the floor with her back to the wall of the van. She held Louisa to her chest, trying to nurse. Javier was asleep on her legs.

"Where are we?" asked Dallas.

Lou was asleep on his shoulder. The baby boy slept too. David was out cold, curled into a ball on the molded plastic floor.

"Tyler," said the conductor. "The Rose City."

"Rose City?" Dallas echoed.

"Used to be, Tyler was the rose capital of the world. City had a long vibrant history of growin' 'em, processin' 'em."

"All right," said Marcus. "Thanks for the ride and the history lesson. We should get inside. This is tribal territory, right?"

The conductor nodded. "That it is. Small tribe here, but there's enough resources they took root. In fact, they call themselves the La Rosa Tribe. See how it's all full circle?"

Marcus thumped the dash with his hand twice. "Let's do this."

Dallas woke up the women and children. They were groggy but aware enough to know what was happening.

Marcus and the conductor exited the van and moved to the rear of the vehicle. Marcus had his pistol drawn. His head was on a swivel while the conductor unlocked the tailgate and swung open the rear doors.

Dallas exited first, and Lou handed him the baby. He shifted the child to one arm and helped her exit with the other. He handed the baby back to Lou and repeated the process with Andrea. The boys were last out of the van.

While the conductor led the women and children into the building, Marcus and Dallas grabbed the packs stuffed with gear and food and took as many weapons as they could carry.

Marcus started toward the door but stopped. "Hey, Dallas, I'm staying here. I don't want to leave the van unguarded with these weapons. Come back and grab the rest. That good?"

Dallas nodded and disappeared inside the place.

Marcus sucked in the dry, warm air of east Texas. This was the part of the state called the Piney Woods, or at least it used to be. More than fifty thousand acres of hardwoods stretched across the Ark-La-Tex, the region where Arkansas, Louisiana, and Texas met at the thick coniferous forest of oaks and pines. Underneath the canopies of those towering trees grew thickets of yaupon and dogwood. Redbud, maple, and elm also grew in abundance.

That was before loggers and then the drought. Now the area looked like what Marcus remembered seeing in books and movies of the German Black Forest after shelling in World War Two a century earlier. There was still some green, some drought-resistant strains of evergreens and succulents.

From where he stood now, in the middle of Tyler at West Elm Street and College Avenue, there wasn't a tree in sight. No grass either. The narrow esplanades that decorated the wide parking lot were barren. Even in the milky dark of predawn, the lack of vegetation was apparent.

Marcus stood watch, listening for movement. On the two-hour drive from the state park, the conductor had warned Marcus of the threats in Tyler. La Rosa was entrenched. They ran both the town and neighboring Longview.

It struck Marcus how people always found a way to take control, to fill the vacuum left behind by whoever had previously failed to maintain power. It was like an immutable law of physics and only bolstered his contention that people weren't inherently good.

There were plenty of good people, but he'd lost hope in the masses, in those driven to self-preservation at the expense of others. He rattled off the long list of malevolent humans he'd come across in his life, and it was a short one compared to what he'd learned about global history.

It wasn't just about war; it was pervasive in the business world. When he'd been a consultant and made the money that paid for the land east of Rising Star, there were always others trying to take from him what he'd earned. There were liars and cheats and those who bent the rules to benefit themselves. They justified it by pointing at others who'd done the same or by suggesting they were novel and brilliant for thinking of it first, executing a plan. Kill or be killed. Darwinian evolution. Eye for an eye. Biblical wrath. It was all the same.

And here he stood on the lookout for the latest incarnation of it, some affiliated group of monsters with a stupid name in search of greater reach, broader power. It made him sick. It would have made him regret leaving his home in Chatham, Virginia, were it not for one thing. Or four things.

Fighting the fight was worth it for Lou, David, the new baby, and even Dallas. It was worth his sacrifice. It was worth facing demons and coping with worsening arthritis. He sucked in another deep breath of the warm air and tilted his head from side to side. His neck cracked like bubble wrap.

The conductor emerged from the building. He was moving quickly, rubbing the top of his bald head with one hand while gesticulating toward the back of the van with the other. "Hey, I'm gonna help you with the rest of the guns and ammo."

Marcus shifted his pack on his shoulder and glanced toward the open door. "Why? Where's Dal—"

"No names." The conductor grabbed a bag loaded with ammo and took a couple of rifles in the other hand.

"Where's the new father?" Marcus corrected himself. "Everything okay?"

"He's dealing with his lady," said the conductor. "She's a little upset. He's trying to calm her down."

The two of them heaved their loads inside the building. A familiar odor Marcus couldn't place hit him as soon as he crossed the threshold.

"Something about books," said the conductor. "She was talking about books."

That was the odor. Books. Marcus inhaled deeply through his nose, relishing the comforting aroma of paper and ink. The smell of a book was something he'd missed. He knew Lou loved them too. But why would they upset her? That didn't make any sense.

The conductor led Marcus through a narrow hallway. It was too dark to see much, and Marcus kept banging into the walls as he moved. Where he could see, he shifted to avoid connecting with anything.

Then the hallway opened into a wide expanse, a single large space. Marcus could hear Lou crying. She sounded almost inconsolable. That wasn't like her. She was passionate, but she wasn't one for tears. Marcus had to admit she'd given birth a few hours earlier, and the hormones raging through her body were probably responsible.

As his eyes adjusted to the dim light filtering in through the windows at the edges of the space, Marcus suddenly understood why Lou was upset. On all sides were floor-to-ceiling bookshelves. There were rows of chairs at tables. There was a large desk at the center of the space, resembling a command center.

This was a library. More specifically, as he read the lettering on the front of the central desk, it was the Tyler Public Library.

His heart sank for her and he found an empty table on which to lay down his gear. Then he crossed the room to Lou and Dallas. Dallas had his arms around her, shushing her. Her arms were wrapped around him, her fingers gripping the shirt fabric on his back.

He almost said something to comfort both of them, but stopped himself. This was their moment. It was Dallas's job to help his wife. He backed up and found Andrea holding both babies. He hadn't gotten a good look at Lou's son.

The conductor cleared his throat to get Marcus's attention. "I'm headin' out," he said. "Got to head back and help with them women in Gun Barrel City. Heard they're all good to go now. Safe and such."

"Where will you take them?" Marcus asked.

"Who knows? They like to be all surreptitious and such. I do what

I'm told when I'm told to do it."

Marcus suppressed a grin at the awkward insertion of the conductor's favorite word. He thanked him again for his help. "See you soon."

"No, you won't."

The conductor waved his goodbyes to the others and left them in the library alone. The door clanged when he shut it behind him. It was a distant metallic sound that echoed through the long hallway, which emptied to the main library.

Marcus crossed the distance to Andrea and held out his arms. It was a hesitant motion from a man usually decisive and sure of movement. "Could I?"

Andrea smiled. "Which one?"

Marcus eyed both babies before his gaze settled back on Andrea. "The boy? I've already held yours."

Andrea shifted her weight in the chair and leaned forward with the baby boy. Marcus stooped and, with both hands, took the child from her. He was wrapped in a cotton shirt. Once he had the child firmly in his arms, supporting the head, he checked behind him.

Lou was still crying. Her sobs, softer now, were muted in Dallas's chest. He was whispering in her ear. Both of them were oblivious to the room around them. David was standing off to one side, a few feet from his parents and between two bookshelves.

Marcus caught David's attention and motioned for him. The boy glanced at his parents, a frightened, drawn expression on his face, and slid past them to Marcus.

Holding the baby with one arm, his head supported in the crook of his elbow, he offered his free hand to David. The boy took it and Marcus led him to a pair of chairs at the other end of the open space.

They were high-backed chairs, the kind you might find in a study or a formal living room. But they were threadbare, the seams torn or popped, the seat cushions missing altogether. Marcus took a seat in one and guided David to the other.

"What do you think about your big brother?" Marcus asked.

David leaned against the oversized arm closer to Marcus. One side of his mouth lifted into a smirk. "Little brother," he corrected. "*I'm* the big brother."

Marcus widened his eyes and dropped his jaw. "Oh," he said, as if he'd discovered something, "you're right. *You're* the big brother."

"I'm older."

"You are older," said Marcus. "And I hear you're a hero."

David studied Marcus. There was no shift in expression. No giveaways. Only a silent appraisal, judgment.

"You think you're funny," said David. "My mom said you thought you were funny. But you're really not."

That drew a genuine chuckle. Marcus bit his lip. "You are your momma's son, aren't you? All spit and vinegar."

Instead of answering, or even fully reacting to Marcus's assessment, David tucked his legs under him and glanced toward his parents. "Why is my mom crying?" he asked. "I've never seen her cry."

Marcus followed David's stare and saw Dallas stroke the back of Lou's head. Then he looked down at the boy swaddled in his arm. "She's thinking of your grandfather, David. Her father."

The boy's eyebrows twitched. "He was David too."

"He was," said Marcus. "He and your mom lived in a library for a while. It was their home. I guess she has a lot of memories about that. This makes her think about that."

"It makes her sad?"

"A little, I'm sure," said Marcus. "Plus, it's been a really long day. She's tired."

"How long will we be here?"

The baby moved in Marcus's arm and brought his hands up to his face. They were balled into tight fists. The kid looked like an angry Winston Churchill.

"Good question," said Marcus.

"I know it is," said David. "What's the answer?"

Marcus looked up from the baby and at David. The kid looked like Lou. It was hard not to be nostalgic with all the kids and babies around, difficult not to reminisce. He realized he'd been doing a lot of that since Dallas showed up on his land a very long five days ago.

Was it only five days? Five days. A lifetime in five days.

Marcus wondered why they'd needed him. He looked down at the new baby again. Was it to play nanny? His eyes, fully adjusted to the faint gray light of the room, found Lou and Dallas.

She wasn't crying anymore. She was whispering to Dallas. His hands were on her shoulders; hers were on his elbows, cupping them.

"Marcus," said David, "what's the answer?"

"I don't know," said Marcus. "It could be an hour, it could be a couple of days, but we're safe here. We've got food, water, and, when the sun comes up, plenty of books to read."

David leaned toward him and Marcus thought he was going to whisper something. Instead, he puckered his lips and planted a soft kiss on the top of the baby's head.

Amidst all of it, there was still this: family. A husband comforted his wife; a boy loved his sibling. Family. That was why he was here.

CHAPTER 11

APRIL 21, 2054, 6:30 AM
SCOURGE +21 YEARS, 7 MONTHS
TYLER, TEXAS

Lou stood at the window, rocking side to side at her hips, holding her baby. She was trying to nurse. It wasn't easy. And it hurt. She winced. Finally the boy latched on and started to feed.

"Hey." Marcus came up behind her. "You okay?"

"I've got a hungry cannibal who hasn't figured out how not to bite the boob that feeds him," Lou said. "So there's that."

Marcus chuckled. "Sorry. Didn't realize. You want me to leave you alone?"

She shook her head. "No, it's okay. Where is everyone else?"

"Asleep."

"Even David?"

"On top of Dallas. They're on the floor somewhere in the children's section. Andrea and her kids are asleep in a chair over by the newspapers and magazines section."

"I couldn't sleep even if I tried, even though I'm exhausted."

Marcus stepped to the window next to Lou. He kept his eyes forward, staring out at West Elm. It was that time of the morning where everything looked like it was filtered through a sepia lens.

Everything blended together and edges blurred. "You've got a cannibal to feed. That's good enough reason to be awake."

"True," she said. "It's not that though. It's the library. It's too much. I want to cry just looking at a book on a shelf. You know, with the little white stickers at the bottom that tell you where it belongs on a shelf? It reminds me of…" She couldn't finish saying it.

"Of him," Marcus said. "I get it. It's totally—"

"No," said Lou. "It's not that." There was no melancholy in her tone; there was concern. "We need to get away from the window." She stepped back carefully, as if a snake were at her feet and she didn't want to disturb it.

"What?" Marcus asked, searching the street in front of him. There was an old church across the road. Next to that was a squat building with an orange roof in bad disrepair. A sign in front of the place indicated it was the Smith County Historical Society.

He stepped closer to the window and looked to the left. Nothing. To the right. Nothing at first. And then he saw them.

Beyond the corner of the church that sat at West Elm Street and South Bois D'Arc Avenue were four men on foot. They were armed. Shotguns? They were zigzagging along the street, peering in windows along one side before crossing the other to do the same. How had Lou seen them so quickly?

"Marcus," she whisper-shouted, "get away from the window."

He took three steps back and turned around to face Lou. She'd already covered up and stopped feeding. The baby gurgled but seemed otherwise content with the abbreviated breakfast. "That's not Pop Guard," she said.

"How do you know?"

"No uniforms," she said. "I bet they're tribal."

Marcus resisted the urge to go back to the window for another look. "Really? You think so?"

"No doubt. If this is a tribal town, nobody else is going to be wandering around armed at dawn, searching buildings."

"Good point," said Marcus. "C'mon."

He led her farther into the space, back behind a collection of shelves with heavy, matching volumes on them. She leaned against one of the shelves, swaying unconsciously while tapping the baby's back with her fingers. He faced over her shoulder, looking at Marcus with a drunk expression on his face. Definitely Winston Churchill. The only thing missing was a homburg and a cigar. He took his attention from the baby and looked through the gap between the top of one row of books and the bottom of the shelf above it.

"I think we can see them from here without them seeing us," said Marcus, "assuming they check the window."

The baby burped and Marcus smelled stale milk. His face soured, but he didn't say anything. He'd never liked that smell. Sylvia had loved it. But she'd also loved the rancid odor of cradle cap and the bizarre enjoyment of picking flakes of skin off Wes's scalp.

"What's the plan?" Lou asked.

Marcus kept his eyes on the window. "For what?"

"If they see us?"

"They won't see us," said Marcus. "If we stay quiet. If we—"

The first face appeared at the window. He was a ginger. A heavy mop of bright red hair below his ears, clinging to his jawline. In one hand he held a Mossberg twelve gauge. He pressed the edge of the other to the glass and used it as a visor to look through the window.

Marcus's pulse quickened. He was faintly aware of the nine millimeter on his hip.

The redhead scanned and squinted, trying to survey the space through the film of bubbling tint on the glass. Then he stopped, focused on something. He pulled his face away from the glass and poked at it, jabbing with his index finger. He said something. Marcus heard him but didn't decipher the words.

"This isn't good," said Lou.

"No, it isn't," said Marcus.

A second man joined the first at the glass. He held his weapon in both hands. Another Mossberg, identical to the one in the ginger's hand.

A third pressed his face to the window. Then the fourth appeared. What did they see?

Marcus pulled back from the shelf and turned his head, trying to find what it was that had the gang's attention. Nobody was visible. Everybody was hidden. There wasn't—

The packs. The rifles. They were on the table at the center of the room. Piled high, covering its wide surface.

Marcus gritted his teeth and cursed.

"What?" Lou asked under her breath. "What is it?"

"Look at the table."

Lou stopped swaying. "Mother—"

"Yeah," said Marcus, "tell me about it."

He and Lou locked eyes. It was like both were looking to the other for an answer.

"So what's the plan, then?" Lou said. "Since they're not going to find us."

Marcus frowned. His pulse thumped at his temples. It was distracting. And suddenly he felt every ache and pain in his body. The base of his neck, his knees, his knuckles, and even a tender spot on the back of his elbow hurt.

He bent over to look through the gap again. The men were still at the window, waving and pointing as they talked over one another. They didn't strike Marcus as tactically aware.

"They're not coming through the glass," he said.

"They could shoot through it," she said.

"They won't waste the ammo," he said, trying to convince himself as much as reassure her. "They'll try doors first. They don't know we're here. They see loot. They're pirates. They want it."

"Good point," Lou said. "Let's wait until they move away from the window. I'll take Dallas. The kids can stay with Andrea. There's a bathroom in the back corner. Well, what used to be a bathroom. It's pretty nasty. But it's got a door that locks. They can hide there."

Marcus looked at the ceiling. "You don't want them upstairs?"

"Better if we all stay together," she said. "We can always fall back to the second floor."

"Or third," said Marcus.

"There's a third floor?"

"An empty computer lab and some offices," said Marcus. "But all of the rooms have locks."

Lou reconsidered. "Okay. Third floor for Andrea and the kids."

"Good," said Marcus. "Then Dallas, you, and me take up positions. They have four to our three. But we have the element of surprise."

Lou nodded and Marcus thought he saw the twitch of a smile. Like old times.

The redhead gave one more squint-eyed look through the window, and the men moved away. Marcus guessed they had a minute until the men started trying the doors.

"Dallas," Lou called. "Dallas, get up."

Marcus moved to the table, grabbed one of the rifles, and pulled out the magazine. He took a full mag from an open pack and palmed it into the semiautomatic weapon. He laid the weapon to the side and did the same to a second rifle.

He thought about how he'd spent the last two hours, the preparations he'd already made. There was little chance anyone other than their next conductor would find them here in the Tyler Public Library, but Marcus had learned long ago that little chances were enough to get a man killed.

There were three entrance doors to the library: an entry from the parking lot, a side door with no handle on the outside, and the main entrance, which faced College Street but was closest to where the quartet had been. That was where they'd try to get inside.

Marcus thought he could wait for them there, right by the entry, and tag them as they broke through the glass doors. However, that presented a bigger problem. Even if he killed all four of them, the sound of semiautomatic rifle fire right by open doors might draw more attention. They needed to lie in wait with the guns.

Dallas joined Marcus at the table. "Andrea took the kids upstairs," he said. "They're going to hide in the computer lab away from the windows."

He had a pink crease along his cheek from where he'd slept. There were puffy, bruised circles under his bloodshot eyes. If a young guy like Dallas looked like hell, Marcus wondered which side of zombie he resembled.

Marcus handed him a rifle as Lou joined them. She reached for a rifle. Marcus held out an arm to stop her.

"I need you at the entrance," he said.

Her brow furrowed. "Then give me a gun."

"Use your knives," he said. "Tag one of them. That's it. Then retreat."

"Why?"

"Just do it," said Marcus. "We don't have time for questions."

Lou issued a sarcastic salute.

"Shouldn't she have a gun?" Dallas asked worriedly. "You know the old saying about bringing a knife to a gunfight."

"I also know the old saying about bringing a feral knife-slinging freak to a gunfight," said Marcus. "Trust me. Your wife is going to be fine."

Dallas and Lou silently exchanged glances. No arguing this time.

"Get on the stairs, Dallas," said Marcus. "You'll have a clean line of sight from there to the foyer. Wait until—"

There was a rattling sound coming from the entrance. The intruders were trying the doors.

"Wait until they clear the foyer, or whatever that brick area is called. Lou, after you get one of them, they'll panic a little bit. They'll be on edge."

"Then we lose the element of surprise," she said.

Another rattle at the door—harder. Metal clanged and echoed into the building.

"Not really," said Marcus. "We have three people, not one. As soon as you get your kill, move to the young adult section. You'll find something there for you. Now go."

Lou eyed both men. She touched her hand to Dallas's face and blew him a kiss. Then she moved toward the entry.

Marcus grabbed the remaining rifle and the pack with ammo. He tossed a couple of full mags to Dallas. They nodded an understanding, and Marcus limped to the DVD and CD section close to the front of the space.

He found a good position behind a spinning wire rack. There were a couple of DVDs still on the rack. One of the movies was *Raising Arizona*. Another was the Steve Martin remake of *The Pink Panther*. Marcus couldn't help but smile as he dropped to one aching knee and lowered his pack to the floor beside him.

He checked and saw Dallas on the stairs. He was using the wooden handrail as a brace for his barrel. He was ready to go.

Marcus lifted his knee off the floor, winced, and again rested his weight on it. His kneecap shifted uncomfortably under his weight. He ignored it as best he could and leveled his rifle, pulling the butt tight against his sore shoulder. He wondered if he'd torn something there. His range of motion wasn't what it should be.

In position for a couple of minutes, Marcus wondered what was taking so long. He expected the thug quartet to shatter the glass doors, clear the shards, and move inside. That hadn't happened.

Marcus considered how odd it was the library was mostly intact. There were a few second-floor windows facing the church that were missing. A lot of the books were on the floors in piles. Electronics were gone. A couple of the bookshelves were disassembled and no doubt used as scrap. But the place was otherwise in good shape. Twenty years after Texas descended into chaos and the library was still standing.

He thought about how the Taliban had destroyed the Buddhas of Bamiyan in the months before 9/11. How in Syria, he'd stood at the same spot at Palmyra where the Temple of Baalshamin once dominated the landscape. ISIS ruined it and another temple dedicated to the ancient god Baal.

Yet the library in Tyler, Texas, somehow withstood the litany of gangs and armies that had sought control of the territory. Until today. Because of him and his party, this place would be in tatters by the end of a violent confrontation. He was sure of it.

He wasn't sure, though, why that confrontation hadn't begun. What were the hostiles doing outside the front door?

Surprisingly, Lou appeared at the spot where he expected to see the first of the intruders. She glanced around the room, locked eyes with Marcus, and hustled across the room toward him. She crouched beside him, holding her belly. Her face was pale, her eyes wide. Sweat glistened on her forehead and in the creases that defined her cheeks.

"There are more than four," she said, heavy breathing punctuating the spaces between her words.

Marcus didn't follow. "What?"

"Men. More than four men."

"How many?"

She wiped sweat from her eyes with the back of her hand. It was then he noticed she held a knife. "I dunno. A dozen?"

Marcus clenched his teeth. "It doesn't change anything."

"The hell it doesn't," she said. "There's three of us."

"Kill two at the door," he said. "Three if you have the knives."

Lou grimaced. She touched her stomach.

Marcus looked down and then stole a peek at the front of the building. He swallowed hard. "What?"

"I just had a baby, Marcus. I lost blood. I'm…"

"What?" he pressed.

"Not myself," she admitted. "I don't know if I can take out three men. My fingers are stiff. I'm weak. I—"

"Half of you is better than all of most," he said. "We can't risk gunshots at the entrance. If there's twelve of them now, imagine how many will scurry out of the cracks when they hear rifle fire in the streets. If you want, I can take the door. I understand. You can head upstairs and—"

Lou sucked in a deep breath and steeled herself. She shot a serious look at the doorway and then at Marcus. "I shouldn't have said anything. I'm fine. I'll do the best I can. I'm not letting you take all the glory."

CHAPTER 12

Lou crouched behind a pony wall that hid her from the front door, the wide entry into the library's first floor behind her. The pony wall, if she stayed low, would provide more than enough cover for her to retreat to her second position, which would form a triangular attack amongst Marcus, Dallas, and her.

The tinting on the front door glass, though bubbling and cracked, provided her enough cover that she was sure they hadn't seen her move. None of the men outside had been close enough to the glass to see anything in it other than their own reflections.

Lou readied herself. She took even breaths in and out, controlling her respiration despite her racing heartbeat. She used her shoulder to wipe sweat from the side of her face and pull back damp strands of hair.

She knew Marcus was right; opening fire as the men came in would force them to open fire from where they stood outside the building. It would draw too much attention. But expertly thrown blades that silently killed or maimed the first intruders would force the firefight deeper into the building, muffling at least some of the shotguns' percussive reports.

She balanced the weight of her knives in her hands, one in each like a juggler preparing to begin her act. They were heavy, forged of steel into one singular piece. The handles were wider than the blades. Opposite the hilt, the blades tapered to fine points. Both sides of the blades were sharpened to a hair's width.

The men fumbled outside. She heard them talking. There was laughter, then shouting. A disagreement over something about entry. She made out only every third or fourth word. But she was ready.

Her chest ached, her lower abdomen was sore, and she was sure there was blood. Yet she shoved those thoughts, those sensations, aside and focused all of her attention on the coming storm.

When the talking outside stopped, the doors rattled again. Then there was a dull, vibrating thud. Another. And then a crack. A second crack and the crescendo of breaking glass filled the room.

Lou waited, listening. When soles crunched against glass, she spun, stood, and faced the intruders.

At the front was the redhead. He held his shotgun backwards, clearly having used the butt of it to smash the front door. The cluster of men behind him was a blur at the fringes of her vision. She waited for the ginger to take two more steps into the space, his eyes not having adjusted yet to the darker interior of what was best described as a small lobby or large vestibule.

Lou brought back her elbow, the knife loose in her fingers, and stepped into a quick throw. The knife flipped twice, slicing through the air and sticking into the jugular notch, the soft dip between his neck and his collarbones.

The second the blade sank into his flesh, Lou flipped the second knife from her left to right hand. The redhead dropped the shotgun and stumbled forward two or three more steps. His boots crunched and he grabbed for the knife, his mouth opening and closing like a fish out of water. His eyes widened and narrowed, watering. His brow twitched and his shoulders hunched.

As he fell face forward onto the blade, Lou unleashed her second throw. Focused on the target directly behind the redhead, she hadn't identified much about him except the position of his body. He too held a shotgun. His head was turned to one side, exchanging some comment with a tribesman behind him.

It gave Lou a wider, fleshier target. She overhanded the knife, coming down across her body like an axe-thrower, and buried the blade into the side of the man's neck beneath his ear.

He slapped at the blade like it was a bee sting and gripped the handle. With a puzzled look on his narrow, bearded face, he yanked the knife from his neck. That was a mistake that dropped him instantly and painted everything near him in bright red.

With two men on the floor before the others had even understood what was happening, Lou still had the upper hand. She reached to the small of her back and withdrew the third blade.

There was screaming and yelling now. Men on their knees. Others searching the relative darkness for the threat that took down two men in less than five seconds.

Lou used the chaos and took a wide step to her left, free of the pony wall's protection. Backlit against the light pouring into the space from the glassless doorway, she picked out a shape. The tallest of the men was easiest to spot. Moving left, she sidearmed the blade, flicking with the grace and expertise of someone born to do it. The flat throw spun like a star and found purchase in the gut of the tall man.

Lou didn't wait to see if it felled him. Instead, she used her momentum to arc away from the threats and toward the open library behind her. The men hadn't yet fired a single shot by the time she turned another corner and ducked beyond the opening that led into the first-floor collection of books, magazines, and digital relics of music and film.

Lou moved quickly to the spot opposite Marcus, where she found a waiting rifle. The first of the shotguns' blasts thundered through her body. She drew the loaded weapon to her shoulder and leaned against a bookshelf bolted to the floor.

A second blast sparked a spray of wooden shrapnel that knifed through the air in front of her. Men, one after the other, poured through the narrow opening, like red ants emerging from a disturbed mound.

There weren't twelve men; there were twenty or more. And the three she'd taken down had only angered the others. They were swarming now, and Lou was convinced there was no way she and her family would survive this.

CHAPTER 13

Marcus was ready when Lou bolted past him. He'd heard the screams and the shouts of confusion moments before her sprint. Then came the first shotgun blast. It tore through the wooden trim framing the entry between the lobby and the library's main floor.

The second shot did the same, and now men were moving through the opening one after the other.

Knowing they were vastly outnumbered, Marcus applied pressure to the rifle trigger and fired a three-round burst at the first target he could home in on.

One down. He scanned left and took down another man. And another. From behind him and to his left, the cracks of identical rifle fire joined his own. Lou and Dallas were joining him in the shooting gallery born from a public library.

The chaotic symphony of the rifles' *rat-tat-tat-tat* and the explosive, bone-rattling blasts from the tribe members' shotguns was deafening and disorienting. Marcus couldn't hear himself think. In truth, he *wasn't* thinking, he was reacting.

This was instinctive and primal. It was something he'd done so many times it was like breathing for him. One after the next, he found a target and hit it.

It was almost as if the tribesmen were unarmed, or so unaccustomed to close-quarter combat that their sheer numbers, which Marcus now guessed was greater than thirty, didn't matter.

Marcus exchanged magazines as a blast rained drywall onto him. He spat the dust from his mouth and leveled his weapon. But the onslaught was over. The remaining tribesmen had retreated. The last of them backed through the entry and fired off one last cover shot before he disappeared.

His ears ringing, nostrils burning from the acrid odor of spent gunpowder, Marcus surveyed the battlefield in front of him. A quick count told him twenty-three men were dead. Another three were alive, although barely. Their heavy breathing, their pained groans begging for help were the only remnant sounds in the room, muffled by the high-pitched din that made it hard for Marcus to hear anything.

The adrenaline still surging through him, he stood from his position and ignored the sharp pains in his joints, the pressure in his knee, and moved to the first of the three twitching men.

Marcus put the muzzle to his forehead and pulled the trigger, fixing the tribesman's fear-laden eyes. The life gone from them, they still stared at Marcus, asking for mercy.

Amidst wide steps that avoided outstretched arms and legs, he moved to the second life-clinger. The man was facedown, his fingers scratching at the floor. His back heaved up and down.

"Lou," Marcus said, pressing the muzzle against the back of the man's neck, "you and Dallas head to the second floor. Now."

He pulled the trigger. Marcus stood over him, watching the life drain from the tribesman, and on the back of his forearm he spotted a bright red tattoo. It was a blooming rose wrapped in thorns, and across it were the calligraphy-styled words *La Rosa*.

The third man had stopped moving by the time Marcus reached

him. He poked him with the barrel. No reaction, no breathing. Blood pooled out from under him, spreading into a dark amorphous pool.

Outside, beyond the entry, Marcus heard more shouting. It was muffled, like everything else, yet he was sure he heard the rumble of an engine, the squeal of brakes slamming hard against rubber tires, the tires sliding across the asphalt.

More men were coming. That was certain. Marcus fell back between two bookshelves and limped hurriedly toward the stairs at the rear of the space. He hit a lever that released the rifle's magazine into his hand and tucked the partially emptied mag into his back, pulling a fresh, fully loaded one from the pack that hung from his right shoulder.

Marcus slapped the new mag into the rifle and reached the stairs. Lou and Dallas had done what he had asked. They were on the second floor now, reinforcing their positions. Marcus stepped onto the spent casings from Dallas's contribution to their firefight. They crunched and bent under the soles of his heavy boots, and he climbed the stairs without the use of the railing. More were coming. It was the story of Marcus Battle's life. More were always coming.

CHAPTER 14

APRIL 21, 2054, 6:53 AM
SCOURGE +21 YEARS, 7 MONTHS
TYLER, TEXAS

Through one of the open windows at the front of the second floor, Marcus used a broken piece of tinted glass to find the muddied reflection of two pickup trucks parked next to each other in the middle of the street. Around them, clusters of men, twenty or thirty in all, stood together, plotting.

He considered using this spot like a sniper, picking off a handful of the men before they could reenter the building, but that would give away their position. He didn't want them knowing yet they were on the second floor. As it was, all hostiles would have to take the stairs. That funneled them into a hallway and created the perfect choke point.

It was the first time in twenty years Marcus was glad the power was out. It meant the tribesmen couldn't use the elevator. They'd have to take the stairs. Marcus angled the shard in his hand to count the men on the street below. Satisfied he had a close approximation, he moved into the hallway, where he found Lou and Dallas shoulder to shoulder near the landing at the top of the stairwell. They stopped talking when Marcus approached. He was keenly aware by the way they averted their eyes he was their topic of conversation.

"Go ahead," he said. "Spill it."

"Spill what?" asked Lou.

"You were talking about me," Marcus said. "Normally I wouldn't care. Not a bit. But right now, I gotta know where your head's at."

"Right now, I'm going to chastise you for ending a sentence in a preposition," said Lou. "That's horrible grammar, even for you."

"I'm flattered," said Marcus. "But seriously, what's up?"

Dallas exchanged a look with Lou and then narrowed his gaze. He took a step toward Marcus. "We should have used this from the beginning," he said of the landing. "They might never have come upstairs. If they had, we'd have gotten them like fish in a barrel."

"Maybe," said Marcus.

Dallas's posture stiffened. He cocked his head to one side. "No maybe about it," he said. "You put my wife, the mother of my children, in danger. You made her the front line and without a gun."

Marcus shrugged. "And?"

Dallas's face reddened. "And? *And?*" His voice grew louder. "You're going to stand here and act like—"

Marcus held up a hand to stop him. "I'm not acting like anything. I'm asking why it's an issue now. First of all, she's fine. Second, you saw what was happening, and you didn't do anything to stop me. I didn't see you volunteering to take the door."

Dallas stepped closer to Marcus, his lips curled into a snarl.

Lou stuck a hand between the two of them. "Now is not the time for this," she said. "We can talk about it later."

"I knew this was a bad idea," said Dallas, venom oozing. "I knew involving Marcus was wrong. Norma was right. We're more likely to die with Marcus Battle around us than we would without him. His help is deadly."

The words stung. In part because Marcus knew they rang true. He *had* put Lou in danger. He *had* ignored her concerns.

Did it matter that he had valid reasons? He'd done it because he thought she was the best person for the job. He'd kept them on the first floor to keep them as far away from Andrea and the children as possible. He'd done it when they thought there were only four adversaries. And then, when Lou told him there were more, there wasn't enough time to change the plan. That would have been more dangerous.

Standing here, all of his justifications were null. Instead of arguing with Dallas, he accepted the charges. Taking a step back, he frowned. He scratched the scruff on his chin, feeling the coarse hair and the wrinkled skin absent its youthful elasticity. He dug the toe of a boot into the floor. "We can do this later," he said. "In the meantime, we need to be on the same team."

They took positions in the wide hallway along the open railing that looked down onto the stairwell. A loud bang echoed from downstairs, followed by the sound of shattering glass.

"They're in," said Marcus. "Heads up."

The stairwell was narrow, enough space for two people shoulder to shoulder. It rose from the first floor and turned one hundred and eighty degrees halfway up. From their positions along the railing opposite a wall, they could see clearly from the mid-ascent landing up the length of the flight to their second-floor landing.

The three of them braced for the advancing tribesmen. Heavy footsteps grew louder. Shouts of disbelief at the first-floor carnage echoed up through the wide well.

The adrenaline surged and Marcus worked to maintain his steady hands on his rifle. His lower back tensed as he leaned in toward the railing.

Marcus was closest to the second-floor landing at the top of the stairwell, the most exposed to any return fire. Dallas was to his right, a few steps to the side. At the end, most protected, was Lou.

Finger on the trigger, Marcus flicked the safety lever into Semi mode. With so many adversaries he knew he had to conserve ammo and make every single shot count. The ringing in his ears had finally diminished. He knew that was short-lived.

Marcus swallowed hard and tasted the dryness of his mouth. Thirst consumed him for a brief second before the first of the tribesmen appeared at the landing, turning cautiously toward the second flight of steps.

Without hesitation, Marcus applied pressure to the trigger. The rifle thumped against his shoulder. He pressed again. Immediately, his weapon drilled twin shots into the target at his rib cage beneath his armpit. The tribesman hadn't even fully turned the corner when the two rounds punctured him and sent him back down the stairs, grunting and staggering.

His momentum sounded like it took more men with him. They cursed and shouted at each other. Marcus glanced at Lou and moved closer to the landing. Then he took a step down. Another. And another.

"Marcus," Lou called out, "don't—"

He ignored her and took another step as two men appeared at the landing. Marcus saw them before they saw him, and he unloaded a half dozen rounds before they'd even pulled the trigger once.

One of them did get off a shot, but it went wide and high, peppering the drywall to the left of Marcus's head with buckshot. A cloud of white dust bloomed beside him, and Marcus took another two steps down the stairs.

Now he could see around the corner, onto the first flight and beyond it onto the first floor. Three men were on the stairs, navigating the dead bodies in their path. Marcus picked them off one at a time. Four shots, three kills. He descended to the landing and kicked aside the arm of a dead man in his way.

Another man appeared between bookshelves and the bottom of the stairs. He had the drop on Marcus and took a pair of shots with a handgun. They missed, both of them slamming into the wall with thick cracks. Their displacement whizzed past Marcus at his elbow before he returned fire with a single shot to the head.

As the enemy slinked to the ground like a blow-up doll losing all of its air, two more men took shots at Marcus. At the edge of the nearest bookcase, their line of sight was poor enough that they both missed. One of them hit the railing in front of Marcus, and splinters of wood exploded at him, pieces cutting his left cheek and temple, barely missing his eye.

He fired back. Even though he couldn't clearly see them, there was enough there for him to find center mass on one and the arm of the other.

The injured one cried out in pain and staggered from behind the bookshelf enough for Marcus to plunk him in the chest. Marcus fired again. The weapon's bolt locked back. His gun was empty. The man stumbled backward and collapsed, his head slapping against the side of the bookshelf with a crack, and he dropped to the floor.

The building was dimly lit. Shades of gray dominated the interior despite the rising sun outside. At this spot, Marcus was exposed. He couldn't see beyond the first row of bookshelves. But whoever was on the first floor looking toward the landing could see his legs. They could disable him with a quick shot and he'd be done. Marcus backed up toward the corner of the landing. This way he could see anyone approaching the stairwell before they'd see him. It was a good spot. He quickly drew another magazine from his pack and saw the wide tear in the canvas bag. It had taken a shot. Marcus shook his head. If it weren't for luck, he'd have died a thousand times.

He scanned the area in front of him, focused, determined. Nobody came. He checked the bodies in front of him. There were nine bodies. Nine. That was all. He replaced the magazine in the rifle and hit the bolt release lever. The gun slammed a new round in the chamber.

Where were the others? He'd counted two dozen. Two dozen and only nine dead? That left another fifteen men. Marcus wasn't great at math, but he knew enough to understand something was wrong.

He started to turn back toward the second flight when he heard a commotion directly above him and Lou screamed.

CHAPTER 15

APRIL 21, 2054, 6:58 AM
SCOURGE +21 YEARS, 7 MONTHS
TYLER, TEXAS

Lou was about to follow Marcus to the first floor when she heard a bang to her right. She'd moved between her husband and the second-floor landing when what sounded like an explosion forced her to stop. It took her a moment in the dim light of the second floor to realize what she was seeing. A man was flying through one of the windows at the landing to the third flight of stairs. His feet filled the space first and he landed awkwardly inches from Dallas.

Then a second, third, and fourth man bounded through the window, barreling onto the second floor. It was like something out of a fantastic novel, pure fiction. Like monkeys flying through the air and dive-bombing travelers at the behest of a wicked witch, one after the other descended upon them. More men were running down the stairs now from the third floor.

Lou screamed for Dallas to move. She lifted her rifle and aimed it toward the dark figures filling the space. Her finger found the trigger and she pulled. Once. Twice. Three times. She hit a pair of them before they set their feet and steadied themselves.

Dallas was knocked to the ground. A man was on top of him,

pinning him to the floor. A second kicked his rifle clear of his grasp.

Lou shifted her aim and fired. She hit the one who'd kicked the rifle, and he toppled back when a second round found his gut. He tripped over Dallas and the tribesman on top of him. The three of them were a heap on the floor. More men advanced.

There were six or seven of them now. Lou took aim. She hit two of them. Four kept coming. Dallas was still on the floor. She couldn't get to him, and she couldn't take a shot or she'd risk hitting him.

One of the men at the landing raised his shotgun. Lou didn't see him quickly enough. He had her in his sights before she could take the first shot.

In that split second, Lou saw a lifetime flash before her. A flicker of images, one after the other, filled her field of view. She tried sucking in a breath but couldn't. She realized she hadn't yet named her newborn. She would never know the child's name.

A loud pop sounded and Lou brought her hand to her chest. She gripped the damp fabric in one hand, the rifle falling to her side. She was light-headed.

Then something strange happened. The one with the shotgun stared blankly at her and dropped, a red stain spreading across his shirt.

"Get back!" Marcus shouted, taking aim at the horde. One after the other he took them down.

Stunned, Lou took a step back before getting her wits about her and lunging forward. She crashed on top of the one holding down her husband, pounding at the back of his head with her fists. He was stronger than her and elbowed her off him. Lou regained her balance and reached for her boot. Pulling free the smallest of her knives, she brought it up and jammed it straight down into the back of his neck.

He immediately went limp. His body shuddered, twitching oddly, before all movement ceased.

Above her, around her, Marcus fought. The sound of gunfire was relentless.

Lou shoved the body off her husband. Dallas was unconscious. His neck was bruised, his mouth hanging open. The gunfire stopped abruptly.

Lou knelt beside Dallas and placed her head to his chest. Then she put her cheek next to his nose and mouth. "He's breathing," she said. "He has a pulse."

The floor around her was littered with dead men. A half dozen of them were splayed out, their limbs and necks at awkward angles. They'd come from the roof, from the third floor.

The third floor.

"Marcus," she said, "the children. Andrea." Her vision blurred; her eyes flooded with tears. They rolled down her cheeks. "The children," she repeated.

Marcus's expression tightened. He dropped to one knee, put the rifle on the ground, and shrugged his pack from his shoulder. With his right hand he fished out a fresh magazine. "Last mag," he said, and with one hand he swapped out the magazines. "I'll be back. They'll be fine. You worry about Dallas."

Lou suppressed a sob. Throbs of pain swelled from low in her gut. She focused her attention on her husband, not sure what she could do for him.

When she heard the voice behind her, Lou thought it was Marcus at first. But the voice didn't sound like his. It was higher pitched and thick with a Southern twang. And what the voice said didn't make any sense.

"Put down the gun," said the rail-thin, stringy-haired man at the landing that led to the third flight of stairs. He was staring at Marcus with his near-set beady eyes. There was a rose red tattoo on the back of his hand.

"I ain't gonna say it a third time," he warned. "Next thing you'll hear is a gunshot and your head explodin'."

CHAPTER 16

APRIL 21, 2054, 7:06 AM
SCOURGE +21 YEARS, 7 MONTHS
TYLER, TEXAS

Marcus didn't like people telling him what to do. He especially wasn't fond of threats that came at the end of a gun barrel. He stole a quick glance at Lou before settling his gaze back on the tribesman who had him in his sights. The tribesman, despite his bravado, looked young to Marcus. He couldn't be more than twenty and was definitely a greenhorn.

The gun trembled in his hand. His eyes, though close set and dark, were framed with apprehension. The kid was more afraid of Marcus than Marcus was of him.

Had Marcus been able to use both hands, he likely would have managed to get off a shot before the punk could do anything about it. If the young tribesman had returned fire, there was a good chance the shot would have missed.

Unfortunately, though, a previous shot hadn't missed. The skin between his left thumb and forefinger was shredded. That part of his hand was called the purlicue. Marcus knew this because Lou had long ago schooled him on odd anatomical terminology she'd picked up from books. Although he'd forgotten most of the words, purlicue stuck. It sounded like curlicue to Marcus.

He was losing blood, not having had time to do anything about the wound, and he wasn't about to hassle Lou over a flesh wound. The injury throbbed. Cold sweat formed at his forehead, behind his ears, and on the back of his neck. He guessed the young gun across from him figured the perspiration was because of him.

"I'll put down the gun," said Marcus, "but I'm gonna need some answers first."

"You're not in any shape to make demands," said the punk. He stressed the first syllable of the word *demand* with a long *e*.

Marcus held up his blood-soaked left hand. Lou gasped. Marcus forced a smile at her and then turned his attention back to the tribesman. "You're right," he said, his voice calm and even. "I'm not in any shape. I can't use my left hand. So there's no way I can shoot you with my right before you'd empty that Sig Sauer into my chest. I'd be Swiss cheese before I take aim."

The punk's eyes focused on the wounded hand, his brow twitching. He glanced up the stairs, where Marcus couldn't see, at Lou, and then back to his target. His hand still trembled. "You need to drop that weapon," said the kid. "I—"

"I will," Marcus said, turning his bloody hand back and forth. "I'm a man of my word. But you need to stay calm and answer a couple of questions. You help me; I help you."

Thick beads of sweat bloomed on the punk's face. He licked his lips and nodded almost imperceptibly. "Go ahead, ask. But if I see one false move, you try anything, I'm gonna shoot you and your woman here."

Marcus didn't bother correcting him. "Are you alone?"

The man hesitated then shook his head. His eyes again darted up the flight of stairs.

"How many?"

The punk frowned. "I ain't answering that."

"Are the kids—"

An impatient shout from upstairs boomed. "What's goin' on down there, Reaper? Is it clear?"

A smile twitched on Marcus's face, but he frowned to mask it. The pain in his hand pulsed with every heartbeat. "Reaper?" he said with as much sincerity as he could muster.

"Hold yer horses," Reaper called upstairs. "I'm clearin' it." Then he addressed Marcus. "You got two more questions. That's it."

"Are the children okay?"

"Fer now."

"And the woman? Her name is Andrea. The children's names are—"

Something flashed at the corner of Marcus's vision, zipping into view, and the man's eyes went wide. The gun fell to the floor. He grabbed at his throat, at the knife sticking out of it to one side. He wobbled, gargled, and collapsed.

Marcus found Lou still huddled over her husband. Her attention turned from the dead punk to Marcus. "Dallas keeps a knife in his boot," she said, "and I was tired of the conversation."

Marcus lifted his left hand and tried putting his index finger close to his lips. He took a couple of quick steps to Lou and crouched, the rifle still in his right hand. "I don't know how many men are up there. I'm guessing three or four."

Lou looked past him and up at the ceiling, as if she could see through it. Dallas coughed and his hand went to his throat. His eyes fluttered open and he tried moving.

Lou touched his forehead and leaned in. "You're okay," she said. "You're going to be okay. But I need to go. Can you wait here?"

Another cough. When he tried speaking, what came out sounded like a raspy squeak.

"Shhh," said Lou. "You're okay. Just lie here for a minute. I need to check on something. Just stay here on the floor."

Dallas reached for her, gripping her wrist, and shook his head. The terror in his eyes told Marcus the man still didn't understand what was happening.

Lou looked over at Marcus for help, her expression somewhere between fear and desperation.

"We'll be right back, Dallas," Marcus said. "It's almost over."

Before he could protest, an impatient voice called from upstairs, "Reaper? We've got to do this."

Lou moved to the dead punk and pulled the knife from his neck. She didn't bother wiping the blade. Turning to Marcus, who stood next to her now, she looked down at his hand. "Can you use that thing?" she asked, tucking the bloody knife into the small of her back and picking up the semiautomatic pistol.

"My hand or the rifle?" Marcus asked as they both took the first step toward the third floor. The landing above them was empty.

"Either," she said. "Both."

"I think so."

He lifted the rifle and held his forearm out in front of him, parallel with the floor. With his right hand he adjusted his grip on the trigger and tucked the butt as tight as he could against his shoulder.

Lou held the pistol with both hands, her elbows bent. She leaned forward into each step as she climbed. Marcus stepped past her, taking the lead.

Unlike the first two floors, there was no open railing, no balustrade on one side that gave someone a view onto the steps as someone walked by them. It was a solid wall on both sides of the steps.

They were a few steps from the landing when a shape emerged. The end of his shotgun appeared before he did. "Reaper, you are gonna—"

Lou aimed. Two quick shots found their target. Still, he managed a single blast, which tore into the wall next to Lou. She shrieked and grunted as the enemy fell forward and tumbled headfirst down the stairs between her and Marcus.

"You okay?" he asked.

"Yeah. I'm fine."

"Let's do this," he said.

They bounded up the final steps and onto the landing. Marcus spun to his left and scanned the open hallway. Lou was at his shoulder, behind him, mimicking the sweeping motion.

It was empty. Together they moved forward, taking long strides. Marcus's vision wavered. Breathing was becoming more difficult. His movements felt stilted, off-balance. He was still bleeding.

Puffing air through his cheeks, he advanced, sweeping past the open door of the computer lab and one of the offices. They were getting closer to the end of the hall.

Lou was to his right. She moved gracefully, especially considering she'd given birth since she'd last had a good night's sleep or a hot meal or a shower. She was a singular woman. He was proud of her.

Had he told her that? He had. Hadn't he? Or had he just told her that her father would have been proud of her? His memory was fuzzy on the subject. The edges were soft on a lot of memories now. Faces were blurry shapes, features only rough caricatures of what they'd been.

He couldn't remember Sylvia's face anymore. Lola's neither. Had Wes's eyes been brown? Green? Or was Sawyer the one with green eyes? Penny?

Marcus wobbled. His shoulder bumped against the wall and he teetered forward. Lou caught his right elbow and steadied him. He nodded at her, blinked his vision back into focus, and pushed toward the door at the end of the hall.

"They've got to be in there," Marcus said under his breath. "I'll go first."

Lou started to argue. "They're my kids. I—"

Marcus bolted to the door, covering the last few feet in an instant. He burst through with all of his might, and the wooden door banged off its hinges. Splinters of wood exploded around him, and the door slammed against the wall behind it.

Marcus leveled his rifle. Lou had her finger on the trigger. Both of them were ready to kill. The room was empty.

They swept in circles, confused. The window at the far corner of the room was open. Outside, the familiar crack of gunfire punctured the silence three times in quick succession. Then another volley of rapid fire echoed from the street below.

Lou beat Marcus to the window. Her gasp worried him. In the orange light of early morning, he saw Andrea holding the two babies. They were in the back of the truck Marcus had seen reflected in the tinted glass. David and Javier were next to her. All of them appeared okay.

Bodies surrounded the truck, lying still where they fell. A man stood at the tailgate, a rifle in his hands.

"Hey!" yelled Lou. "What are you doing with my kids?"

Swinging quickly, he lifted the rifle toward her. She raised her hands over her head then tossed the gun out the window. It bounced off a fire escape and slapped the ground three stories below.

He lowered the rifle, but kept his finger close to the trigger. He motioned to the truck bed. "These are your kids?"

"Two of them," Lou said. "The other two are hers. She's Andrea."

"We've met. I'm your new conductor. You'd better hurry. We'd best get a move on before reinforcements show up. La Rosa won't take kindly to your lack of hospitality."

CHAPTER 17

APRIL 21, 2054, 8:20 AM
SCOURGE +21 YEARS, 7 MONTHS
ATLANTA, GEORGIA

Rickshaw stood outside the cell. The lead from his West Virginia team was next to him. The soldier's heavy lids struggled to stay open even as he stood there. He startled when Rickshaw slapped him on the shoulder.

"Good work," he said to the soldier. "You made excellent time."

"Thank you, Captain. Do you need anything else?"

Rickshaw looked through the door at the ragged man chained to the stainless-steel table in the middle of the cell and shook his head. "No, I can take it from here. Get some rest. You look like hell."

"Thank you, Captain."

In his mind, Rickshaw replayed the message he'd received just before leaving his office to come to the cell. It was from a superior, reminding him of his failures, failing to recognize his successes, and warning him he was running out of time.

"If you can't find the Harbor," it had said, *"we'll get someone else who can. And if you can't put a stop to the fugitives who break our laws and then find refuge outside our sphere of influence, we'll get someone else who can."*

Rickshaw had replied to the message, "Understood."

That was the only thing he could say. His superiors had long proven they were immune, if not allergic to, excuses. He'd learned from them the value of constant pressure, how the threat of painful consequences was more effective than the application of them. He knew that if he didn't accomplish the task they'd assigned, and do it on his own without their assistance, he'd be out of a job or worse. Pop Guard captains didn't grow old if they were ex-captains.

Rickshaw used the biometric scanner, waited for the door to whoosh open, and stepped into the cell. Inside the room on either side of the door were two guards. Neither of them said anything to Rickshaw when he entered, but they stood straighter as he passed. They lifted their chins, pulled back their shoulders, and tightened their grips on their weapons.

"I hear you've come a long way to see me," said Rickshaw. "I appreciate the effort."

He pulled back a chair, pulled his Ruger Blackhawk six-shooter from his hip, and set it on the table. He flipped his duster wide with his wrists and sat down with a flourish.

The prisoner hung his head low, his chin to his chest. Rickshaw noticed the beginnings of male-pattern baldness. A thinning circle of hair spiraled outward.

"Have they offered you anything to drink? Are you hungry?" asked Rickshaw. "I'm sure we can get you something."

Without waiting for a response, he snapped his fingers. "One of you get this man some water. Maybe a piece of fruit. Fruit is a delicacy. It's the least we can do."

The guards exchanged nervous glares before both of them moved toward the door. One stopped and the other pressed his eye to the scanner. The door whooshed open. It wasn't shut yet when the prisoner spoke.

"I don't know anything that can help you," he said. "I already told your people that."

The man didn't look up as he spoke. His voice was soft but firm.

It hinted at a reluctant defiance. Rickshaw chuckled. He flexed his fingers and the knuckles popped. The series of snaps echoed in the room.

"*My* people?" said Rickshaw. "We're all the same people, friend. We're all in this together. I'm on your side here. If I weren't, you'd know it."

Rickshaw reached for his weapon. He flicked the barrel with his index finger and the weapon spun like a top on the stainless-steel table. He waited until it stopped, the barrel pointing at the prisoner.

"As for whether or not you know anything that's useful," said Rickshaw, "I'm going to be the judge of that. I think it's arrogant of you, almost disrespectful, to think you know what I'll find useful and what I won't."

The prisoner lifted his head and glared at Rickshaw. His thin face was unshaven, the beard blotchy and hidden underneath grime and blood. His shaggy brown hair was cut short, and his nose was long and thin. It also might have been broken. There was swelling along its side, and dark, bruise-colored crescents gave his eyes the appearance of a raccoon. At least it reminded Rickshaw of what a raccoon might look like. He hadn't seen one in so long it was hard to remember.

"I'm not on your team." The prisoner sneered, one side of his chapped lips lifting higher than the other. "And I'm not your friend."

Rickshaw chuckled again and planted his elbows on the stainless-steel table, pointing at his prisoner with a wagging finger. "That's a delayed reaction," he said. "You okay in the head? Did they rough you up a little too much on the way here from West Virginia?"

"I don't have anything to say. You killed my wife. You killed my friends. Even if I knew something, and I don't, I wouldn't tell you if my life depended on it."

Rickshaw couldn't resist the broad grin that spread across his face. It was too good a lob not to smack it out of the park. "Your life *does* depend on it," he said and motioned around the cell with one hand.

"I thought all of this made that abundantly clear. I wouldn't bring you here, offer you water and fruit, play nice, if I didn't think your information is worth the effort."

A sour look appeared tattooed on the prisoner's face. He didn't react, only sat there glaring intently and with malice at Rickshaw.

The captain decided to take a different tack. Time was essential. The abandoned harbor at Greenbrier made that apparent. Whatever information this man held, it most likely had an expiration date. Rickshaw slapped his palms on the table and stood. The prisoner shuddered but was otherwise unmoved as the captain slid the gun into his hand and moved around the table.

"Let's do this," he said, "since you seem unaffected by my hospitality and my charms. And since you're convinced you don't know anything of value, I'm inclined to be a little more aggressive."

The door whooshed open and a guard appeared with a bowl of red grapes and a glass of water. His rifle was slung over his shoulder. He stood in the open doorway, evidently unsure of what to do.

Rickshaw, who was now standing next to the prisoner, nodded at the guard and eyed the table. The guard scurried across the cell and set the bowl and glass next to the prisoner's hands. He backed away, his attention on Rickshaw, and unslung his rifle, resuming his position at the door.

"The timing isn't great," said Rickshaw, pointing the gun at the snack, "but I'm a good guy. I'm fair. I did make the offer. It would be rude if I took it away from you. You answer my questions and it's yours."

The prisoner didn't move, his gaze somewhere in the distance beyond the walls of the cell. His hands were clasped, fingers laced, and he didn't strain against the binds. His forearms rested on the table, his elbows hanging off the edge of it.

"Grapes are drought resistant," said Rickshaw. "They don't take a lot of water. Same as pomegranates, figs, dragon fruit. While I don't have any of those more exotic offerings for you, I can attest that the grapes are delicious. They have seeds in them, so be careful not to—"

"I don't want your grapes," the prisoner seethed. "I don't want–"

Rickshaw backhanded the prisoner, slapping him so hard spit flew from the man's mouth. He grunted and looked up at Rickshaw with surprise, his cheek turning red. His eyes were suddenly wide with fear.

Rickshaw bent closer and spoke in a low, even tone intended to induce more terror than a yell. "Where is the Harbor?"

Stunned into silence, the prisoner licked a spot of blood from the corner of his mouth and shook his head.

"Where is it?" Rickshaw demanded. "This is only going to become more unpleasant for you. Less grapes and water, more pain and blood."

Rickshaw backhanded him again, along the other side of his face. The strike whipped his head away from Rickshaw. The surprise of it had him whimpering now. Rickshaw could tell the prisoner was trying to keep himself composed, trying to stay in control, but was losing the internal struggle.

"Where is it?"

The man sputtered and spat blood onto the table. It bubbled in a sticky splotch next to his arm. The metal cuffs dug into his wrists. His fingers were balled into fists, his knuckles white.

"Where is it?"

He shook his head and looked up at Rickshaw. He said something, but it was inaudible.

"Speak up," said Rickshaw.

"They moved it," he said. "I don't know where to, but it happened a few weeks ago."

Rickshaw reached out toward the prisoner with his free hand. The man flinched, his body rigid.

"See?" said Rickshaw, stroking a bright red cheek with the back of his hand. "Was that so hard?"

The man trembled, his eyes flitting around the room as if looking for help that wasn't coming.

"What's your name, friend?" asked Rickshaw. "I'm Greg. My friends call me Greg."

The man's face twitched. The question seemed to throw him. It was part of Rickshaw's method. With a man who'd gone from rabidly defiant to compliant so quickly, this was the next step.

"Blair," said the man. He was drooling now.

Rickshaw sat on the edge of the desk and smiled. "Blair. That first or last?"

"First."

"Last?"

"Evans."

"Blair Evans," said Rickshaw, trying out the sound of it. "Okay then, tell me, Blair, where did they move it?"

Blair's brow furrowed and he shook his head. "I don't know. I told you that."

Rickshaw frowned. "You also told me you had nothing of value, nothing in which I'd be interested."

"I don't know," said Blair. "Everything is a secret. Only people who need to know are told things. I wasn't told things like that."

"Things like that?" Rickshaw asked, arching an eyebrow. "So you were told *things,* just not things like where the Harbor is."

Blair swallowed hard. He looked down, flexing his hands against the binds. He'd slipped up, and both he and Rickshaw knew it.

The captain held up his revolver and opened the cylinder. He emptied it into his palm and then put one round into the weapon. He spun the cylinder. "You need to reevaluate what you think I might find of interest, Blair," he said. "And you need to do it fast."

Blair stared at the revolver with wide, frightened eyes. "What are you doing? Are you gonna shoot me?"

"That depends on you," said Rickshaw.

The captain stood and turned around. With one hand he gripped Blair's wrist at the metal cuff. He held it there, flat against the table, while the prisoner struggled and pleaded.

Rickshaw pressed the barrel into the back of Blair's left hand and pulled the trigger.

Click.

"You're crazy!" said Blair. "You're out of your mind. I don't know anything! I don't—"

Click.

"Please!" Blair begged. "Don't do this. There's nothing I can—"

Click.

Tears streamed down Blair's flushed cheeks, tracing lines in the grime. He struggled against Rickshaw's grip but couldn't free himself.

"Okay!" he said. "Okay! I know something. I overheard some things, things I wasn't supposed to hear."

Click.

"Stop!" he cried. "There's a place in Atlanta where they coordinate, where they plan. I know a place."

Rickshaw lifted the revolver and let go of Blair's wrist. The prisoner sank in his seat, the tension leaking from his body like air from a punctured balloon. He sobbed, his shoulders bouncing up and down.

The captain walked around the table and lowered himself into his chair. He reached out and slid the glass of water to the blubbering prisoner. "Take a drink," said Rickshaw. "Calm yourself, Blair."

Blair reached for the glass. He lowered his head toward his chained hands and hesitantly took a sip. Then he gulped it empty, wiping his mouth and nose on his shoulder.

"Tell me more about the place in Atlanta," said Rickshaw. "Tell me everything you know."

CHAPTER 18

APRIL 21, 2054, 8:30 AM
SCOURGE +21 YEARS, 7 MONTHS
PUTNAM, TEXAS

Norma lifted the brim of her hat and wiped the sweat from her forehead. The heat beat on her back as she rode east, away from the sun. She eyed the full canteen hanging from the side of her saddle. It was calling her.

"Don't wait until you're thirsty," said Rudy, riding alongside her. "You're already dehydrated at that point. No offense, but I don't want to be picking you up off the highway."

They were saddled on the backs of two of the poachers' horses. A third trailed behind them, serving as a packhorse, loaded down with extra supplies, water, food, and weapons.

"We've only been riding for two hours, Rudy. We've got two days until we hit the wall. I don't want to waste it."

"If you're drinking it, it's not waste."

Norma relented and lifted the canteen. She took a couple of healthy swigs and offered it to Rudy, who declined.

"I had some a couple of miles back," he said. "I'm not as cautious as you are."

"How are you holding up?" she asked.

"Good. It hurts, but I'm good."

"Where does it hurt?"

He smiled broadly. "Everywhere."

Norma blew him a kiss and shifted her weight in the saddle. Her boots pressed against the stirrups. She was as comfortable as she could be on someone else's horse. They were riding along the edge of the interstate, headed due east.

They'd started on the asphalt but decided it was better for the horses to walk on the dirt that stretched in all directions around the thin gray line of highway that ran from Pecos to Latex and beyond.

Aside from the heat, it had been an easy ride so far. As long as Rudy was okay, she was good. The sounds of the horses' shoes on the hard earth and the sway of her body in the worn leather saddle lulled her into a trance. Her mind drifted.

Rudy whistled occasionally, sometimes he hummed, but he didn't intrude. He didn't ask her what she was thinking or try to strike up a conversation laden with small talk. He knew her so well, she thought. He was her other half and she knew she was his.

It was his life, as much as anyone else's in Baird, she'd tried to protect by asking Marcus to leave more than a decade earlier. Rudy was loyal to Marcus. The venerated Mad Max, the crazy soldier who'd beaten back the Cartel in the legendary battle at Palo Duro Canyon, had led him on a suicidal rescue mission that recovered her, Gladys, and Gladys's sister.

"We owe him," Rudy had said too many times to count. "I owe him. I can't just walk away from him."

Norma had known that Rudy would never leave Marcus. He'd give his life, if that's what circumstances dictated, in favor of abandoning the reluctant, brooding hero.

"He couldn't keep his family alive," she'd told him. "Either of them. What makes you think he can keep an entire town safe? And if you're by his side?"

It was a callous thing to say. Norma had known that the moment she'd said it. She'd seen the hurt in Rudy's eyes, the disappointment spread across his face like darkness at sundown.

Rather than push her husband to leave Baird, to leave Marcus, she did what she thought was her only viable option. It had been the only thing she knew to do that would keep her husband, their friends, and their family safe.

Though that action hadn't bothered her then, it did now. As they rode east toward the coast all these years later, her conscience wore at her. It was time to come clean.

"I have something to confess," she said, her words cutting through the warm air and ending the long minutes of silence they'd shared.

Rudy stopped humming and glanced at her. "Confess?"

"It's something I did," Norma said. "Something I probably shouldn't have done. Looking back, I definitely shouldn't have done it."

Rudy's expression tightened. His eyebrows knitted, and he turned his body toward her. He eased his horse to keep even with Norma's. "That sounds serious."

Norma sucked in a deep breath. The warm air filled her lungs, and she held it there for a long moment, nodding on exhale. "Yes, it's serious. And I was wrong. I thought I was right. I really—"

"What did you do?" Rudy cut in with a hint of worry. While his tone wasn't accusatory, nor was it sympathetic.

"It's two things, really," Norma said. Her heart pounded in her chest. The rapid pulse in her ears was almost deafening. Her palms were sweaty against the leather reins. "All those years ago, when Marcus left Baird, you remember how I said something about him not coming back?"

"I remember," said Rudy. "You said something about him knowing his value elsewhere. We were arguing with that guy Harold, the one who gave him the truck. It was Harold, right? Died of a heart attack a few months later?"

"It was Harold," said Norma. "And yeah, I hinted Marcus shouldn't come back. But that wasn't all I did."

Rudy frowned. He reached for the saddle horn and gripped it. "What do you mean?"

"I gave him a note before he got in the truck and drove off. Well, when Lou was trying to give him her Astros cap, I put the note in his bag. He didn't see me do it. I don't know when he actually saw the note."

"What did it say?"

Norma swallowed and looked down at the horse's thick black mane. It was easier to do that than look her husband in the eye. "It asked him not to come back. In no uncertain terms, I laid out my case for why I didn't want him around my family, why I thought he was a danger to us. His insistence on ending things violently, on making every solution a permanent one when I thought it wasn't necessary, only served to put us in danger."

"You'd already made that clear," he said. "Why did you need a note? What else did it say, Norma?"

Rudy's voice didn't change in volume or octave. He was as calm as if they were talking about the weather. Still, her words caught in her throat.

"I didn't put anything else in the note. I appealed to his affection for Lou, suggesting it was better for her if he wasn't around."

Rudy's expression wasn't one of anger, nor one of shock. It was something akin to sadness or, worse, disappointment. She hadn't seen that look on his face before. In all their years together, Norma thought she'd seen every facial tic, heard every tone of voice. Apparently, she hadn't.

"There's more," she said.

Rudy pressed his mouth into a flat line. He shifted his hips in the saddle and winced. He stole a glance at the path ahead then leveled his gaze back on Norma.

"I didn't think he would keep in touch," she said. "I'd made it clear I thought his distance was a good thing for all of us. But he's a good man, I know that. And he wouldn't abandon us even if he didn't come back. His last letter…I…I intercepted it and I wrote back to him. I asked him not to write anymore, not to communicate at all. I told him it was too hard on Lou and that forgetting him would be best for all of us."

Rudy shook his head. "Why would you do that? Why would—"

"I thought it was best. I was afraid he'd come back, especially if Lou got pregnant. If she and Dallas had children, I wanted them to have a childhood. I knew he'd bring the violence with him. I knew it. So I did what I thought was the right thing to protect us. To protect you, to protect Lou, Dallas, all of us."

It sounded worse said aloud. The thing she'd done, keeping Marcus from them, was selfish. It wasn't what she'd intended. She'd thought she was being the opposite of selfish, whatever that was. Yet hearing the words come from her mouth, articulated to her husband, only made what she'd done appear worse.

Rudy sucked in a deep breath and hitched. He winced again, grunted, and turned his head away from her, studying the brown haze that hung low in the sky to the east.

Norma studied him as best she could from the perch of her saddle. He wasn't typically a hard man to read. Being together as long as they had, she could read him like the back of her hand. But from the side, his face almost expressionless, she couldn't tell what he was thinking. Her chest tightened.

"Say something," she said. "Please."

Rudy rubbed his jaw and raked his fingers along the underside of his chin. He adjusted his hips in the saddle and squinted. While it was only a few seconds, each one was agonizingly drawn out into super slow motion. Norma's vision blurred. Tears again. She hadn't cried so much in years.

Her horse loped after the long, warped shadow cast ahead of them. Norma felt as hollow as that gray version of herself. Maybe she shouldn't have said anything. She'd coped with the guilt of her actions long enough—reflected in Lou's sad eyes, in David's tiny hands and toothy grin, in Dallas's anger for the man who'd abandoned his wife.

Norma thought the confession, an admission of past sin to the one person in the world in whom she could confide without judgment, would lighten her load. It hadn't done that so far.

Finally, Rudy sighed and spoke. "I can't say I agree with what you did."

Norma sensed a "but" coming. That gave her hope.

"But," he said, "I know you, Norma. In my heart I'm positive that everything you do has good intentions. I don't think you have a mean bone in your body."

She dabbed at the corners of her eyes with her index finger and blinked away the sheen of tears.

"Our lives haven't been easy since the Scourge," said Rudy. "This world, our world, has deteriorated into a place where people pick and choose their morality to suit their circumstances. You've never done that. You've always done the best you can to be good, to do good."

The tears welled again. This time they weren't from guilt. They were a product of the ridiculous love she felt for her husband.

He held her gaze for a moment before looking ahead. Eyes narrowed, he wiped his brow with his sleeve. The shadows in front of them were shrinking as the sun lifted higher into the sky. The orange hue had given way to a pale blue that was hazy at the edges.

"What you did for Gladys?" he asked rhetorically. "Her sister? Having them live with us for as long as they did? It was so generous. I wouldn't have done that."

She smirked. That was a generous lie. He'd been every bit as willing to house the women as she'd been. He'd given them the space to work through what the Llano River Clan had done to them. She'd been less patient, pushing them to engage, to be a part of their extended family.

"Then the way you helped Gladys with the railroad? All of the people you've helped get to safety at great risk to yourself? Don't tell me you're not the most selfless person you know."

He was the most selfless person she knew. There was nobody even close except maybe Marcus. The more she thought about Mad Max, the more she understood his sacrifice, his reluctant heroism.

"It's going to work out," Rudy said. "I promise. It's all going to be okay."

He offered her a twitch of a smile at first. Then it spread into a grin. He clicked his tongue at the horse and maneuvered it closer to Norma. Wincing, he reached out with his hand and touched her leg.

With the reins still wrapped around it, she placed her hand on his and squeezed. She blew him a kiss. He blew one back.

Rudy raised his eyebrows. "Now," he said, dipping his chin, "as for that other crap? The poacher? Let's not think about that. What's done is done. We have to move forward. And I have a feeling there are more people who are going to need killing."

Norma clenched her jaw. He was right. She knew it.

CHAPTER 19

APRIL 21, 2054, 8:45 AM
SCOURGE +21 YEARS, 7 MONTHS
ATLANTA, GEORGIA

Sally clutched her chest. Dark blood, her blood, seeped through her fingers, painting the back of her hand bright red.

In front of her, a dark figure aimed the weapon at her. Smoke drifted from its barrel, tendrils swirling before they dissipated into the darkness of the night.

She pulled her hand from her body. The soaked cotton of her shirt stuck to her palm. Looking down, all she could see was a small circular tear in the fabric. She felt nothing. How could so much blood come from something so tiny, so painless? Yet it flowed almost as if someone had sliced her jugular.

Her pulse pounded. Her knees weakened.

"Why?" Sally asked the dark figure. She lifted her gaze from the gushing wound to settle on the dark figure.

The figure laughed. It was a guttural laugh, the kind she expected to hear from a storybook villain, not a real person. The figure stepped from the dark into a light Sally hadn't previously noticed.

The blood pooled at her feet now. It seeped through her boots and squished between her toes. She tasted it in her mouth, warm and coppery. It was thick in her throat and on her tongue. The air was humid and acrid. The sharp odor of gunpowder stung her nostrils.

Her balance wavered. She was light-headed.

How had this happened? Where was she? The street beneath her feet was cobbled stone. The stones were wet with rain.

Rain?

When had it rained?

The buildings were close on either side of her, their pale brick and mortar aged, moss-covered, and rust-stained. Gutters clanked with the rhythm of dripping water. The sky above, only a sliver of it visible beyond the tight gap between the tall buildings, was milky. There were clouds. Clouds. Rain. Blood. None of it made sense.

She blinked the figure into focus and had to blink again to be sure her eyes weren't playing tricks. The woman in front of her took another step closer and fired another shot from near point-blank range.

"Gladys!" Sally shouted. "Gladys, no!"

The world went black.

Sally shot up in bed. Soaked in sweat, she tried catching her breath. Her hands grabbed at her chest, searching for the wound, the blood.

The light in her room flicked on, and Gladys stood in the doorway in a pale blue nightgown, the skin under her arms sagging. Her eyes were bleary and appeared smaller. The wrinkles on her face were deeper somehow. "Are you okay?" she asked. "Were you having another nightmare?"

Sally leaned against the wall behind the bed, propped up by the three pillows under her back. Her breathing was ragged. She patted her chest, searching for a wound that wasn't there.

Gladys glided into the room and sat on the edge of the bed. The mattress springs creaked and the bed shifted. "Can I get you something?"

Sally shook her head. "No, thank you. I'm okay. I think."

"What was it?"

Sally didn't understand the question. "What?"

"The nightmare," said Gladys. "What was it about?"

Sally swallowed hard. The explosion of adrenaline, of raw fear, was fading. She sank against the pillows and her spine pressed against the wall. "I don't know," she said. The dream, as vivid as it had been moments earlier, was foggy now.

"You called my name," said Gladys. "But you were asleep. You were dreaming about me?"

Sally searched her mind, digging for snippets of the dream like a word on the tip of her tongue. "I was in an alley," she said. "It was raining. Or it had rained, I can't remember. I just know the street was wet. There was the sound of rain in the gutters."

Gladys flashed a smile. Her crow's feet deepened. "That sounds more like a dream than a nightmare. Rain? I can't remember the last time we had real rain. Three months ago? Six, was it? I can't recall."

Sally looked through Gladys, into the haze of the dream. Her hand went back to her chest. She clutched the shirt, gripping it in her fist, and tightened her hold on it. "There was blood," she said absently. "Blood was everywhere. I was bleeding, I think. I could taste it."

"You were hurt?"

Sally nodded. She licked her lips.

"It was only a dream," said Gladys. "It wasn't real."

It still felt so real. There was the faintest taste of copper in her mouth, like the remnant flavor of last night's dinner. She let go of her shirt and blinked back to the moment. "What time is it?"

"Close to nine o'clock," said Gladys. "I've been up for an hour. Do you want some coffee?"

"Please," said Sally.

Gladys smiled and slapped Sally's leg, making Sally jump. "Sorry," Gladys said. "Didn't mean to startle you. I just—"

"It's okay," said Sally. "I'll meet you in the kitchen."

Gladys got up from the bed. The mattress creaked again. She

glided from the room, her nightgown flowing behind her like a cape.

Sally pulled the thin covers back and swung her legs to the side of the bed. Her bare feet touched the cool floor and she sat there to collect herself, her thoughts.

The nightmares were getting worse. They'd started a year earlier. Or was it two years? Sally couldn't remember the first one. Not exactly. And it wasn't that the violence was worse or that she was less able to save herself in each subsequent iteration of the dreams, it was that they felt more real. There was a latency when she awoke from them, the sensation that what had happened somehow manifested itself in the real world.

She knew that wasn't the case. A nightmare was a nightmare was a nightmare. None of it was real, even if the dampness under her arms and her still quickly palpitating heartbeat suggested otherwise.

Sally lifted herself from the bed and stood solidly on the floor. Her nose itched. She scratched it and crossed the room to the door. She glanced back at the unmade bed, thinking about the blood in her dream, and turned out the light.

The strong aroma of coffee greeted her even before she stepped into the kitchen. Gladys liked to make the coffee strong. Every morning she said coffee wasn't coffee if it didn't make you feel like you could blast off into space.

Two mugs were steaming. One was cupped in Gladys's hands. She blew on it with pursed lips. The other mug was on the counter. Sally picked it up by the handle and the steam puffed onto her face. It reminded her of the smoke she'd seen swirling from the barrel of the gun in her dream. A shudder rippled through her body.

Gladys had a book open on the counter. She'd obviously been awake for a while, despite the exhaustion etched on her face.

Sally was eager to forget the nightmare despite its images cementing themselves in her mind. Changing the subject seemed like a good option. She jutted her chin at the book. "What are you reading?"

Gladys set the mug on the counter and picked up the paperback. Using her thumb as a bookmark, she flipped over the book to study the cover. The pages were yellowed and some curled at the edges. To say the book was dog-eared was a dramatic understatement.

"It's a western," she said. "*Judgment Day* by a guy named G. Michael Hopf. It's an old one. Came out in 2019. What is that? Thirty-five years ago?"

"You read westerns?" asked Sally.

"I guess I'm not the target audience, but coming from Texas, I've got an affinity for a good dusty yarn. Good versus evil, that sort of thing. And there's a lot of revenge in westerns. I like that."

Gladys winked at Sally. A smile edged onto her face; the parenthetical wrinkles that framed her mouth deepened and widened.

Sally tasted the coffee. It burned the tip of her tongue. She winced, blew on the mug, and tried it again. "What's Texas like?"

Gladys raised an eyebrow. She folded a corner on a page and closed the book. Running her hand across the cover in the same way she pressed the wrinkles from her dresses, she seemed to consider the question as if to choose the right words. "That's a complicated answer."

Sally took another sip of the coffee. The steam dampened her nose and cheeks.

"Texas was the most beautiful place on Earth," said Gladys. "The ocean, mountains, rivers, wide-open spaces, large cities, friendly people, diverse population…"

"Was?" asked Sally.

Gladys shrugged. "Before the Scourge it was all of those things. Afterward…" Her focus softened. She shook her head and chuckled. "People used to say, only partly in jest, Texas could secede from the rest of the United States and be its own country."

"It was its own country once, wasn't it?"

Gladys nodded. "It was a lot of things. On the floor of the rotunda in the state capitol, there used to be the emblems of all of its affiliations. It was a territory of Spain, France, and Mexico. It was part of the United States and the Confederate States of America. And then, of course, after beating back Santa Anna at the battle of San Jacinto, it became its own republic."

Sally toasted Gladys with her mug. "You know a lot of history."

Gladys flashed a smile. "Had to learn it in school when I was little. We even had to learn the Texas Pledge."

"Texas Pledge? Like the Pledge of Allegiance we used to say?"

Gladys nodded. She lifted her chin and put her hand over her heart. "Honor the Texas flag," she recited from memory. "I pledge allegiance to thee, Texas, one state under God, one and indivisible."

"Whoa."

"I know. I loved it. There was a real pride in being a Texan."

"Was?" Sally asked again.

"Everything changed so rapidly after the Scourge. People got desperate. They did desperate things. Then the government spent a ridiculous amount of money building the wall, which I never really understood. All it did was solidify the Cartel's grip. Then it was a string of power-hungry groups that took control one after the other. It really was the Wild West. Still is, I think. The cities are now under gang control."

"The tribes?"

"Yeah," said Gladys, her gaze distant again. "They're no different from the Cartel, the dwellers, the Llano River Clan. They subjugate women and children. They murder innocents."

Both women sipped from the mugs. The steam was gone. Sally relished the hint of sweet in her black coffee. She let it sit in her mouth for a moment, washing over her tongue, before she swallowed.

Gladys put her hand on the book like a witness swearing on a Bible. She blinked and stared at Sally. "That's why I like westerns," she said, flattening the warped cover of the paperback. "The good guy always wins in the end, and the bad guys get what's coming to them. There is no shortage of karma in westerns. That's not how the real world works."

"No, it's not," Sally said. "I get it. I wish I read more. It would be a good escape, and certainly healthier than a bottle of whatever."

The women toasted each other. Gladys downed the rest of her coffee, then motioned for Sally to follow her from the kitchen. "Bring your coffee with you."

Sally took the mug with both hands and tried to match Gladys's glide through the hallway to a door she hadn't entered before. Gladys stretched onto her tiptoes, reached up to the doorsill, and pulled down a key. She stuck the key into the lock, turned it, and pushed open the door.

The room was dark and cooler than the rest of the house. Goose bumps pimpled Sally's skin as they moved into the space, and Gladys shut the door behind them. There was the faint hum and buzz of electronics. Gladys flipped a light switch and Sally's eyes adjusted.

Along one wall was a desk. A banker's lamp, the kind with a green glass shade, sat on one corner. It was off, but the main components sitting next to it were powered up. There was a piece of paper taped to the desk containing a list of numbers and letters.

Sally pointed at the collection of boxes and wires. "What are those?"

"My connection to Texas," said Gladys, "and beyond."

"Are they radios?"

Gladys rolled back the wheeled chair at the desk and sat down. Using her heels, she scooted close to the desk and touched a couple of buttons on one of the components. She turned a couple of dials. There was a headset plugged into one of the boxes. Gladys unplugged it, drew a microphone closer to her, and pushed the button at its base. She held it down with her fingers.

"This is GFAGA5," she said. "Is anyone monitoring this frequency?" She let go of the key and glanced back at Sally. "Questions?"

"Too many to count," said Sally.

Her eyes danced across the collection of electronics. There were wires that ran along and under the table, snaking up the wall into holes in the ceiling. There were pieces of faded paper with typed letter-number combinations taped to the wall next to the wires, and hastily scribbled notes on the papers in red and blue magic marker. Sally saw the blue marker sitting on its end on the desk next to the banker's lamp.

Nobody responded on the radio. Gladys repeated the call. Twice.

Sally was dumbstruck. She'd always wondered how the railroad communicated long distances without the Pop Guard monitoring their messages. This was the answer. She had no idea how the radio technology worked, but it made sense this was how they did it. It was relatively anonymous, it was transient, and it could get a message to someone far away almost instantaneously.

The radio crackled. A man's voice broke through the static.

"Hello, GFAGA5," he said. *"This is HR29BR. We hear you."*

"Copy that, HR29BR," said Gladys. "Checking status."

"Who is that?" asked Sally. "Who are you talking to?"

Gladys didn't answer her before the voice responded in a high-pitched tone.

"Status is good. New arrivals today. More tonight. When is the special delivery?"

"On its way shortly," said Gladys. "I'll update. FYI, Texas connection is off-line. Establishing new link soon."

The response was immediate. *"Copy that, GFAGA5."*

"Talk later," said Gladys.

She turned a knob on the face of the component and the volume lessened.

"That was the Harbor," Gladys said. "Had to check in. They moved a few weeks back, and things have been tenuous since then."

Sally's eyes widened. "Where is it?" she asked. "Where am I headed?"

Gladys curled her lips over her teeth and studied Sally. She spun the chair to face her and rubbed out the creases in her nightgown. Then she rolled back to a shelf on the wall perpendicular to the desk. Sally was so focused on the electronics, she hadn't noticed the shelf until now.

Gladys pulled a thick, folded piece of paper from the shelf and placed it on the desk. Rolling back to face the flat surface, she unfolded the paper. Sally realized it was a map.

Gladys pressed the map flat, working its folds, and then traced her finger along the face of it. Sally stepped closer to her and eyed the multicolored chart. It was a representation of the United States as it had been before the Scourge. Some of the creases were torn along their seams.

Various locations were marked with blue, hand-drawn stars. There were lines traced atop highways or interstates. Some of them were precise; others looked shaky.

Gladys's finger stopped and she tapped the map with her finger. It was pointing at White Sulphur Springs, West Virginia. "It was here. It was a great location; somewhat secluded, underground, decent security. Winters were tough, but with the bulk of everything being in a bunker, that wasn't much of an issue."

Sally bent over. "You moved it?"

"Yes. We were compromised. There was the possibility that the Pop Guard might find us there. So we packed up and moved out."

"Where are you now?"

Gladys slid her finger along the map, tracing the route from White Sulphur Springs. She tapped the new location. "Here."

"There?" asked Sally. "Really?"

Gladys nodded. "I know, it's an unusual choice. We have our reasons though, one of them being ease of access."

"Or lack of it."

"Exactly the point," said Gladys.

"Is there a bridge?"

"No. Long gone."

Sally scratched her chin. "Then how do you get there?"

Gladys chuckled. There was a hint of condescension in her tone. "Boat."

Sally's face grew hot and her cheeks flushed. "So I'm taking a boat?" she asked. She'd never been on a boat before.

"You're taking a boat," said Gladys. Her expression hardened. "Assuming you make it that far."

CHAPTER 20

APRIL 21, 2054, 9:00 AM
SCOURGE +21 YEARS, 7 MONTHS
LATEX, TEXAS

"Thanks for the first aid," Marcus said to the conductor. He was in the passenger seat of the eighteen-wheeler.

"Happy to help." The conductor shifted gears and pressed the accelerator. "That's a nasty wound. Is the aspirin helping?"

"Some," said Marcus. "Thanks for that too."

He held his left hand across his chest above his heart, which helped to lessen the pulsing pain that synced with his heartbeat.

The driver thumped on the steering wheel, a percussive rhythm that filled the silence between them.

"I didn't know they had many of these left," said Marcus, trying to make conversation.

He was in too much pain to sleep. Plus, they were getting close to the wall.

The conductor's bushy black eyebrows lifted into distinctive arches, almost reaching his hairline. His Roman nose crinkled. "Any of what?"

"Trucks," said Marcus. "I'd think the diesel alone would be prohibitive."

The conductor chuckled, his Adam's apple sliding up and down his throat. "When you transport for the government, diesel is the least of your worries."

Marcus loosened his seatbelt across his chest with his right hand and turned toward the driver. He wasn't sure he'd heard the man right. His ears were still ringing from the firefight. "You work for the government?"

He thumped out a crescendo on the steering wheel and nodded. "That I do. Perfect cover, right? Nobody suspects a government trucker is working for the railroad."

"So you transport a lot of people?"

"Enough."

"Why do you do it?"

The driver shrugged. He downshifted and the cab lurched. Marcus tightened his seatbelt.

"I don't know," he said, "why are you here? You don't have a dog in the hunt. These babies ain't yours."

Marcus took a deep breath and exhaled through his nose. "I've got a dog in the hunt," he said, using the man's vernacular. "That's family."

He smiled, reached for a thermos with his right hand, and popped the top with his thumb. He took a swig of whatever was in it and winced as he swallowed. Then he offered it to Marcus.

Marcus thanked him but declined.

"No offense," said the conductor, "but none of those folks in the back are your family. I mean to say, maybe you're close to them, but you're not blood."

"How do you know that?"

"'Cause you didn't deny it. Plus none of 'em look anything like you. Not a bit."

Marcus glanced out the window at the landscape. Dense thickets of dead pines raced by. They were evenly spaced, planted for logging decades earlier. Then they died.

"I'll take money from the government if they're willing to give it," said the conductor, "and I'll use their equipment against them."

"Why do you do it, though?" Marcus asked. "It's a big risk."

The conductor winked, his smile now wider on one side of his face. Marcus was convinced there were a dozen smiles and he regularly alternated between them.

"Anything worth having is risky," the conductor replied. "And I don't like what they're doing."

Marcus tried moving his thumb in the tight wrap the conductor had wound around his hand. A jolt of electric pain sparked along the right side of his hand. He stopped moving the thumb.

Both hands on the wheel, the conductor leaned in and spoke as if in confidence, his breath washed in moonshine. "You know this overpopulation thing is a red herring. Since when is there a population problem when two-thirds of the world died off a generation ago? That makes no sense. It's a false flag."

Marcus didn't think the conductor was using either of the terms correctly, but he didn't bother arguing the point. It was moot.

"This is about power," he said. "It's about control. The truth is, the government *wants* people to have too many babies. Then they can come along, take the extras, and indoctrinate them. It's no different from what those damned tribes are doing here in Texas."

Marcus nodded. "I've heard that."

"It's true. One hundred percent. I don't like it. I don't like what it does to families. It's some Eastern Europe fascist baloney, if you know what I mean."

The conversation stalled when the truck dipped over a rise in the road and a wall loomed ahead of them a half mile up highway 1999. It wasn't *a* wall. It was *the* wall.

The tension stiffened in Marcus's joints, his chest tightening with unconscious apprehension.

The wall.

No matter where he saw it, or crossed it, it was the bane of his existence.

"Now, you let me do the talking," the conductor instructed. "I've done this a thousand times. They're going to stop us, I'm going to have to show them the cargo in the trailer, they'll look at my manifest, I'll bribe them, then we'll be on our way. It's as simple as that."

"Bribe them?" Marcus asked. His attention was on the wall as it grew larger, looming closer to them. "You work for the government, so do they, and you have to bribe them?"

"We may work for the government," said the conductor, "but we also work for ourselves. Every hauler like me always has a little extra in the trailer, stuff we sell on the black market. It's expected. If we don't, it's suspicious, so we bribe them. It's a wink, wink, nudge, nudge thing."

Marcus thought of the old Monty Python skit. It'd been among his digital collection in the solitary years after his family died. He smiled, picturing the comedian Eric Idle and his elbow jabs.

"Say no more," said Marcus.

The conductor laughed and slapped his thigh. His seat bounced on its shock absorbers and he downshifted. Once they reached the wall, an armed guard stood in the middle of the highway, holding up a hand to stop them.

Another soldier adjusted his helmet and tugged the strap across his chin. Eyes forward, he marched deliberately to the driver's side window of the truck, motioning with one hand for the conductor to lower his window.

The conductor, his omnipresent grin brightening his face, complied and reached for a tablet charging underneath the center console. A couple of taps and swipes across the screen made it glow. "Here you go," he said, handing the tablet to the soldier as he climbed onto the running board beneath the driver's door. "Everything should be in order."

Without a greeting, the soldier leaned on the door and took the tab with his free hand. He studied the display, his eyes shifting as he read. After a minute he handed the electronic device back to the conductor and tapped the side of the door. "Okay, you know the drill. I'll need the engine off, you and your passenger at the back of the trailer with the keys."

"Sure thing," said the conductor. His affability seemingly genuine, he turned off the engine.

The truck rumbled, coughing itself into silence. The conductor motioned for Marcus to exit the passenger-side door and then used his shoulder to push his way through his.

Marcus opened his door with his good hand, forgetting to undo his seatbelt. He tried getting out and found himself stuck. It took him a second to realize what was holding him in place, and he reached across his body to unlatch the buckle.

It took effort to get to the ground, but he managed without losing his balance. The jump jarred his knees, and Marcus knew he was doing more harm than good on this trip. His body didn't much like him at the moment. He limped toward the rear of the eighteen-wheeler, walking along the edge of the highway, carefully sidestepping the crumbling edges of the asphalt, and maneuvered around the wide tailgate of the trailer to the rear of the vehicle.

The guard was already in the cargo area, standing with his back to the conductor. He checked the crates, lifting lids, picking through contents of random containers. After a few minutes he turned toward the conductor, cocked his head to one side, and pointed at Marcus. "What happened to his hand?" he asked. There no hint of emotion in his voice, no compassion. If anything, suspicion punctuated the question.

"He can answer for himself," the conductor replied, with a glance at Marcus. "He can talk."

"So talk," the soldier deadpanned. "What happened to your hand?"

Marcus wasn't giving him any more than he needed. He was going to play coy to the conductor's Chatty Cathy.

"Accident," he said simply.

The soldier took a step toward the trailer's exit. "What kind of accident?"

"Stupid one," said Marcus. "It's embarrassing."

"Embarrass yourself, then," said the soldier. His tone had gone from suspicious to condescending. He clearly liked his authority.

"Sliced it open on the loader. I was checking the hydraulics. Wasn't watching what I was doing, tore it open between the thumb and forefinger. Hurts a lot."

The soldier stared at Marcus for a moment longer than was comfortable, then thumbed toward the front of the trailer behind him. He redirected his attention to the conductor. "I'm gonna need to check back here," he said. "Leave the door open. Try anything funny and it's a big problem."

The conductor raised his hands in surrender. "Do what you need to do."

The soldier tapped the side of his helmet, and a white light illuminated at the center of it. He walked deeper into the truck, disappearing amongst the boxes and draped containers.

Marcus shot an uneasy glance at the conductor, who shook his head imperceptibly and, maintaining his grin and keeping his eyes on the soldier, whispered, "Don't worry about it. This is for show. He won't look too carefully."

"You sure about that?" asked Marcus. "He seems to be thorough."

"They all do this. They've got nothing else to do at these checkpoints. This kills time as much as anything else."

"As long as that's all it kills."

The conductor stifled a laugh. He stuffed his hands into his pockets, puckered his lips, and started whistling. It was an unfamiliar tune, something Marcus imagined was made up.

Several long minutes later, the soldier returned to the back of the trailer and tapped off the light on his helmet. He climbed down, landing hard on the asphalt. Marcus noticed the soldier, whom he'd initially pegged for someone in his mid to late forties, was closer to thirty. He might not even have been that old.

A thin whip of a mustache grew above his upper lip. It was a pitiful attempt at facial hair, though not nearly as weak as the patchy mange of a beard that spread across his cheeks and along his soft jawline. Was everybody young? Or was Marcus really that old? It was a combination of both, he figured.

The soldier cleared his throat. "I saw a couple of…irregularities…in the back there," he said. "But it's something I think is fixable."

There were the words he was speaking and, more importantly, the ones he wasn't saying aloud. He shot glances at both of them and raised his eyebrows such that they disappeared under the brim of his helmet.

"Sure thing," said the conductor. He pulled a small pouch from his front pocket and offered it to the soldier with a handshake.

The soldier took the pouch and nodded. Without even looking at the contents, he released his grip and weighed the pouch in his hand before shoving it into a pocket at his thigh. He flashed a smile that evaporated instantly. "Okay then," he said. "We're all good here."

Five minutes later, they were in Louisiana. The conductor was tapping on the steering wheel and whistling.

"What did you give him?" asked Marcus.

"Drugs. That's all they want. Every last one of them."

"Drugs?"

"Yep," said the conductor. "Legal drugs, illegally obtained. Typically it's uppers. They need something to keep them alert during their long shifts, and coffee ain't in the supply it once was. With the drought, it's harder to come by coffee than it is allergy or ADD medication."

ADD. Attention deficit disorder. Marcus hadn't thought about that since he'd taken Adderall as a kid. "Is that even a thing anymore?"

"ADD?" asked the conductor. "Who knows? But the drug is good for narcoleptics, so it still gets made overseas. The government imports it, doles it out judiciously. Us employees, we can get whatever we need. And as truckers, they want us awake and driving as many miles as we can handle. No union or FMSCA regulations like there were before the Scourge."

"You don't look old enough to have been a driver before the Scourge," Marcus noted.

The conductor laughed and shook his head. "I wasn't; my dad was. He drove long haul for years, had his own rig. I learned how to drive a stick and double clutch in his truck."

Marcus humored him. "Did you?"

"Imagine that," said the conductor. "A kid knows how to drive a truck before he can drive a little old Chevy. Funny, right?"

"Funny, yes."

They sat in silence for a few minutes; then Marcus glanced over his left shoulder toward the bunk in the back of the truck. "They're okay back there?"

The conductor shifted into a higher gear and refocused on the road ahead of them. They were heading due east toward Shreveport. "Of course. That secret compartment is pretty handy. And I've done this enough I've got it outfitted pretty good."

"It looked comfortable," Marcus admitted. "Spacious enough, I guess."

"Oh yeah," the conductor said with pride. "I could fit ten in there if I had to. I've had to do it, actually. Three families at once. That breaks the railroad protocol, you know. We're really not supposed to handle more than a half dozen at a time. But sometimes necessity dictates we break the rules."

Marcus pictured the eight-foot-square space and its pair of twin bunks bolted into the ceiling and floor. There were pillows, blankets, a stack of books, and a mini-fridge that ran off the truck's power.

"They've got plenty of water," the conductor said. "I think I've even got some tangerines from Florida in there. They're fine until we get to where we're going."

Marcus sank a little into his seat and plucked at the belt running diagonally across his chest. He rested his left hand against his chest. The throbbing was now a solid, constant ache. His eyes were getting heavy. "Where exactly is that?"

"Where exactly is what?"

"Where you're taking us?"

The conductor drew in a deep breath, shifted gears, and exhaled with a puff of his cheeks. He pinched the bridge of his nose and knuckled his eyes, rubbing them. "Not sure I can tell you that."

"Is it all the way to the Harbor? Is that why you can't say?"

"Oh no," he said with an overly dramatic shake of his head. "No. No. No. I'm not taking you to the Harbor. That's someone else's job. Heck, I don't even know where the Harbor is. Plus, I have to stick to my work route. I can't stray from that or my government bosses would get suspicious."

"It exists though?" Marcus still had his doubts. "The Harbor *is* real?"

"Yes," said the conductor. "It's real."

"Why can't you say, then?"

The conductor glanced at the display in the dash. His fingers danced along the top of the steering wheel. Now the motion was more like a pianist flitting his fingers along the keys instead of a drummer thumping out a rhythm on the taut skin of a bongo head.

"C'mon," Marcus said. "Who am I gonna tell? We're not using names. We don't know our final destination. You work for the government. What does it—"

Marcus had an epiphany. He smiled and wagged a finger on his right hand.

The smile disappeared from the conductor's face. His head snapped to Marcus, to the road ahead, and back to his passenger. His brow furrowed. "What?"

"I know where we're headed," said Marcus. "It's obvious."

"Is it?"

"Yes," said Marcus. "You work for the government. We're headed to Atlanta."

CHAPTER 21

Rickshaw held his hands under the stream of hot water. His skin was pink and felt raw from the scrubbing. He turned his hands over and curled his fingers in toward his palms. There was still blood under his fingernails. He still couldn't figure out how he'd gotten blood under his nails.

That wasn't entirely true. He knew how it had happened.

After more than ten hours of interrogation, Blair had cracked. More accurately, Rickshaw had cracked him open.

He grabbed the shriveled bar of soap from the dish on the sink's edge and passed it between his hands, creating a healthy lather. Then he held it in one soapy hand while he raked the fingers from the other across it, digging into it. He repeated it with the opposite hand and then plopped the bar back onto the ledge.

The hot water stung as he ran his thumb along the beds of his nails and under the nails themselves, trying to pry loose the remnants of Blair's gore. It was tedious. He sighed. He'd done this to himself.

There wasn't a need to get as violent as he had with Blair, who was relatively forthcoming. It was that last little bit of information he wouldn't divulge that had driven Rickshaw to exact the sort of pain usually reserved for higher value targets.

In the end he'd put the poor man out of his misery, though not before Blair gave Rickshaw what he wanted.

It was a strange thing, being an interrogator. It was stranger still to enjoy it as much as Rickshaw did. Even though extracting intelligence wasn't in his job description, it was something he did with relish. It allowed him to explore both the depth of his intelligence and cunning, while at the same time delving into the darkest corners of his soul. He could play psychologist and antagonist, friend and foe, liberator and captor, judge, jury, and executioner all within the span of a few hours.

Rickshaw turned off the water, content to leave specks of dark blood trapped underneath his jagged nails, and then flicked the water from his raw hands. From a hook on the wall, he pulled his duster and slid into it one arm at a time. He adjusted the collar and looked at himself in the mirror above the sink, winked at himself, and moved to the hallway outside the restroom. The soldiers waited for him, standing at attention. They were in uniform, armed, and expressionless.

"You ready?" he asked them collectively.

"Yes, sir," they said in unison.

"You have the address?" he asked the tallest of the five, a guard named Krespan.

"Yes, sir," said Krespan. "It's logged into global positioning."

"Let's go," said Rickshaw.

The guards saluted and fell into rank order as they marched along the hallway toward the transportation bay. Rickshaw walked behind them, his mind lingering on the last bits of information Blair had given him. He tightened his jaw thinking about it. It was infuriating.

They wound through the labyrinth of secure corridors until they reached the bay. Krespan unlocked it with a scan of his eye and finger, then held the door for the others to pass through. Rickshaw thanked him as he moved past the soldier.

Krespan was a good man. There was kindness in his eyes, a humor in his laugh, that didn't exist much anymore. Rickshaw sometimes wondered if Krespan was too good for the work of the Pop Guard. Still, he'd always done as Rickshaw asked. He never questioned authority. He used his rank judiciously, rarely pressing an advantage over lesser soldiers. It almost made Rickshaw untrusting of the soldier despite having no legitimate reason to doubt him.

Krespan let the door close behind Rickshaw and hustled past the captain to lead the formation. They were on the bottom level of the multistory garage. It was hot in the concrete structure. The smell of exhaust and motor oil was almost overwhelming.

Though much of the Pop Guard's fleet was solar electric or electric-fuel hybrid, there were plenty of older vehicles that relied on fossil fuels. The maintenance work on those trucks and SUVs was completed on that level.

Rickshaw noticed several of them in various states of disrepair as they worked their way across the bay toward their vehicle. The captain tried taking short, shallow breaths to avoid inhaling the noxious odors, which turned his stomach. Blood and gore he could handle. Exhaust and motor oil, not so much.

"Where is this thing?" he snapped, his voice echoing against the solid surfaces of the structure. "Why wasn't it pulled around to the door?"

Krespan kept his pace. "Sorry, sir, it's the newest of the fleet. It's the fastest, but I wanted to keep it charged as long as possible."

Rickshaw rolled his eyes. Another few steps had him at the side of a black van. It was oddly shaped, more rounded than squared. Krespan stood at attention and slid back the van's cargo door on the driver's side of the vehicle.

The four men in front of Rickshaw climbed into the crew hold, angling their rifles to accommodate the space, and they found their seats on benches that ran the length of the hold on both sides.

Krespan slid the door shut.

"Sir," said Krespan, "let me get your door. I—"

"No need for that," said Rickshaw. "Get behind the wheel. I can open my own door."

Krespan saluted Rickshaw and hopped into the driver's seat. He was buckled, the engine running, and the van was in gear by the time Rickshaw opened his door.

The captain climbed into the front passenger seat and aimed the air-conditioning vents away from him. Despite the heat, Rickshaw didn't want the cold air blasting on him. Krespan tapped the display at the center of the dash and the stream of air dissipated.

"Sorry about that, sir, I—"

"Just drive," said Rickshaw. "We don't know how time sensitive the intelligence might be. Let's get there."

Krespan nodded, wide-eyed, and took his foot from the brake. The van accelerated silently and he steered it out of the bay, up a gradual incline, and onto the street. He swung the wheel, the tires chirped on the asphalt, caught, and the van jerked forward.

"As fast as you can," said Rickshaw.

On the central display, a map of their location glowed against the dark cabin of the van. At its center was a green, strobing dot that represented the van. Surrounding the dot, a spiderweb of streets and highways crisscrossed the screen in all directions. Rickshaw tapped the screen, and the display shifted from an overhead view of their navigated path to one that more closely resembled a three-dimensional representation.

Krespan had both hands on the wheel, his eyes fixed on the road ahead. His face reflected the blue glow from the dash display in front of him.

"How fast are you going?" asked Rickshaw.

"Forty-five."

"Faster," said Rickshaw.

"Yes, sir."

The sudden acceleration pushed Rickshaw back against his seat. The men behind him grumbled. His weight shifted when Krespan slowed, steered onto Peachtree, and accelerated again. Rickshaw turned his attention from the navigation display to the window. His nose touched the glass and he watched his breath plume and evaporate.

Beyond the glass, they zipped past the modern Atlanta. Trash littered the streets or spilled from trash cans set at the ends of driveways. Buildings were dark or dimly lit. People stalked the sidewalks alone or in small groups. They kept their heads down, their hands stuffed in their pockets or gripping the hands of companions.

They slowed again and Rickshaw looked up at the twin spires looming over him. He'd never been inside Cathedral of Christ the King, but he'd heard it was beautiful. The stained glass was remarkable and particularly beautiful in an area succumbed to neglect and blight.

The large doors to the church were propped open. As they passed, Rickshaw stole a look into the sanctuary beyond. The soft glow of candlelight, either real or artificial, was welcoming. There was a small part of Rickshaw that would have enjoyed a detour inside the cathedral. He'd like to see what kind of people still prayed, still knelt before their God, and were thankful for what they had, wanting of more, or both.

He sucked in a breath and exhaled. The sound that accompanied the sigh surprised him, and he coughed to mask it. His fog of breath evaporated and he turned back to the screen.

They were almost there. Three blocks.

"No mercy here," he said to the men in the back of the van. "I don't want any hesitation. There might be young women, children, we don't know. Regardless of what we find, act decisively."

The men agreed. Krespan nodded his understanding of the orders.

"There is one person I do not want harmed," he said. "No matter what, it is imperative she survives and we have her alive. She is an incredibly high-value target. I cannot stress that enough."

"Yes, sir," the men said.

"I do not know her appearance except that she's a white woman," said Rickshaw. "She's older, looks like a grandmother. My guess is she's the only one there who will fit that description."

"What is her name, sir?" asked Krespan.

"Her name is Gladys. She runs the whole damn thing. We grab her, we might put an end to the railroad once and for all."

CHAPTER 22

APRIL 21, 2054, 9:00 PM
SCOURGE +21 YEARS, 7 MONTHS
ATLANTA, GEORGIA

Sally heard the air brakes squeal and hiss outside the safe house. Through the window she saw it edge to the curb across the street. She let go of the white sheers and stepped back into the room. It was time.

Gladys was standing in the foyer, swiping the wrinkles from her long skirt and adjusting the tuck of her blouse. She offered Sally a smile and picked at the stray hairs at her forehead. If Sally didn't know better, she'd think the woman looked nervous.

Sally tugged on the waist of her pants, sliding the button to align with her navel. Then she moved from the parlor to the foyer.

"That's them, right?" Sally asked. "The truck?"

Gladys nodded. "It is. I was on the radio a few minutes ago. They've come from Texas. They're the special group of folks who'll be your last charge."

"Texas?" Sally looked toward the door as if she could see the truck through its solid mahogany. "Are you serious?"

"I'm serious," said Gladys. "My old friend is there. She sent them this way. I think they took a path similar to the one I took a few years ago."

Sally stared at Gladys, trying to fix eye contact. Was Gladys serious? The look of confusion and disbelief must have been obvious. She'd heard Gladys mention Texas when they were on the radio with the Harbor. But she didn't put two and two together and Gladys hadn't connected the two at the time.

"They drove through Latex," she said. "That's an actual place in east Texas. They rode through Shreveport, Louisiana, the Talladega National Forest, and then on into Atlanta. It's a ten- to twelve-hour drive from the wall."

Sally still wasn't sure what to think. In all of her years, she'd never conducted a trip for someone from Texas. She'd heard of people fleeing the territory, especially since the Pop Guard amped up its patrols.

"*The* wall?" she asked.

"*The* wall," said Gladys. "It's a—"

A strobe of headlights flashed through the transom above the front door, and Gladys's expression flattened. "Come on," she said. "That's the signal."

Gladys led Sally away from the foyer and deeper into the house. It was a maze of hallways into a part of the first floor Sally hadn't explored. They passed a laundry room and a walk-in pantry with its door open. A light flickered in the pantry, casting an eerie effect on the cans and boxes of dry goods on the shelves inside.

Gladys swung open a narrow door and flipped a switch on the wall. Without checking to make sure Sally was behind her, she descended a narrow set of stairs into a basement that Sally had no idea existed until now.

Sally pounded down the unfinished wooden steps, her hand gliding along the handrails affixed to cinderblock walls on both sides of the stairs. They reached the bottom of the steps and Gladys swung to her left. She wove between pieces of cherry furniture half-draped in sheets, old bicycles wrapped in chain link and padlocked to a support beam in the middle of the space.

There were boxes labeled with black marker, random tables covered in paper maps and laptop computers. Some of the computers were off, while others glowed with their home screens asking for passwords. Black power cords and orange extensions snaked across the floor, plugged into large multi-outlet boxes affixed to the cinderblock walls.

The farther they traveled the space, the danker and cooler it became. The faint odor of mildew tickled Sally's nose.

"Where are we going?" she asked, trying to keep up with Gladys.

The older woman was surprisingly spry and sure-footed. She kept maneuvering amongst the clutter, not answering Sally's question.

The more they walked, the clearer it became they were no longer directly underneath Gladys's home. It wasn't possible. They'd walked too far.

She noticed then that the walls weren't cinderblock anymore. Now they were red brick, sandwiching thick zippered layers of grout from floor to low ceiling. They were definitely under some other structure.

Gladys slowed and turned left again. She pulled a set of keys from a pocket in her long skirt, flipping through them until she found one she took between her thumb and forefinger. They were at a door. It was narrow, half the width of a normal door, and Gladys struggled to slip the key into the deadbolt above the knob.

It stuck. Gladys cursed under her breath and wiggled the key. Finally it clicked and she turned it.

"Come on," she said and tugged open the door, pulling it into the basement. "Almost there. Switch places with me."

Beyond the door was another staircase. Sally stood at its bottom step for a moment while Gladys locked the door behind them. They climbed quickly, Sally almost out of breath. Her heart pounded from the speed with which they moved and the excitement of the secretive adventure.

Their shoes pounded on the wooden steps as they ascended in the dark. The keys in Gladys's hand jingled. When they reached the top of the staircase, the older women nudged past Sally and drew another key. Without the benefit of light, she managed to fit the key into a lock. It clicked and the door opened.

They walked through it and stood in a brightly lit kitchen decorated in white tile, red fabric, and black-lacquered cabinets. It had the look of a diner from the 1950s, like those Sally had seen in photographs and old movies.

"Where are we?" asked Sally.

"It's all a precaution," said Gladys. "Can't be too careful. We never know who's watching."

They moved from the kitchen into a hallway. The home's floor plan was a mirror of Gladys's place. They hustled through the hall toward the parlor, on the opposite side of the space in Gladys's home.

"Wait here," said Gladys. "All of this is going to happen quickly. You ready?"

Sally nodded.

"All your supplies are loaded. Food, water, contacts. You're good to go. You okay?"

Sally was not okay. Her heart was racing, her throat was dry, her head hurt, and she wanted to puke. "I'm fine."

Gladys nodded. Sally was sure the woman knew she wasn't fine. The flat glare barely covered the vaguest hint of sympathy or pity. Gladys turned and moved swiftly from the parlor to the front door. She peeled back the lace sheers covering the sidelight of frosted glass next to the door and then stood on her tiptoes. Her fingers against the door, she looked down her nose, shifting her head as if trying to peer through a small slit that only gave glimmers of what lay beyond.

Another glance toward Sally, another nod, and she lowered herself. She balled her hands into fists and straightened her arms, appearing to psych herself up for what was to come. Her tension eased and she flexed her fingers, then pressed out the creases in her dress.

Gladys unlocked the door at the handle, a deadbolt, and a chain. She stepped back, away from the door, and folded her arms low across her chest.

No sooner had she moved out of the door's swinging arc than it burst open. Three, four, five people were suddenly in the foyer. Or was it six? Their dark figures merged together with ambient light from the street, making it difficult to see the details of their faces. Even Gladys was virtually unrecognizable. Outside, the hiss of air brakes and the rattle and rev of a powerful diesel engine cut through the still air. There was a loud clunking sound, and what sounded like a large truck lumbered away.

"Close the door," said Gladys. "Hurry."

One of the figures, a man, pushed the door shut. He locked the handle, the deadbolt, and pulled the chain. Gladys motioned for the group to follow her. They passed the parlor and moved toward the kitchen.

Sally watched them as they moved past her with stolen glances, flashes of smiles, or weary expressions of fatigue or distrust.

Two men, two women, and two children. The two women held babies. At least Sally thought they were babies. The women held the tiny bundles in their arms like newborns, and the bundles were small enough to be newborns.

This was not what Sally expected. Eight people now depended on her. Eight people. That was more than she'd ever guided before. No conductor would handle eight passengers at once. It was too sloppy, too risky, too much to control.

It was hard enough, as she'd proven within the last week, to transport a much smaller passenger load. What was Gladys thinking?

Sally stood there, stunned. Her stomach churned and tightened into a cramp before a surge of hot acid raced up her throat. She gagged and swallowed it before it reached her mouth. She didn't want to do this. Her gut, upset as it was, told her not to do this. But she was committed. Wasn't she? There was no time to think. Not now that they were here. Not now that Gladys was hustling them toward their transportation. Not now.

In the words of so many people in and out of her life over the years, she thought, *It is what it is.* She'd always hated that saying. It defined a sense of destiny or fate beyond self-determination. And while it was true that Sally regularly believed the cosmos was out to get her, she always rationalized that others had it worse. She had a roof over her head, she had a job that made a difference, and she controlled her own fate. If she wanted to alternate stupors and hangovers to get through her life, that was her decision. Nobody made that choice for her.

The irony of it, perhaps, was that as she forced herself to march along the hallway toward the kitchen, this was not really her choice. She'd joined the railroad to make her own choices, to help others make their own choices for their families, and here it was taking that away from her. What was worse, she'd let them do it.

Sally swallowed again. The sour aftertaste of bile stung her throat. Her mouth was dry, her tongue thick. A chill ran along her spine and radiated outward. Perspiration formed on her brow. She wiped her sweaty palms on her shirt and exhaled, not realizing until she did that she'd been holding her breath. Her heart was racing as she stepped into the kitchen. For the first time, she got a clear look at her passengers. Gladys began to introduce them. She spoke with the rhythm of a child anxious to tell an absent parent about her day. Sally hadn't seen Gladys so agitated. The woman pointed at the oldest in the group.

"This is Marcus," she said. "Is that right?"

It surprised Sally that Gladys would use their names. That wasn't part of the protocol. No names, no addresses, no backstories. That way everything was compartmentalized. If anyone was caught and interrogated, there wasn't anything they could reveal that might compromise the railroad, its conductors, or any of its leadership. Maybe none of that mattered since this was her last mission. She was their last conductor. Gladys had made that clear when she'd revealed to her the ways in which they would get out of Atlanta and north and east toward the Harbor.

The old man, with his pain expression and leathered face, rubbed his chin. He took off his black cowboy hat and ran his hand across the top of his head. His short-cropped hair was more white than dark. He had age spots at the temples and in front of his receding hairline. He seemed to hesitate too, as if he understood the typical anonymity of the railroad and its participants.

"Yeah," he said. "I'm Marcus. This is Dallas, Lou, their kids, Andrea, and her kids."

Even before he said their names and referenced them individually, Sally recognized they weren't two couples, as she'd originally thought. Marcus looked more like a grandfather than a dad. He clearly wasn't with Andrea. She stood on the opposite side of the group. She didn't make eye contact with anyone but her son. He was gripping her side and she was quietly reassuring him.

The way Dallas stood protectively next to Lou made it obvious they were together, and their son was between them. He was the spitting image of his father but with his mother's olive complexion.

"I'm…" Sally hedged and swallowed. Then she figured it didn't matter. "I'm Sally. I'm your conductor."

The old man smiled. The deep creases on his face, which reminded Sally of the perpetual ones on Gladys's dresses, stretched. He had a kind face, an honest face. But his eyes…his eyes told Sally something different than did his smile.

There was wisdom in those eyes, yet it wasn't the kind of wisdom that came exclusively from experience. It came from pain. It came from loss. It came from guilt.

Sally recognized the pain, the loss, and the guilt in Marcus's eyes because it was so familiar to her. She saw it whenever she looked in the mirror.

"We know each other, don't we?" Marcus said. "I recognize you."

Sally didn't know him. Then she saw Gladys smile and realized the question wasn't for her.

"We do," Gladys said. "It's been a little while, but yes. My sister and I lived with you in Baird. Well, we lived on the same property as Norma and Rudy."

A flash of recognition brightened Lou's face. She pointed at Gladys and shook her finger. "I remember you," she said. "I *knew* I knew you, I just couldn't place it. You and your sister used to join us for dinner. You did chores around their house."

Gladys nodded. "Marcus and Rudy, and you, Lou, rescued us from the Llano River Clan."

Sally's head was spinning. These people knew Gladys? They lived with her?

"It *has* been a while," said Marcus. "And your sister?"

Marcus searched the room as if the woman might magically appear, raising his eyebrows questioningly.

Gladys shook her head and lowered her chin. "It's just me," she said. "And my railroad."

"Well," said Lou, "it's good to see you again. This time you're rescuing us."

"I hope so," said Gladys. "That's the plan."

"You've *got* a plan, right?" asked Marcus. "I'm assuming we need to move along? We're not standing here because you're about to offer us a late-night snack, are we?"

Sally wasn't sure if he was talking to her or Gladys. It could have been either of them or both. Sally answered. These people were *her* charge now. They were *her* passengers. And as much as she had no power, she was in control.

She cleared her throat. "Yes, we have a plan."

Marcus raised an eyebrow. He was either doubting her or asking for details.

"What is it, then?" Lou asked. She held a bundle close to her neck and was swaying, rocking her child. Her tone was harsh and definitely edged toward doubting.

"We have a truck waiting," said Sally. "It's stocked up, ready to go."

"Is there fuel?" asked Marcus.

"Plenty," said Sally. "Enough to get us where we're going."

"Where exactly *are* we going?" asked Lou. "We've traveled pretty far already. Almost all of it was in the dark about what's next."

Gladys clapped her hands together, a party host looking to play mediator. She chuckled nervously. "All in due time," she said. "Right now our focus needs to be on getting you—"

There was a loud banging noise coming from the front of the house. Someone pounding on the front door. Everyone looked at Gladys, then at Sally, then toward the hallway that led to the entry.

"Are you expecting someone else?" asked Marcus.

Gladys's brow furrowed and she shook her head. The jackhammer fist heel on the door pounded. Again. And again.

"We need to go," said Sally.

"What if it's the last conductor?" asked Dallas. "What if he's warning us about something?"

"Then we need to go now regardless," said Marcus. He jutted his chin toward Sally. "Where to?"

Sally exchanged a knowing look with Gladys, who nodded almost imperceptibly. Then the conductor started back toward the door that led to the basement.

Another volley of heavy pounding reverberated. It sounded as if the door might explode from the hinges.

"You remember your way back?" asked Gladys.

"I'd better," said Sally.

"I'll hold off whoever it is. Don't worry about me. And, Sally?"

The banging stopped.

"Yes?"

"You can do this."

A knot thickened in Sally's parched throat. She mouthed, "Thank you," to Gladys and waved at the others to follow. They moved in a cluster. Only the movement of feet shuffling along the floor, the brush of bodies against one another, the rhythm of their breathing made noise as they quickly headed down the stairs.

Sally stood at the door, waiting for the last of them to pass, shut the door behind her, and descended into the dark basement, hoping she could recall where exactly she needed to go.

CHAPTER 23

APRIL 21, 2054, 9:10 PM
SCOURGE +21 YEARS, 7 MONTHS
ATLANTA, GEORGIA

"They're in there," Rickshaw growled. "I know they're in there." He pounded on the door again. The heel of his fist hurt, each knock vibrating through his hand and up his wrist.

Krespan stood behind him on the stoop. The others were at the bottom of the stoop, on the sidewalk in front of the brownstone.

"Krespan, you saw what I saw, right? A bunch of people, at least one with an infant, run inside this place? It was this place, right?" He jabbed his finger at the door. He wanted to put his fist through it.

"Yes, sir," said Krespan. "I saw them. Six in all, sir. There were definitely four adults. Two of them were children."

Rickshaw turned back to the door. "That's what I thought."

He raised his fist to bang again when the sounds of locks clicking on metal stopped him. The door cracked, a metal chain stretched taut between the door and the frame. An older woman in a short-sleeved, ankle-length dress peered through the gap.

"Hello," she said in a congenial voice. "May I help you?"

"Open the door," said Rickshaw.

The woman grimaced. Rickshaw could tell she was feigning confusion.

"I'm sorry?" she said. "It's very late and I'm tired. Your banging frightened me and—"

Rickshaw tuned her out. He could play the game. He could go back and forth with her for several minutes. He could have his team aim their weapons at her. He could break through the door. It was solid wood. But it wasn't a single piece. There were four inlaid pieces of decorative wood at its center. They were weak points.

He wasn't interested in playing games. He balled his hands into fists and flexed them. The knuckles cracked. He refocused on what she was saying.

"...was cooking a late dinner, and I think it's best if you—"

With lightning speed and thunderous force, Rickshaw lowered his shoulder and drove it into the door at its open edge. It burst inward, the chain breaking away at the jamb. The woman flew backward, stumbling as Rickshaw's momentum carried him into her.

He landed on top of her, and the force of his weight pressed the air from her lungs, leaving her gasping and wheezing. Rickshaw used her shoulders to push himself up into a plank position and planted the toes of his boots against the floor. He looked down at her. Her eyes were wide with shock and pain. She gasped like a fish suffocating beside its bowl.

He rolled off her and got up. His men were at the stoop. None of them had come into the house. The brass chain swung like a pendulum on the door. The jamb was splintered where the locking bar had ripped free.

"Get in here," he snapped at his men. "Close the door. Pick up the woman."

The men did as they were told. Two of the soldiers held up the woman underneath her arms. She was still gasping, her head hanging limply on her neck. Her dress was torn at the shoulder.

Rickshaw scanned his surroundings and pointed toward the

parlor. "Take her in there," he said. "Krespan, you come with me."

Rickshaw spun away from the woman, believing it would be a few minutes before she could answer any questions. He needed to find the others—four adults, two children, two infants.

"You check all the doors. Open them one by one. If they don't open with a turn of the handle, figure out an alternative. Those people couldn't have gotten far. Find them."

"Yes, sir," said Krespan. The soldier saluted him and checked a door right next to them. It was a coat closet.

Rickshaw marched toward the kitchen at the end of the hallway. The room was too clean to be a kitchen. And at the same time it was too dirty.

There was no grease on the stove, no fingerprints or smudges on the stainless steel. There was no evidence the lady of the house was cooking dinner. But there was dust everywhere. A thin layer coated everything in the room. Everything except where it was recently swiped clean along the edges of the engineered stone countertop at the center of the kitchen. Then he looked at the floor. There were boot prints. Not so much prints, really, as they were the remnants of dirt that shook loose from soles in the partial imprints of boot treads. There were people here. No doubt.

Rickshaw spun around like he'd missed the people by a fraction of a second, like they were standing behind him, snickering at his lack of situational awareness. His body tensed and he stomped through the kitchen, blindly searching the large rooms of the first floor.

He bounded up the stairs, clearing empty room after empty room. The rooms weren't only empty of people, they were absent furnishings and light fixtures. The only decorations at all, aside from peeling wallpaper or chipped paint, were the same doily sheers that blocked the sidelights next to the front door to the house. They hung in front of the windows to each of the rooms, pulled closed.

The rooms themselves were stuffy, the air dusty. He could taste it in his mouth even as he breathed through his nose. Nobody lived here.

He holstered his pistol and raced down the stairs to the parlor. The woman was sitting in an oversized chair, two guards flanking her. The other two were at the entry to the parlor, standing watch.

Rickshaw snapped at both of them, "What are you doing?"

The guards looked at him, puzzled. Neither of them responded quickly enough.

"Go help Krespan," Rickshaw barked. "You're doing nobody any good standing here. Like we need four armed men watching this woman. Use your heads."

The men ducked their chins like scolded dogs and hustled from their posts. Rickshaw twisted his neck from side to side. Small pops of air crackled as he took in a deep, calming breath. He adjusted his duster and eyed the woman, stepping confidently toward her and effecting a broad, cheerful smile intended to be as intimidating as it was anything else.

"Hello," he said. "I think we got off on the wrong foot. I'm Captain Greg Rickshaw with the government's Population Guard."

Rickshaw held eye contact as he sat down on the sofa across from her chair. He flipped the duster back and sank into the soft, worn cushion. Using his palms, he pushed himself onto the firm edge of the cushion, relying on the furniture's frame for support. The woman's nose was bloodied. There were smudges of it on her upper lip and chin, a spatter of it on the front of her dress. She sat stone-faced with her hands clasped in her lap.

"And you are?" he prompted.

The woman said nothing. One thumb ran across the other. Her legs were crossed at her ankles.

Rickshaw put a hand to his chest. "I'm sorry," he said, a lilt in his voice. "I didn't mean to injure you. That was an unfortunate by-product of my forced entry. Collateral damage. It happens."

The woman's lip twitched. She separated her hands and used her fingers to press flat her dress. Her eyes never left his.

Rickshaw sighed. "Where are they?" he asked, searching the woman's face for any reaction, however small.

The woman raised her eyebrows. "Who?"

"I know they were here," he said. "I know you said you're cooking dinner or whatever, but they were in the kitchen. Now they're gone. Where are they?"

Her eyebrows relaxed and her mouth flattened into a straight line. "I don't know what you're talking about."

Rickshaw frowned. "That's a shame." He stood, flipped aside the long tail of his duster, and unsnapped his holster.

Her eyes fell to his hand on the revolver. He watched her as he moved around the table between them. Then he motioned to his guards.

"Grab her hands," he said. "Hold one flat on the table."

He twirled the gun in his hand. The woman struggled against the two much stronger men. Her placid expression tightened; her face squeezed with worry. She grunted protest and balled her fists. Her body stiffened; the tendons in her neck strained.

"No, no, no, no, no," she said, resisting. Her back arched. The nostrils of her bloody nose flared.

The men restrained her nonetheless. One held her at the neck, pushing her forward. The other held her wrist at the table. She struggled against their force. It was futile.

Rickshaw checked the cylinder and spun it. Then he reached down and pressed the barrel against the back of her fist. "Where are they?"

She didn't answer. Instead, the woman struggled and fought against her captors.

Rickshaw shrugged. "Okay then." He pulled the trigger. The hammer snapped. *Click.*

The woman relaxed for a brief moment and tensed again. He didn't have time for this. He couldn't let this interrogation take its course over the hours he'd usually employ at headquarters. There was urgency here. Every second that passed meant the people, the infants, were getting farther and farther away.

This woman, who he assumed was Gladys, could help him derail the underground operation bent at undoing his good works. However, that could wait.

"Where are they?" he asked again with the same intonation, soft, assured, deliberate.

The woman gritted her teeth. Her nose started bleeding again.

Rickshaw pressed harder into the back of her hand, blanching the skin white. He pulled the trigger. *Click.*

The woman let out a spit-laden breath. Her body relaxed for an instant before she tried to free herself again. It struck Rickshaw as odd that she'd keep struggling. Even if she managed to free herself from the two guards, where would she go? What would she do?

The human mind was an amazing creation. It worked in ways Rickshaw had only begun to understand. He did know a lot about the inducement of fear and how it forced people to do things, to say things, to react in ways a rational person would not.

"Where are they? If you—"

Krespan burst into the room, breathless. "Sir," he said, "we found where they went."

Rickshaw eyed the woman again and winked. "I'll be back."

He followed Krespan from the room, his revolver in his hand, calling to the guards, "You can let go of her. Keep an eye on her. I'll be back."

He and Krespan wound their way back through the kitchen to an open door. It was narrow and taller than the other doors. As he approached, Rickshaw could see it led to a set of stairs that descended into a basement. Krespan led him down the steps and into a dimly lit space with low ceilings and the dank odor of mildew and red clay.

They turned right and Krespan guided Rickshaw amongst boxes

and discarded household goods. Rickshaw noticed they'd traveled too far to still be underneath the brownstone from which they'd descended.

"Where are we?" he asked.

"This leads to another house," Krespan said. "There are stairs leading there. The other two guards are there."

"How far?"

Krespan pointed ahead with the barrel of his rifle. "Up here. Almost there."

Krespan turned right and started bounding up the steps, taking them two at a time. Rickshaw followed his lead, his boots hammering on the stairs as he climbed toward this new house.

He reached the top and entered the kitchen. It looked almost identical to the one from which he'd just come, but it was backwards, a mirror of the other house. This one had clearly been used.

The faint scent of coffee and cooking oil permeated the space. Rickshaw looked around. Despite the evidence of people having been here, he didn't see any people.

"Where are they?" he asked with the same tone he'd used with Gladys.

"Follow me," said Krespan.

They maneuvered their way through the house, racing along corridors and through large rooms until they reached an open door that led to a garage. The garage door was open. One of the guards was on the concrete floor, motionless, a pool of blood leaking from under his back.

Rickshaw marched past the body, not checking to see if the guard was alive. He kicked away the rifle and sent it skittering across the floor. The other guard was standing in the short driveway, his rifle raised at an invisible target farther up the street.

"What is this?" Rickshaw demanded. He stood with his boots shoulder width apart, his attention split between the guard on the driveway and Krespan.

Krespan was kneeling next to the prone guard. "He's dead."

"I don't care about that," said Rickshaw. "I care about the fugitives. What happened?"

Krespan got to his feet and met Rickshaw in the driveway. There was dim light from the moon and the lone functioning streetlight on the block.

"We found the door open," said Krespan, "the one leading from the basement to this house. I sent the two guards ahead and came back to get you. So—"

"Then stop talking," said Rickshaw. He rounded on the other guard. "I need to hear from someone who knows what happened."

The guard lowered his rifle. He kept both hands on it and aimed the muzzle at the ground. "They were still here when we got into the kitchen. We could hear 'em. They were loading up into a truck."

Rickshaw tensed, one hand curling into a fist. With the other he adjusted his grip on the revolver.

The guard swallowed hard. "We tried to stop 'em, sir. They got the drop on us. We both fired. I think I hit the truck, but there was–"

"How many were there?"

"Eight."

"Eight?"

"Four adults, a couple of kids, and I'm pretty sure there were two babies."

Rickshaw loosened the fist and held up two fingers. "Two babies?"

The guard nodded, his eyes darting between Rickshaw and Krespan.

"What was the vehicle?"

"A big silver truck," said the guard. "Chevy, I think. Four door, big bed. It had a tarp over it held down by bungees. I—"

"Which way did they go?"

The guard pointed in the direction he'd been aiming his rifle. "They can't be more than—"

The bullet drilled through his skull and dropped him before he finished the sentence. Rickshaw held the revolver out for an extended moment. Then he lowered it and flipped open the cylinder. From his pocket he pulled out a handful of rounds and loaded them, one by one, into the weapon.

He turned to a slack-jawed, wide-eyed Krespan. The soldier appeared frozen into place, the human model for a stone carving or wax figure.

"Fifty-fifty shot," Rickshaw said. "Pretty good odds. For me, not for him."

Krespan leveled his gaze at Rickshaw. "Why did you do that, sir?"

"He let them get away. I don't need somebody like that working for me. Plus, it felt good. It's a release. You get it, Krespan?"

He nodded, but Rickshaw knew the guard didn't get it. Krespan followed orders, but he wasn't cut from the same cloth.

"C'mon," he said. "Let's get the woman and take her with us as we give chase."

Krespan's brow wrinkled. "Give chase, sir?"

Rickshaw chortled. "Yes. We're not letting them get away."

The captain led his subordinate back through the house and down the stairs into the basement. He knew that in the big scheme of things, chasing a random group of newly proclaimed fugitives shouldn't be a priority. Not on the surface, anyhow. But given that this group of men, women, and children had made a stop at the home of the purported ringleader of the railroad, there must be some value in them.

If Gladys would risk her entire operation to save these people, two things were clear. One, she had a connection to them. And two, they were definitely headed toward the Harbor. He could feel it.

Adrenaline surged through his body as he weaved his way across the basement toward the steps that led back to the first house. The big strong guard kept pace. Rickshaw felt Krespan on his hip. The heavy plunk of his military boots on the floor matched Rickshaw's own gait.

They climbed the steps with the same vigor and speed as before. Rickshaw led them through the kitchen. His revolver was holstered now. He dragged the fingers of his right hand along the dusty countertop, leaving clean streaks behind.

His duster billowed behind him as he moved with purpose into the hallway. Then he stopped cold.

Rickshaw held up his hand and stopped Rickshaw. The two stood in the hall. A gurgling sound came from the parlor. A rifle lay on the floor, half of it in the hallway. The front door to the house was open.

The captain motioned for Krespan to move forward, and the two of them inched toward the parlor. Rickshaw unsnapped the strap on his holster and drew the revolver. He spun it in his hand and held it up, ready to fire.

The gurgling sound grew louder as they approached. The closer they got, the more it sounded like a man choking.

Rickshaw reached the wide opening that led from the hallway into the parlor and swung around with the revolver leveled waist high, sweeping the room.

The woman was gone. Two men were on the floor. One of them stared blankly at the ceiling, his throat torn open. The other was on his side, his legs and arms twitching. His hand gripped a knife at the corner of his neck. It was driven to the hilt. He was the source of the gurgle, the choking sounds that sent chills up and down Rickshaw's spine.

"Check the door, Krespan. See what's out there."

He moved to the dying man on the floor and crouched beside him. He held a finger to his lips and then put his hand on the man's shoulder. "Shhh," he said. "Stop fighting it. It's over for you, brother. It's over."

Then he twisted the knife and withdrew it from the man's neck. It *was* over.

Rickshaw wiped the blade on the guard's uniform and studied it. It wasn't a big knife, the blade no more than three inches. But it was serrated on one side and sharpened to a fine edge on the other. He folded it into its grip and stood, stuffing it into his pocket.

Krespan came back into the house and stood in the hall. He pursed his lips and shook his head. "She's gone, sir," he said. "I don't see any trace of her."

CHAPTER 24

APRIL 21, 2054, 9:30 PM
SCOURGE +21 YEARS, 7 MONTHS
ATLANTA, GEORGIA

"Did you kill him?"

The question lingered in the truck's cab. It hung there amongst them, three in the front and four crammed into the back.

Marcus took off his hat and put it on the dash in front of him. He leaned against the front passenger's door, giving himself as much hip room as possible. Dallas was in the middle between Sally and him.

"It was a clean shot," said Marcus. "So the chances are good."

Sally gripped her hands on the wheel. "Good that he's alive, or good that he's dead?"

Marcus scratched his neck. The stubble was irritating his skin. "Depends on your perspective, I guess."

"He did what he had to do," said Lou. "If he hadn't returned fire, they'd have caught us."

Marcus shifted in his seat. He didn't like being this close to Dallas. Days without a shower hadn't done him any favors.

Sally checked the rearview mirror, presumably to glare at Lou. She twisted her hands on the wheel again, tightened her grip, and

168

accelerated onto the highway. The truck bounced against a pothole the size of the Volkswagen from Gun Barrel City.

David squealed in the back seat. Or it could have been Javier. Marcus wasn't sure. They were in the middle, next to each other and between their mothers. Both women held their infants against their bodies.

"I'm just saying," said Sally, stealing glances at everyone in the truck, "that if they are dead, they're all the more likely to come after us."

"I'm just saying," mocked Lou, "that if we hadn't gotten out of there, none of this would matter. What did you say your name was?"

Sally changed lanes to avoid another pothole. She glanced in the mirror. "Sally. And you're Lou?"

"Why are you doing this?" asked Lou.

"Doing what?"

"Helping us?"

"I'm a conductor," said Sally. "It's what I do."

That answer seemed to satisfy Lou, at least enough that she didn't ask any more questions. She turned her attention to her newborn. Marcus heard the suckling sound of a newborn trying to learn the art of feeding.

The truck bounced when the tires struck a wide divot in the road. It wasn't really a pothole, it was more of a crease that spread from one side of the concrete to the other and was essentially unavoidable. Sally jerked the wheel. The bright white fan of the headlights shifted their illumination of the road ahead and settled again.

Marcus was surprised at the state of disrepair of the roads here. The last time he was in Atlanta, more than a decade ago, it hadn't been this bad. And technology had only improved, hadn't it? Clearly, the government had other priorities.

They were headed northeast. Marcus only knew that from the electronic compass on the dash. He adjusted his hips again and leaned on the door. His eyes settled on the zip of the fading white dashes separating the highway's two lanes.

He squinted, focusing on the lines appearing at the edge of the headlights' reach and disappearing underneath the front of the truck. He smiled, remembering how, as a child, he would do this and pretend he was in a spaceship traveling at light speed.

It was especially fun on newly paved asphalt, which was virtually black and gave the impression that he was surrounded by darkness. In his head he would make laser noises or maybe the sounds of explosions as his spaceship, an X-wing fighter from *Star Wars* or a Cylon Raider from *Battlestar Galactica,* fought off the enemy. Fighting the enemy in his head was so much more fun than doing it in real life. Nobody got hurt, and he was absent guilt or regret.

He was lost in thought long enough that the women and kids in the back were asleep. Even the infants were snorting contentedly. That was a blessing.

Only Sally and Dallas were awake.

Dallas nudged him back to the moment. "Hey."

Marcus gave Dallas a side-eye, which he hoped would tell him he wasn't interested in talking. It was either too dark in the cab for him to see it or Dallas ignored it.

"You awake?" Dallas asked.

Marcus knew that Dallas knew he was awake. This dude was a man-child. Marcus sighed, as would any exasperated parent. He regretted not having put his hat on his head and pulling it low over his eyes. He could have used the sleep, and it would have stopped a conversation he didn't want to have. He hadn't had the forethought, so he relented.

"Yeah," he said. "What's up?"

Dallas leaned in, eliminating the modicum of space between them, and lowered his voice. A waft of his rank odor wafted into Marcus's nose. "I've gotta get something off my chest."

Marcus considered making a Lou-quality snarky comment, but

thought better of it. He shrugged. "Go ahead."

"I know Lou wanted you here," said Dallas, "and I—"

Marcus sighed. "Are we doing this again?"

Dallas put up a hand. "Just let me finish. I'm trying to be a man about this."

Marcus snorted then apologized. "Sorry."

Dallas flexed his jaw, likely restraining himself from saying something that would derail whatever his point was. He closed his eyes for a moment and then continued. "Back at the library, you really put my wife in danger."

Perhaps sensing the tension building in Marcus's body, Dallas held up his hands and shook his head. "I'm not saying you meant to do it, I'm just asking you to remember why you're here. You're here to keep us alive. This is not a revenge mission. It's not a rescue mission. It's an escape."

Marcus relaxed. The kid had a point.

"I love Lou more than anything in this world," Dallas said. "I mean, I know you love her too, in your own way. She's like a daughter to you. She looks at you like a father. You're her hero. Really. And I don't begrudge you that, Marcus. The two of you have been through so much together, a two person-wrecking crew."

"That was a long time ago," said Marcus. "We—"

"It was as recent as the library," said Dallas. "And before that, she did it to herself in Gun Barrel City at the reservoir. I couldn't stop her. She doesn't listen to me like that. You know how strong-willed she is."

Marcus smiled. He knew.

In the glow of the dash, Marcus noticed the glistening sheen in Dallas's eyes. The kid's voice was shaky.

"But there was no need to have her take the door at the library," said Dallas. "You could have done that. From here on out, until we get to the Harbor, I'm asking you to consider her safety first." Tears rolled down Dallas's cheeks. He wiped them away with the back of his hand and kept talking. "Please, she listens to you. She idolizes you. My world is Lou and our kids. *Please*."

Marcus studied Dallas's face, as much as he could in the relative dark, and then stared out the front windshield at the white dashes disappearing underneath the truck. The fan of the headlights arced across the width of the highway.

"You're absolutely right," he said. "I should have taken the door. In all truth, Lou should have been upstairs protecting Andrea and the kids."

Dallas rubbed his hands on his pants. He sniffed and wiped his nose.

"When this is said and done, rest assured, I'll head back to Virginia and you don't have to worry about me."

Dallas huffed a sarcastic laugh. "Huh. For a minute there I was impressed. You listened to me."

"But what?" asked Marcus.

"You had to take a nice sentiment and flip it. Now you're being a martyr," said Dallas. "That's appropriate."

Marcus considered it. The kid was more intuitive than he'd understood. Maybe, despite his ripe body odor, he was good for Lou. He had, after all, taken care of her all of these years. She loved him, he clearly loved her, and his anger at Marcus was born of that love, of his desire to protect her from hurt even if he knew that the only person Lou believed was capable of impenetrable protection was Mad Max.

"That's fair," said Marcus. "I hear you. You're right, I probably wallow too much. That comes from living by myself. You tend to be inside your own head a lot. I'll work on it."

Dallas's brow twitched and furrowed. He frowned, like he wasn't sure what to make of Marcus's admission.

"I'm serious," said Marcus. "I'll do a better job. However long I'm with you. Okay?"

Dallas's face relaxed. He scratched his chin and rubbed his hands on his pants again. He sniffed, crinkling his nose. Finally, he nodded. "Deal."

"Hey, guys?" said Sally.

Marcus had forgotten she was there, too focused on the conversation with Dallas. "Yeah?" he said, leaning forward to look past Dallas.

"Are you done with your male bonding?"

Marcus and Dallas exchanged glances. Neither of them said anything.

"Because we need a plan," she said. "There's no way we're getting to where we're going without resistance."

Marcus grimaced. "I thought you had a plan."

"I do," Sally said, "but we all need to be on the same page or it isn't going to work."

"How about you tell us where we're going?" asked Dallas. "That might be a good start."

"I shouldn't say exactly where," she said.

"Why not?"

"It puts too many others at risk," said Sally. "The Harbor is home to a few hundred people. I don't want to put them in danger. And if we don't make it, it's better that..."

"Plausible deniability?" asked Marcus.

Sally snapped her fingers and pointed at the road ahead. "That's it. Plausible deniability. If you don't know the exact location, you can't tell anyone else where it is."

Marcus watched her for a moment. She continually twisted her hands on the wheel, leaned forward then back, shifting uncomfortably in her seat.

"You don't know where it is, do you?" he asked. "They didn't tell you either."

Sally's head snapped toward Marcus, her eyes wide with surprise.

"If we get caught," said Marcus, "you get caught. So you don't know."

Sally clenched her jaw. She swallowed hard enough that her throat moved. She wiped her forehead with the back of her hand. "No, they didn't tell me."

CHAPTER 25

APRIL 21, 2054, 9:40 PM
SCOURGE +21 YEARS, 7 MONTHS
ATLANTA, GEORGIA

"Well, this is clever," said Greg Rickshaw. "Very clever."

"You think this is how they communicate, sir?" asked Krespan. "How they make the railroad work?"

They were standing in front of a table loaded with electronics. It wasn't a cheap setup. Rickshaw imagined they'd purchased most of it on the black market. The government wasn't much for letting people use radio bands. It was too difficult to monitor.

"That's a good guess," said Rickshaw.

"Don't these people understand that we have laws for the betterment of everyone?" asked Krespan. "We have population restrictions for a reason. We fight so hard aginst conspiracy for a reason. It's for the good of the whole."

Rickshaw glanced over his shoulder and studied the good soldier. He nodded at Krespan while marveling at his belief in the system. He'd bought into it hook, line, and sinker.

The government needed people like Krespan. It had to have naïve purists like him to function. If everyone knew the real reasons for their heavy hand, it would collapse. That was why stopping the railroad was so important.

It wasn't about the children or even the flouting of the laws. It was the seeds of discontent it sowed. It was the whisper in the alley, the note passed under the table, the wink and nod on the street corner. The railroad was a freight train. The louder it got, the closer it was to barreling through everything in its way, leaving it in tatters.

"Have you thoroughly searched all of the rooms?" he asked his subordinate.

Krespan shook his head. "Not yet, sir."

"Why don't you do that while I figure this out? I might get lucky and glean something from it."

Krespan saluted. "Yes, sir." He spun on his boot heel to search the rest of the brownstone.

They'd come back here, entering through the garage, after the truck and Gladys escaped them. Rickshaw wasn't about to go back to headquarters empty handed. He'd lost four men and been outsmarted by an elderly woman.

Rickshaw pulled out the chair and sat down. He flipped aside his duster and studied the equipment in front of him.

"Computer," he said out of habit and hoping it would work, "are you there?"

He waited. There was no response. He cursed under his breath.

Rickshaw knew it was unlikely this place had a central computer, but given the railroad's success and Gladys's obvious craftiness, it was worth a shot. Absent the computer, he'd have to do this the old-fashioned way.

He rubbed his hands together and then flexed them in and out. Knuckles cracked and the stiffness loosened. He sighed and scanned the equipment. He pulled the chain on the banker's lamp, and the dim yellow light warmed to a soft glow. Next to the lamp was a piece of paper with a list of random letter and number combinations.

As good as he was with the state-of-the-art offerings in the headquarters, these much lower-tech devices were a mystery. He rolled in the wheeled chair and picked up a set of headphones, adjusted them for his head, and slid them over his ears.

He spun a volume dial to the right. Then he pushed a button, which appeared to be a power toggle. A low hiss of ambient noise filled his ears. He put his hand on a desktop microphone, which he assumed was the way to communicate.

There were knobs and dials, which looked as though they controlled the transmission frequency. He didn't want to mess with them. Changing the preset conditions might only serve to eliminate the one shot he had at learning something.

He pushed the button at the base of the mic and spoke into the wire mesh at the mouth of it.

"Hello?" He let go of the key, waited, and pressed again. "Hello. Is anyone there? This is railroad business."

There was a hiss and a crackle. Then a static-laden response leaked from the headphones and Rickshaw smiled.

"This frequency is clear," said the voice. *"Hello."*

The next part of the message wiped the smile from Rickshaw's face.

"This is HR29BR." It was a man's voice. *"Who is this?"*

Rickshaw didn't know who he was supposed to be. His eyes darted across the equipment. He spun in the chair, looking for any sign or clue as to how he should respond. Of one thing he was sure; he couldn't say he was Gladys. That would end the conversation and maybe send an alarm.

"This is HR29BR," the voice on the other end of the radio transmission repeated. *"Who is this?"*

Rickshaw cursed under his breath. He cupped the headphones with his hands and dropped his elbows onto the table. An invisible timer was counting down in his head. He knew he didn't have but a few seconds to respond with something credible.

He eyed the radio, the mic, the banker's lamp, the—

Next to the lamp was the piece of paper he'd glossed over before. On it was written a collection of number and letter combinations. He noticed one of them, near the bottom, was HR29BR.

Rickshaw ran his finger up and down the list of numbers and letters. They were call signs. How had he not recognized this?

He had to pick one. Which one? Which one? Clenching his jaw, he traced the identification at the top of the list. It was as good as any of the others. Rickshaw thought he might as well spin the cylinder of his revolver and pull the trigger.

Rickshaw pressed the mic key. "Hello, HR29BR," he said. "This is G-F-A-G-A-5."

He released the key and listened. With his eyes closed, he awaited the response. His pulse thumped in his neck. Rickshaw didn't like this feeling. His stomach lurched. There was something about not being in control that made his skin itch.

"Hello, GFAGA5. We weren't expecting a transmission. Everything good on your end?"

Rickshaw considered his response. His accelerated heartbeat made him uncomfortable. A lot was riding on this conversation. He had to skillfully extract information without revealing his real identity. Intelligence gathering was a much different task without the benefit of chains and a game of Russian roulette. It wasn't nearly as satisfying.

He pressed the key. The static in his ears went silent.

"On schedule here. Assets are in position. How about on your end?"

It struck Rickshaw that whoever was on the other end of the transmission seemed unconcerned about talking to an unfamiliar voice, yet they didn't pick up on it. At least not yet. He assumed there must be multiple people using the system. How many radios did the railroad have? Was this how they were so successful at communicating their movements, how they stayed one step ahead of the Pop Guard?

"On schedule here," he said, lifting the octave of his voice. "How's the weather?"

It was a silly question on its face. The weather was always dry. Rain came once every few weeks in some regions, not at all in others. Rickshaw hoped that the description of the weather might give him some clue as to where the transmission originated. Maybe he could glean some clue as to which part of the railroad this was and where it operated.

There was a long pause this time. Static and high-pitched waves of sound danced in his ears. He pushed one of the headphones back. The side of his head was damp with sweat.

"Weather is the same. Windy offshore, though."

Offshore? Had Rickshaw heard that correctly? His eyes scanned the desk, his fingers hovering over the mic key. He pressed it. "Repeat, please? I didn't copy you, HR29BR."

The response was almost immediate. *"Weather is the same, but it's windy offshore."*

He *did* say it. That was a clue. It was a clue in the eye of a needle amongst a thousand needles in a haystack, but it was a clue.

His eyes absently skittered across the desk again. Rickshaw searched his mind for the next question. What could he ask that might narrow the coastline? He had Pop Guards patrols up and down the Eastern Seaboard. He could direct all of them east to the shorelines, the beaches, the ports, the harbors.

The harbors.

His eyes widened as he stared at the piece of paper on the desk underneath the banker's lamp. The letters glowed in the soft light, calling him, offering him answers to questions he didn't realize he had.

There it was. HR29BR. HRBR. Harbor. He was talking to the Harbor.

Rickshaw rolled back in the chair and darted his eyes around the room, then pushed his hands on to the chair's arms to stand. When he did, the headphone cord stretched and pulled. The headset flipped from his head, dragging across one ear, and whipped at the end of the cord. It dangled, twisting, from the edge of the desk.

He laced his fingers behind his head, walking in a small circle, pacing in the room. Rickshaw wasn't sure what to do next. If he could extract a little more information from the Harbor, he could tell his superiors where to shove their ultimatums.

Should he tell them what he'd learned already? Give them a status update?

No. None of that. He would solve the problem first. He would end the railroad. He would expose the Harbor. Only then would he tell them.

His eyes focused on the volume meter on the transceiver. The needles were bouncing. Someone was talking. His brow furrowed, his hands went to his ears. He realized he'd lost the headset. Rickshaw scrambled back into the chair, rolled himself forward, and put on the headset.

"…there? Do you copy?"

Fingers trembling with excitement, he pressed the key. He exhaled slowly to even his breathing and responded, "I'm here. Apologies, HR29BR. Got sidetracked here. Any other details for us? Asset allocation?"

He let go of the key, releasing the soft strain into his ears before the Harbor communicator responded. It was short. It was exactly what Rickshaw needed.

"Low-country assets all good. Standing by."

Rickshaw's finger hovered over the key. His mouth hung open as he considered how to respond. He moved his hand away from the mic and took off the headphones. He didn't need to say anything else. He knew exactly where to go.

The captain stood, adjusted his duster, and flexed his fingers. He stepped from the radio room and into the hallway. "Krespan!"

The soldier appeared within seconds, standing at attention. "Yes, sir?"

"Connect with all of our patrols within a one-hundred-mile radius of Charleston, South Carolina," he said. "I want them all converging on Charleston."

Krespan saluted. "Yes, sir. Right away. Should I let headquarters know?"

Rickshaw put a hand on Krespan's shoulder. He shook his head and offered a wry smile. "No. We're going to take care of this and offer a wonderful surprise to HQ when it's all over."

Krespan smiled. "You found the Harbor? It's in Charleston?"

Rickshaw nodded. He knew that the "low country" was what South Carolinians called the southern coastal region of their state. He couldn't be sure that Charleston was the exact location of the Harbor, but he knew it was close. And if he could get enough of his assets into position, they could torture their way to the precise location.

Once they had the Harbor under their control, they'd have a gold mine of information. Every single person there had traveled the underground railroad to get there. Even if individuals could only offer snippets of intelligence, he could piece enough of those snippets together to get the bigger picture. He'd get names, locations, methods of transportation.

"Yes," he said to his aide. "We've found it. More or less. Now get the troops headed in that direction. We're joining them. We've got to get going. I want this thing over yesterday."

CHAPTER 26

APRIL 21, 2054, 10:00 PM
SCOURGE +21 YEARS, 7 MONTHS
ATLANTA, GEORGIA

Gladys pushed on the trapdoor and eased it up slowly. The well-oiled hinges slid open and she peeked out from the subfloor bunker.

In truth, it was more of a cubbyhole than a bunker, but it provided enough space for six people should the Pop Guard come calling. It was in the hallway between the kitchen and the door to the radio room of her house.

She'd run to it as soon as she'd escaped the hapless, unsuspecting guards watching her two doors down the street. Gladys's first instinct was to run as far away as possible. But where would she go? It was better to go home and wait it out, especially since her gut told her Rickshaw would come back.

Gladys had been surprised to see the dead men in front of her house. One of them bled into the street from the edge of her short driveway. The other was motionless in her garage. Had Marcus and his group killed both of them during their escape? Gladys remembered how efficiently violent he could be. Despite his age, he'd obviously retained his lethality.

She climbed from the hiding place and brushed the creases from her dress. The front door was open. She walked the short distance to the foyer, stepping past the dead soldier half in the hallway, and pushed the door shut. She locked it.

"All right," she said with a huff, "where to begin?"

First she checked the dead body in the parlor and was disappointed to find her Huse hand-forged folding knife was missing. It had come in handy more than once. She cursed under her breath and marched to the kitchen. Angrily, she rummaged through the drawers and cabinets, looking for a backup knife, but couldn't find one. It would have to wait.

Back in the radio room, she rolled herself to the desk and lifted the headset. She adjusted the volume on the transceiver and pressed the mic key. Whatever they'd communicated to Rickshaw had given him the impression he knew exactly where to go to find the Harbor. Now she had to know what they'd revealed, and she had to warn them. If Rickshaw had time to gather enough of his armed patrols and they hit the coast before her people were ready, they'd be slaughtered.

The Harbor answered immediately when she called. The man on the receiving end of her transmission was floored. Through the static, she could hear the guilt, the fear, the worry in his voice.

"It's not your fault," said Gladys. "You couldn't know he'd have access to the equipment or our handles. I should have installed a fail-safe code."

Gladys couldn't believe she hadn't done that. All of her operatives had codes in the field, safe words that would tip off others to danger. How had she not done the same for radio communications between the Harbor and her?

After years of doing this, of living on the edge and in the shadows, she'd learned from her mistakes. Then she'd course-corrected and improved the function of her clandestine operation. Would she get the chance to learn from this? Or would the Pop Guard and their mother government finally get the best of her?

Her mind raced as she discussed plans with the Harbor. How had Rickshaw found her in the first place? Had he followed Marcus, Lou, Dallas, and the others here? Had it been a happy accident or coincidence?

No, she thought. *There's no such thing as coincidence.*

Someone had tipped off Rickshaw and his goons. Someone had told them where to look, where to find her.

Rickshaw had clearly known, even if he hadn't said it, she was in control. Did he know her name?

Gladys suddenly felt ill. Her stomach roiled. Her head ached with the thick pulse of a building migraine. Planting her elbows on her desk, she put her head in her hands. The adrenaline surge from the last hour was waning. Exhaustion rippled through her body and she wanted to sleep, close her eyes and dream good dreams. Yet there was too much work to do. There was too much riding on the next twenty-four hours. She couldn't stay here; she had to be there. She had to find a way to the coast, to the low country, to the Harbor.

"We can get you here," said the voice on the other end of the transmission. *"There's a supply transport leaving soon. I have an address. You could beat him here."*

Gladys gathered herself and leaned back in her chair. "Don't give me the address," she said. "I know where the transports pick up their goods. Just let them know I'm coming. Don't let the truck leave without me."

"Roger that," said HR29BR.

Gladys swallowed hard. She pressed her hand to her stomach and suppressed the urge to vomit. Her temples were throbbing. She took a deep breath, held it, and blew it out like a long kiss through puckered lips. Her fingers again found the mic key.

"I'm on my way," she said. "Don't start the fight without me."

CHAPTER 27

APRIL 22, 2054, 4:00 AM
SCOURGE +21 YEARS, 7 MONTHS
TUSCALOOSA, ALABAMA

"I was always more of an Auburn fan," said Rudy. "Don't ask me why. Maybe I liked that they were the underdog."

"Underdog?" Norma leaned back to stretch her torso. It was stiff from sitting for too long.

"I mean, compared to Alabama and their juggernaut, everybody was the underdog before the Scourge."

"Not Clemson," she said.

"True. But Auburn definitely was."

They stood outside the train station. Above them was a simple green sign that announced their location. To their left were the tracks; ahead of them was an empty parking lot.

"How long before he's here?" asked Rudy. He leaned on a cane, his shoulders stooped with exhaustion. "I'm getting tired. Sort of need a rest."

Their bags were at their feet. Norma eyed her husband. He did need to rest. She'd asked so much of him to travel this far, to travel at all, really. But he was healing. That was good. Instead of telling him that, she smirked.

"Who said it's a he?" she asked. "Why can't our conductor be a woman?"

Rudy didn't miss a beat. "Oh, it could be," he said. "I just figured a man would be the only one stupid enough to meet us here in the middle of the night."

Norma chuckled. It was good to laugh. And her husband could still make her laugh. "Touché," she said. "I don't know where *he* is. But he knows we were on that train, so it shouldn't be long."

Norma was turned, her back to the lot, to talk with Rudy. Her eyes drifted past him to the building at the edge of the tracks. The old brick station resembled something out of nineteenth-century England, complete with a two-story turret at its center. It was something her grandmother would have called a conversation piece.

The air was cooler here. Spring hadn't quite sprung as much as it had in Texas. Though in west Texas there were only two seasons: summer and almost summer.

"I think I see him," said Rudy. He motioned behind Norma with his chin. "Big truck?"

Norma turned to see the bright twin headlights of a large truck. Its engine rumbled and the brakes squealed as the driver downshifted. The beams flashed at them. She used her hand like a visor to shield her eyes.

A quick scan of the parking lot told her it was otherwise empty, as best she could tell. There were a couple of workers inside the building, but they hadn't stepped outside since the train pulled out of the station and headed for Birmingham.

"I'll go check," she said.

"I'll go with you," said Rudy. "Hand me a bag, please."

Norma frowned at him. "No need to be chivalrous. I can handle it."

Rudy smiled. His teeth shone in the lights. "I know you can handle it. I don't want you leaving me alone here."

He winked. She smirked and handed him a bag. The two of them crossed the lot toward the driver's side of the truck.

"How are we going to know?" asked Rudy.

"We'll know," said Norma.

The truck's engine idled. Heat from its machinery rolled off the cab in waves. The smell of diesel was pungent and stung the back of Norma's nostrils. She coughed and shook her head free of the fumes.

At the driver's side door, she reached up and banged on the metal. It echoed in the parking lot; Norma stopped after the first few hits. Then she knocked softer. It was a pattern of knocks. While it wasn't "two shaves and a haircut," it was a code nonetheless.

The driver rolled down the window. His thick forearm rested on the open sill and he leaned his head out the window.

A burly man, he looked to her like the photographs of loggers she'd seen in books about the Pacific Northwest in the twentieth century. He had a large handlebar mustache and a wiry beard that almost looked like an uncoiled Brillo pad. His eyes were pinched between the folds of his full cheeks and heavy brow. He wore a wool beanie despite the weather. His left ear bore a black gauge earring the size of a quarter.

"I've never seen the Llano River," he said. "But I hear it's disgusting this time of year."

Norma gave him a thumbs-up and glanced back at Rudy. "It's him."

Rudy mumbled, "Llano River? Really?"

The driver dropped his arm from the sill and slapped the outside of the truck like it was the hindquarters of a thoroughbred. He dramatically jerked his head toward the passenger side of the truck. "Climb on in," he said. "Let's get on the road, eh?"

They clambered into the truck and the driver shifted into gear. He worked the truck backward and then forward until they were on the road. Norma sat in the front. Rudy was in a comfortable jump seat in the back positioned at the center of the truck's cab.

The truck smelled like mint and sawdust. Norma noticed a cup in the center console. Dark liquid sloshed around inside the plastic. The driver had a wad in his left cheek.

"Chewing tobacco?" asked Norma. "I didn't know that was available anymore."

The driver shifted gears and glanced at Norma. He smiled, some of the juice leaking onto his lips from between his teeth. She could see it in the glow from the dash.

"Everything's available if you know where to look," he said. "You should know that, Norma."

"I thought we weren't using names," said Rudy. "Isn't that part of the deal on the railroad?"

The driver accelerated and the truck lurched forward, the seats bouncing on their shocks. "This isn't technically the railroad. I'm just giving you a ride, you know?"

"Then why the spy stuff when we met?" asked Rudy. "The special knock, the inside joke about the LRC?"

"Old habits die hard," he said. "And this was arranged by the railroad. So there's that, you know?"

"I'm Rudy."

The driver offered a salute. "I'm Nolet."

"You Canadian?" asked Norma.

Nolet raised an eyebrow. His meaty hands twisted on the wheel. "That a problem?" The question was playful.

"No," said Norma. "I've just never met one."

"One what?"

"A Canadian."

That drew a belly laugh from the big truck driver. He grabbed the cub and spat out a healthy gob of chew and cleared his throat. "Sorry about that."

"What's so funny?" Norma was on the verge of laughter too, despite being clueless.

"You said it like I'm a unicorn," he said, "or an American beer."

Rudy leaned forward as far as he could and said, "Canada is in America."

Nolet chuckled and wagged his hand. "Meh. Not anymore. This place here, the lower forty-eight, or however many states still exist, are a far cry from Canada. That's why my people closed the border."

"The border between the US and Canada is closed?" asked Norma.

"It's not really the US, now is it?" asked Nolet. "But yes, aside from the straggler who manages to get through, it's closed down to northern-flowing traffic."

Norma put her hand to her chest. "I had no idea."

Nolet shrugged. He picked up the cup and spat into it as politely as possible. "How would you? You've had your hands full south of the wall, from what I hear. Plus, the government doesn't go around advertising you can't get to Canada. If people knew that, it would cause a problem."

Rudy asked, "A rush of people?"

"That." Nolet nodded. "Especially the twice pregnant folks, eh? But also people knowing that Canada closed its borders makes people question why. It creates demand where there wasn't any before. Like Cuban cigars used to be. Honduran were always better, but when you Americans couldn't get Cubans, they became the forbidden fruit."

It made sense. Norma hadn't given any thought to the world beyond her own, beyond the daily life-and-death struggle of her family, her extended family, and those who needed the railroad.

"Is there a railroad?" she asked.

The husky Canadian scratched his belly and then the back of his neck. He raked his fingers through the wiry tendrils of his beard. "You mean other than the one you know about?" He said the word *about* like he was saying "a boot."

Norma nodded.

"Of course," he said. "There are railroads for everything if you know where to look."

"Everything?"

"Everything," he repeated and waved his hand in the air as if swatting away flies. "You name it, there's a way to pay to get out of it. I know of three routes that get you to Canada. Four can get you to Mexico, though it's no better there now. Then there's your own little endeavor."

"It's that bad?" asked Rudy.

"Did you ever read George Orwell or Margaret Atwood? Aldous Huxley?" asked Nolet. "I liked Atwood. She was a Canadian."

"I read a couple of Orwell books in school," said Norma. "*Brave New World*? Is that Huxley? I read that too."

The trucker nodded. "Yes, that's the one. Well, mix 'em all up like a nice plate of poutine and you got what's going on in your world right now. Toss in a little bit of religious extremism, add social oppression, a pinch of reproductive control, a dash of conditioning, and that's *your* America."

"It's not *my* America," said Rudy.

The trucker sighed. "It's somebody's. That's the truth."

They rode in silence for a couple of miles. The truck vibrated against the rough highway, heading east. Although the occasional truck or car zipped past going west, traffic was virtually nonexistent. It was the middle of the night, the predawn hour when most were asleep no matter where they were.

"You two can get some sleep," he said. "There's a bunk big enough for two back there behind your seat, Rudy." He motioned over his shoulder with his thumb.

Norma glanced behind her husband but couldn't see the bunk. The space behind the driver's cab was large though.

"I'll go for a few more hours," said Nolet. "Then I'll find a place to stop, take a catnap myself. Then we'll make the final stretch."

"Final stretch?" asked Rudy.

Nolet exchanged a quick glance with Norma. "Did you tell him?"

"Tell me what?" asked Rudy.

Norma turned to address him. "Our next stop is the Harbor. We got the express flight."

CHAPTER 28

APRIL 22, 2054, 6:30 AM
SCOURGE +21 YEARS, 7 MONTHS
CHARLESTON, SOUTH CAROLINA

"What do you mean the boat's not here?"

The strain in Marcus's voice was evident in each word. His fists were balled, the blood vessels in his neck bulging beneath the wrinkled skin.

He held his hat in one hand and jabbed at the air with the other. His anger was directed at nobody and everybody. But really, it was aimed at Sally.

"What kind of plan is this?" he asked. "We're standing here at the end of the line. And you tell us we're meeting a boat. There's no boat."

The seven of them stood in an open area between what used to be tennis courts and a building that appeared to be a former yacht club. Beyond the yacht club was a deteriorating but apparently functional series of wood plank docks and slips.

"Can't we go somewhere else?" he asked. "Wherever the boat actually is? The longer we're standing here, the longer we're exposed."

Sally visibly bristled at the tongue-lashing. She started to say something a half dozen times, but Marcus followed one question with the next and didn't give her a chance to respond.

When he finally took a breath, she crossed her arms in front of her, jutted her hip to one side with attitude, and ignored the blinding headache that pulsed behind her eyes.

"Do you have a magic wand?" she asked, a bite in her tone.

Marcus wasn't sure what to make of it. He didn't say anything. He held onto his grimace though.

"Well," Sally pressed, "do you?"

Marcus felt Lou staring at him. Dallas and Andrea too. Even David was awaiting an answer. He could feel it. "No."

"Neither do I, Marcus," she said. "I can't make a boat appear out of thin air. I'm not on the boat. I'm not the captain. All I can do is plan to have the boat here. I did. Well, Gladys did. But it was planned and—"

In the distance, the squeal of tires on pavement interrupted the conversation. It was a block or two away, Marcus figured. A moment later, the rev of an engine told him the vehicle was getting closer. It was coming fast. It was coming for them.

"We need to get out of here," Marcus said. The anger in his voice was gone. This was concern. Flat, unadulterated concern.

Sally's posture shifted. She visibly tensed.

"Now," said Marcus.

Sally bolted past the tennis courts to the truck. Dallas already held the infant. Marcus picked up Javier. Andrea had her infant pressed tight against her. Lou took David's hand and urged him toward the truck.

They piled in and Sally pushed the ignition. The truck's engine turned over and she shifted into gear.

The truck was already moving when Marcus slammed his door shut. He reached into the glove box in front of him and pulled out a nine-millimeter pistol, dropped the magazine out of the gun, and pulled a fresh one from the glovebox. He racked the slide and loaded the first round into the chamber.

"Why'd you do that?" asked Sally. "You had plenty of bullets left in that other—"

"First, drive," Marcus said. "Second, you can never have too many bullets. Take a right."

"First," said Sally, "you shoot; I drive. Second, the water's to the left."

"I know," said Marcus, "but the people chasing us are to the left."

"I like her," said Lou from the back seat.

Sally rolled the wheel to the right and the truck leaned as if it might tip. Everyone crashed to the left of the cab. Marcus held himself with stiff arms against the dash.

"Do you know your way around here?" asked Sally.

"No better than you," said Marcus.

"A no would have been fine," said Sally.

"I *really* like her," said Lou. "I mean *really*. I misjudged—"

"Not now, Lou," Marcus said. "Dallas, roll down your window. Get your sidearm. You might need to provide cover on that side."

Sitting behind Sally, Dallas nodded his understanding and quickly did as Marcus instructed.

"How much gas?" he asked Sally. "Turn left."

She braked and turned left. They were headed north on Concord Street. A long waterfront park stretched between them and the water.

"A half tank?"

She accelerated and then braked again suddenly. It was a dead end. Left was the only option. Everyone slammed forward. David shrieked. One of the babies started crying.

"Mother of—" Marcus clenched his teeth. "Turn left. Make a quick right and then go north again."

Sally turned left, right and then left. Her foot punched the gas pedal and the truck's thirsty engine responded. They surged ahead.

"The boat's back there," said Sally. "Why are we—"

"The boat wasn't there," Marcus said. "Maybe it will be, but it isn't yet. We need some distance between us and whoever's looking for us."

Dallas interjected, "Pop Guard."

Marcus shifted and looked back at Dallas. His window was down. The wind whipped through the back of the cab, whistling as it passed.

Dallas motioned out the window with his head. "They're a couple of car lengths back."

Sally checked the rearview. It was useless with the tarpaulin-covered collection of goods heaped into the truck's bed. She stole a glance at her side view and then Marcus's.

"Are they closer than they appear?" she asked.

Marcus rolled down his window and pivoted awkwardly, twisting his lower back. He saw the vehicle giving chase. Actually it was two vehicles.

He sank back into his seat. With a jab of his finger, he aimed left. "Turn up here. It's one-way."

Sally slowed, but only a notch, willing the truck to the left and onto Queen Street. They powered past a large sign for the Old Slave Mart Museum and sped up, passing Washington Square on their right.

"What are we doing?" asked Sally. "Where are we going?"

"They're gaining," said Dallas.

"Lou, Andrea," said Marcus, "get down as low as you can. All of that gear in the back will act like a barrier between you and whatever comes this way if they open fire."

Andrea shrank down with her infant and pushed Javi lower too. The boy was whimpering along with the baby. At least the wailing had subsided. Somewhat.

Lou wasn't as compliant. One of her eyebrows arched higher than the other. Her glare intensified. "Get down? Are you serious, Marcus? I'm not some shrinking violet you can—"

"He's right," Sally cut in. "Protect that baby."

Lou grumbled and hunched down, taking the baby and David with her. "I don't like you anymore," she said flatly. "You had me. You lost me."

Dallas checked his wife with a knowing simper. He puckered his lips and blew her a kiss.

Lou widened her eyes, fluttered her eyelashes, and pretended to catch it on her cheek. She grumbled again.

Marcus marveled at her. In the midst of this she hadn't lost herself. Lou was Lou regardless of what was going on around her. He eyed David and then the infant in Lou's arms. They were in good hands. They'd stay that way if he could help it.

One of the Pop Guard vehicles, a gas-powered sedan, revved its engine and edged closer on the driver's side. Dallas stuck his arm out the window. A loud pop followed the crack of a single gunshot. Wheels screeched and the loud bang of metal colliding with something brought Dallas back inside the cab.

"One down," he said.

"Make a right up ahead," Marcus said. "Try not to make it until the last possible second."

Sally nodded, her white knuckles wrapped around the steering wheel. Leaning forward in her seat, Marcus thought their conductor looked every bit the first-time driver getting tested at the DMV. She had that same intent look on her face as the frightened sixteen-year-olds who'd queue up for a chance at judgment from both the testers and their peers.

Marcus didn't know why he made that connection in this moment. He hadn't considered it for decades. But there it was.

The truck swung to the right. It fishtailed, drifting on the rough pavement. Sally got it under control and accelerated out of the turn, heading north again.

The open window forced a thrumming in the cabin. Tiny tornadoes of air caused waves of pressure that filled the cabin with a *whump, whump, whump*. The resonant sound was so loud one of the infants started crying again.

Dallas talked over them. "I had no idea there were so many gas-powered cars and trucks outside Texas."

Sally checked over her shoulder at Andrea, who was behind Marcus. She pressed a button and lowered the passenger-side rear window. The warbling stopped. Her hands again found nine and three on the wheel.

"Refineries in Louisiana," said Sally. "There are also some along the Delaware River. Virginia has some too. When Texas went off—"

"No time for a history lesson," said Marcus. "Roll down your window."

Sally pushed her button and the window lowered. Marcus did the same.

The wind whipped through the cabin, swirling, muting everything else. The air was salty, heavier than in Atlanta or in west and central Texas. It was like Louisiana, but without the odor of bayou rot.

The second Pop Guard vehicle was closing in. It too tried to make a run along the driver's side, but instead of pulling even, it zipped past them. Dallas got off a couple of shots, although nothing hit.

The tinted windows of the car revealed nothing but vague shapes of the presumably armed men inside. Sally pressed the gas, accelerating to keep the car from passing them completely. But the car was too quick. It put half a car length between them and started to merge in front of them.

"Hold on," Sally warned.

She slammed on the brakes, coming out of her seat to step hard on the pedal. The truck's tires screamed against the road. Smoke curled around the truck. Everybody pitched forward. Marcus hit his shoulder on the dash. Hard. He grunted, a push of anguish from his lungs.

Sally slipped the truck in reverse and backed up through the cloud of smoke, which filtered into the cabin. Andrea coughed. So did David.

Sally braked again, not as hard, and spun the wheel to the left like she was playing roulette. Then she jerked the truck into drive and made a fast turn.

"We're heading back to the water," she announced. "The boat has got to be there by now."

Another Pop Guard vehicle was ahead of them. It was coming straight for them, on their side of the road. Sally swung the wheel again and headed south. Right into the path of another Pop Guard patrol.

Marcus leaned forward, using the large side-view mirror for balance. His right side strained, his back tightened, but he gripped his weapon with both hands and set the heels of his hands on top of the mirror's thick molded plastic frame.

They were closing fast. Seventy-five yards separated them.

He tucked his head into his armpit and yelled to Sally, "Aim for it! Straight for the car!"

Fifty yards.

Confusion flashed on her face for an instant, although she didn't question him. Her hands shifted on the wheel and Marcus felt the vehicle jerk beneath him. He wobbled but held his spot.

Forty yards.

"Hold it," Marcus said.

Lifting himself up, he leaned in. His finger found the trigger. He aimed, fired.

Twin pops cracked through the windshield of the oncoming car. There were twenty yards between them.

"Hold it!" he shouted.

A third round spiderwebbed the glass and the car jerked to one side, then the other. Then it peeled off the narrow road and slammed into the thick trunk of a dead magnolia. An instant later they sped past the smoking heap of a car. Half a body stuck through what was left of the front passenger's side windshield.

Marcus's face was windblown, eyes glossy, skin reddened. He

puffed his cheeks and exhaled. "Alright," he said. "We know they'll keep coming."

Sally stayed the course. South on Franklin Street. The road curved hard to the right when they passed Broad Street. Now they were on Savage.

"Where does this go?" asked Marcus.

"I don't know," snapped Sally. "I got here the same time you did, remember?"

Marcus checked behind him. Lou was comforting David while holding her infant. She was anxious. He could see it in her eyes. She wanted to be in the fray. Slinging knives, pulling triggers, doing bad things for a good cause.

Andrea's eyes were closed. She had her mouth pressed to her infant's ear. She was soothing the child, whispering and shushing. Javier was playing with the buckle end of the seatbelt he wasn't wearing, seemingly oblivious to what was going on around him.

"Another one," Dallas said.

Savage converged with another street that ran south into a Y intersection. The Pop Guard patrol was even with them and appeared willing to sideswipe them at the mouth of the intersection.

Sally saw this, looking through Marcus's window. She pressed the gas and the truck surged ahead.

Marcus leaned from the window, his elbow on the sill, and took a shot. Then another. The rear driver's side passenger window shattered. The tinted glass peeled away and hung by threads of glass along the side of the car. It flapped and banged and revealed a man clutching the side of his throat. His wide eyes were a mixture of shock and fear.

Beyond the dying man, in the back seat, another guard returned fire. The pops were hollow sounding, like the cap bombs Marcus used to slam at the ground as a kid. One of the rounds drilled the door next to Marcus's head and buried itself in the headrest. Foam padding bloomed behind him and Andrea shrieked, startling her baby.

Sally beat the car to the Y intersection and headed south on Rutledge. The car nipped the back of the truck and the rear slipped. But Sally maintained control as the truck wobbled from side to side.

"We're running out of road," she said. "Left or right at the dead end? Left or right!"

Marcus didn't know. Either way, they'd be on the lone road that ran along the southern edge of what was essentially a flat peninsula.

"Either," he said. "Just make a choice."

Sally went left. She drove away from the Hazel Parker Playground, where they'd stationed themselves for the rendezvous with the boat, and was heading east now. The Pop Guard patrol was at their bumper. Marcus's side-view mirror shattered. Glass sprayed into the cab and caught the side of his face.

He grimaced and swiped at his face with a heavy hand, the grind of grain-sized fragments raking across his skin. His fingers came away streaked with red and he cursed under his breath.

Sally was driving along Murray Boulevard, and turning left wasn't the right way to go. It ended at an abandoned US Coast Guard Station. There was a sharp right-hand turn. It was blocked. Two Pop Guard patrols were positioned behind their vehicles like police staffing a barricade at the end of a long chase.

Sally braked hard again. She slipped the truck into reverse and started driving backward along Murray. With the rearview mirror useless and Marcus's side view shattered, she tried aiming the truck with the help of her side view. The truck wove backward.

Bullets from high-powered rifles peppered the hood, clinking off the metal and fiberglass. Rounds thunked into the windshield. Marcus leaned out his window again and returned fire, more for cover than anything else.

In the rear seat, facing the opposite direction, Dallas opened fire on a new threat. A large passenger van was barreling toward them.

They were trapped. Then Sally swung the wheel wildly, and the truck, almost tipping onto its side, made a left-hand turn in reverse and headed north on Rutledge.

The respite was short-lived. They were trapped again when the van made a right. Behind them, at the next intersection, was another blockade. They were caught. There was no avoiding it.

Sally stopped the truck and slid it into park. She looked over at Marcus, her eyes wide. There was something in them that apologized for not finishing the job. Marcus saw the familiar haze of pain and loss in her eyes when she opened her mouth to speak.

Then a bullet slapped into the side of her head. Her body jerked awkwardly and she slumped against the open driver's window, the back of her head banging against the sill. The truck's engine idled at a low purr. Sometimes people didn't get happy endings no matter how much they deserved them.

CHAPTER 29

.

The sudden death of their conductor startled Marcus. Instinctively, without fully processing what had happened, he swept the weapon toward the spiderwebbed windshield.

The van was stopped in front of them, its passenger-side door open. A man in a leather duster stood behind it, a rifle leveled at the truck, at Marcus.

"Weapons out. Then everyone out," he said. "Now."

"What do we do?" asked Dallas.

Marcus glanced at Sally's limp body slumped awkwardly in her seat, her mouth agape, her shirt bunched at her waist. He said a silent prayer for her. Although he hadn't prayed in a long time, it felt right.

"We do as the man says," said Marcus. "I don't think we have a choice."

"The hell we don't," said Lou.

"Lou," Marcus said, "you have to think of your kids."

"I am thinking of them."

"Toss your weapons from the truck," said the one in the duster. "Do it now. Then get out. I'm giving you until five. Then I'm—"

Marcus tossed his weapon through the window. It bounced off

202

the asphalt into the sandy dirt beside the road. Dallas did the same on the opposite side of the truck.

The duster-wearing soldier stood up taller behind the open door. He lowered the barrel, angling it downward as if it were the lever that pushed him higher in his stance. Another man, bigger in frame and in a Pop Guard soldier's uniform, opened the driver's door and stepped from the van.

"That can't be all of 'em," said the soldier in charge. "Two handguns? Doubt it."

His voice carried in the warm air. It was resonant, controlled, the voice of a man who was used to giving orders. Marcus had listened to a lot of men and women in his time who affected the same verbal posture. There was something psychological about the way they issued commands.

"My hands are empty," said Marcus. He raised both of them, fingers spread apart. "We've got more weapons. There are rifles in the bed."

Keeping his rifle aimed on Marcus, the soldier on the driver's side said something to his commanding officer Marcus could hear but didn't understand. It was spoken softly enough that it sounded like a murmur of slurred words. The commander nodded.

"I want all of you out," said the one in charge. "There are two men?"

Marcus nodded. "Yes."

"Men first," said the man in the duster. "Slowly, hands where I can see them. You first, then the one in the back."

Marcus kept one hand up and opened the door with the other. He nudged it wider with his shoulder and stepped from the truck onto the road. His hat was on the floorboard. It had fallen from the dash during their failed attempt to avoid exactly what was happening now.

The soldier in charge tilted his head to his right, Marcus's left. He jutted his chin in the same direction. "Step to the side," he said, "away from the truck."

Marcus did as he was told. He sensed the presence of more weapons aimed at him. He glanced behind him. He was right. Two Pop Guards stood about fifty feet back. They had him in their sights.

On the opposite side of the truck, without waiting for instructions, Dallas did the same thing. He opened the door, stepping away from the truck. Fingers spread, he held his hands high above his head.

Marcus shrugged. "Now what?"

The man in the duster tossed his rifle into the front of the van and slammed shut the door. The whack of metal on metal echoed.

At his sides, his fingers flexed in and out, in and out. It injected Marcus with the same shot of adrenaline he'd absorbed in the moments before gunfights on the streets of Baird. The young gun would wiggle his fingers, flex his hands, as if he were engaged in some peacock ritual before mating.

Marcus couldn't help but smile at the showmanship as he strode forward. His posture was straight, shoulders back, but he walked with an unmistakable swagger. This man not only issued orders, he carried them out. He was the kind of alpha male that Marcus both appreciated and loathed. Maybe that combination of emotions was because Marcus recognized it in himself.

The soldier stopped in the center of the road and set his booted feet shoulder width apart. He whipped back the duster, revealing a revolver at one hip. A thick leather gun belt sat cockeyed on his waist. Despite the seriousness of the dire situation facing them, Marcus couldn't help himself.

He snickered, immediately pressing the smile flat, and sucked in his breath. No need to poke the dragon.

The man flexed his hands. A brow arched questioningly above one eye. "Something funny?"

"No."

He pursed his lips into a pout, nodded slowly, and motioned toward the truck. "I'm Captain Greg Rickshaw. Population Guard.

But I guess you knew that second part."

Marcus didn't respond.

"Followed you here from Atlanta," he said. "You're the ones who rushed out of Gladys's place, right?"

Marcus's silence answered the question.

"Two women?"

Marcus nodded.

"Leave the women out of it," said Dallas. "Take us. Let them go."

"Quiet, Dallas." Marcus looked over the top of the truck at him. "Not now."

Dallas frowned. He looked away from Marcus and eyed the ground.

A smile curled on Rickshaw's face. He shot a look at the soldier on the other side of the van. "How gallant," he said. "Isn't it gallant?"

The soldier nodded, although Marcus sensed a hesitancy in the soldier, like there was something he didn't like or didn't trust.

"We all know the women are why we're here," said Rickshaw. "More to the point, the women and their children are why we're all here. Frankly, I could shoot you dead in the street and it wouldn't affect anything. It wouldn't even be a ripple in a pond, a flap of a butterfly's wing." His gaze shifted to Marcus. He lifted a hand and held up four fingers. "Two children and two infants?" It was more of a statement than a question.

Marcus nodded. "Yep."

"I want the women out of the truck," he said. "Again, one at a time. Hands up and such."

"They're holding babies," said Marcus.

Rickshaw sucked in a deep breath. His nostrils pinched when he did. He nodded slowly, mulling over the next step. "That's fine. It keeps their hands full. They can't do much with an infant in their arms, now can they?"

"I guess not," said Marcus.

Rickshaw lifted his right hand, palm up, then curled his fingers inward, motioning for the women to get out of the truck and move toward him.

"What about the older children?" asked Marcus.

"We'll deal with them in a moment. This is my rodeo, cowboy, so hold your horses."

Clenching his jaw and resisting the urge to say or do something he'd regret, Marcus nodded. He pivoted. The heel of his boot ground against the road. Through the cracked windshield, he looked past the slumped body of their conductor and locked eyes with Lou.

She nodded and said something to Andrea, who shook her head, her stressed features pinched with resistance. Lou remained calm, her flat expression evident through the glass.

"They might want to hurry," said Rickshaw. "I ain't got all day."

Marcus turned away from the truck and toward Rickshaw. He flashed a smile. "If this isn't your first rodeo, then you know it can be tough to get a bull through a gate. Give it a minute."

Rickshaw stiffened, flexing his hands at his sides. His fingers clenched into fists and relaxed.

Behind Marcus, the doors creaked open. He dragged his glare away from the sadist and fixed it on his friends.

From one side of the truck, Lou slid out and found her footing behind the rear passenger door. Andrea was a mirror image on the driver's side.

Behind them, the Pop Guard soldiers positioned at the blockade lifted their aim. They tracked both women independently.

Marcus stood still. He said nothing as the women met each other at the front of the truck.

Dallas whispered something to his wife. She offered him a weak smile but kept moving past him. Dallas looked like he wanted to run after his wife, but his better judgment held him in place and forced him not to do something stupid.

"Bring the babies here," said Rickshaw. "I got car seats in the back. I'm gonna need you to strap them in for me."

He held out his hands and wiggled his fingers. It reminded Marcus of a cheerleader in the late twentieth century. Spirit fingers? Was that what they were called? He'd never been much for cheerleaders. Yeah, they were athletic, but he could never get how they could smile and drive pom-poms into the air in support of a team down twenty with less than a minute to play.

"I've got a little arthritis," said Rickshaw. "Makes it difficult for me to work the tiny buckles and straps."

The women exchanged looks. Andrea hesitated. Lou nodded at her and the two of them walked forward, shoulder to shoulder.

From the truck, one or both of the boys whimpered. One of them called for his mother.

The women marched deliberately, step by step, toward the van in front of them. As they approached Rickshaw, he held up a hand.

"Whoa, slow your giddyup." He shifted to look at Marcus. "Did I say it right, cowboy?"

Marcus tightened his jaw. He balled his fists. His fingernails, which he'd meant to trim before leaving his home in Virginia, dug into the calloused flesh of his palms.

Andrea was trembling. Even standing still, she wasn't standing still. Marcus knew the woman was brave. She was strong. But everyone had a breaking point and Andrea was obviously nearing hers.

"Let me see the child," said Rickshaw. He extended his arms and stepped closer to Andrea. "I'm not gonna hurt it."

Andrea curled her shoulder inward, her hold on the child tightening. She shook her head.

"I'm not asking," said Rickshaw.

"Take mine," Lou said. "You can hold mine."

Rickshaw studied both women. He stepped to the side and faced Lou.

"Lou," said Dallas, "what are you doing?"

Lou handed Rickshaw the child. "He's a boy. He's strong. He'll be a good soldier someday."

"Perhaps," said Rickshaw.

He took the child with both hands. But instead of cradling him, he scooped him under his arms and held him up with his legs dangling. The wrapped fabric that swaddled the child fell away. The baby was nude. He kicked his legs and started to cry. His pink skin reddened except for the skin around Rickshaw's fingers; it was blanched white.

Rickshaw held the child at arm's length with a grip altogether unfriendly. There was nothing paternal in this man and very little that was human.

"Sir," said the guard at the van, "I can take the child. There's no need—"

Rickshaw spun around to face the burly man, the child still at arm's length. His little body swung with the momentum of Rickshaw's turn. His cry, which was like a lamb bleating, was more of a wail now. The child's legs were drawn tight to its body.

Dallas's face was drawn with fear. Lou's was pinched with anger.

"Krespan," Rickshaw snapped, "I don't need you to get a conscience here. Do your job. Don't suggest how I do mine."

Krespan's face knotted with confusion; then it shifted into realization. His eyes darted wildly, not focusing on anything. Marcus thought the soldier was searching his soul.

"In fact," said Rickshaw, "your job is to kill that woman and her child."

Rickshaw was looking at Andrea. Andrea looked at Rickshaw, then at Lou, then at the guard. Marcus was certain she'd take off running. She didn't. Instead, the brave woman was frozen in place. She wasn't shivering anymore.

"Sir," said Krespan, "I don't think I can do that. We don't kill children. That's not what—"

Rickshaw spun around. "Are you disobeying an order?"

"No, sir," said the soldier. "But—"

"Fine," said Rickshaw. "I'll do it."

Rickshaw marched to the truck. He set Lou's wailing baby on the front seat. The boys in the truck were crying. Dallas looked pained. Marcus searched his mind for some way out of this. He didn't see one.

And then he did. This was it. After a lifetime of conquering demons, one in a leather duster was going to be his undoing. This would be his end.

Marcus charged forward. Unarmed, he raced as fast as his stiff joints would carry him. If he could draw attention and fire his way, that might give the others a chance to defend themselves. The world slowed as he jumped into action.

Three bounding steps into his charge, the guard at the van swung his weapon toward him. Then he jerked, his body twisted, and he disappeared behind the door, falling to the ground.

Rickshaw had shot him. Then he spun to Marcus, leveling his revolver directly at him.

Marcus was sunk. He'd take a direct hit. There was no avoiding it. He charged forward nonetheless. He was committed.

Beyond the barrel of the revolver, Marcus noted the grin on Rickshaw's face. He heard the children's cries, tasted the sweat dripping on his face, felt the sting of it in his eyes.

Two more steps and the muzzle flashed. An instant later a familiar, air-sucking heat pierced his side. Marcus twisted, his body absorbing the force of the bullet, but he kept running. Only two or three more steps and he'd tackle him. One more shot, though, and he'd never make it.

That shot never came.

As Marcus reached him, ready to take a final hit before diving onto his killer, a blur of swift movement shot from the left edge of his vision. Then the soldier was on the ground, flat on his back.

Lou was atop him, her hands at his chest. And then they were above it, clasped. The glint of blood-soaked steel beneath her hands reflected the sunlight for a brief moment before she plunged the blade again into Rickshaw's chest.

Marcus reached them as the man dropped his revolver. Marcus dove for it, then spun around and yelled for Dallas to take cover.

Dallas dove into the truck's front seat at the instant the barricade guards on the other side opened fire. Bullets zipped past Marcus. They dinged into the van's open passenger door, shattering the windshield.

Andrea was on the ground, covering her child. She was trying to find a safe place.

Marcus ran to her and put his body between her and the incoming fire. "Get in the van!" he yelled at her.

When she didn't move, he repeated his order. She acquiesced and started crawling awkwardly, the baby in one arm.

Marcus returned fire. Three more shots. Then the revolver was empty. He was trapped.

"Get back here!" yelled Lou. "Now!"

The staccato of semiautomatic rifle fire followed her command. She was standing behind the driver's side of the van. She had Rickshaw's rifle and was emptying it at the barricade.

Hunched over, Marcus ran toward the driver's side. Andrea was there. So was the guard named Krespan. He was holding the baby in his lap. Andrea had his rifle.

Marcus gave them both a confused glare and ducked beside them. "What is this?"

"He's good," said Andrea. "He's hurt, but he's going to help us."

Krespan's voice was weak. His chest heaved. Blood soaked through his uniform at the spot where his shoulder met his neck. That arm hung at his side. "There's more in the back," he said. "More guns."

Krespan was pale. The color had drained from his face. He was sweating and his lips were blue. He was losing a lot of blood.

"You're bleeding," said Andrea. Her eyes were wide and focused on the wound in Marcus's side.

"I'm fine," he said. "We'll deal with it later."

Marcus climbed into the van and maneuvered his way into the cargo hold. Behind him the cacophony of the gunfight was louder. Andrea was returning fire.

They had to end this and get away. The longer it went on, the more Pop Guard reinforcements would show up. Then they'd never have a chance.

Marcus found a rifle and checked the mag. It was good to go. He climbed over Lou's baby and out the passenger's side. Lou was in front of him, still picking her targets. There were at least three dead soldiers at the other end of the street fight.

Marcus stepped around the door, rifle pulled tight to his shoulder, and tilted his head to take aim. He counted another six men.

"Get behind the wheel," he said to Lou. "Get Andrea and the guard."

"What about you?" she asked. "And Dallas? The boys are in the truck."

"Get in the van and back away," he said. "We'll follow in a minute. Head southeast. Do it now."

Marcus picked off the first of the six targets as he advanced. Another round drilled into his side, almost exactly where the first it him. An explosion of pain sparked through his body. He hitched and gritted his teeth to fend off the swell of agonizing heat. He took out another guard. And another.

Now he was at the open door to the truck. He was almost there.

Behind him, doors slammed. Tires squealed. An engine revved.

Good, he thought. *Lou listened for once.*

Marcus used the driver's side door for cover and took out a fourth and fifth guard. He couldn't find the sixth, but he was there. Short bursts of semiautomatic fire cracked. Bullets dinged off the truck's exterior.

"Dallas!" Marcus yelled. "Get behind the wheel!"

It wasn't a yell, really. It was a hoarse attempt at yelling. Marcus didn't recognize the sound that came from him. It was soaked with pain, with the inability to breathe normally.

Sweat drained from his scalp and down the back of his neck. Although the throb of the wounds at his side almost doubled him over, he held his position. He scanned the barricade for the sixth soldier, who was hidden beyond his line of sight.

The barricade was getting bigger. Another pair of Pop Guard patrol vehicles joined the party. Four men from each spilled onto the streets, their weapons raised.

"Dallas," Marcus said; then he stopped. Sally's body was on the ground beside the truck. Only the door separated him from the conductor's graying corpse.

Dallas was already behind the wheel. He was trying to crank the engine. It didn't start. "Get in, Marcus."

"Get it started first," Marcus said.

"I'm trying. It won't turn over. It says there's no key."

"No key?" Marcus wasn't sure if Dallas could even hear him over the percussive blasts from the newly engaged Pop Guard.

No key. No key. Where had the key—

Marcus squatted at the door. He dropped onto his knees and then lay prone on the ground. Bullets ricocheted off the asphalt near him. They pounded into Sally's body, shaking her otherwise unmoving body with every strike.

Marcus reached under the bottom of the open door and felt blindly for her body. He touched fabric. Was it her shirt? Her pants? The flesh underneath was thick and muscular, but there was fat there too. It had to be her leg.

"It won't start," Dallas said. "What do I do?"

"Hang on," Marcus said.

A bullet drilled into Sally's body next to Marcus's hand. He flinched but quickly resumed his search. His hand was on her thigh. He groped until he found her pocket. There was a bulge.

Marcus dipped his fingers into the pocket, between the pieces of cotton. When she'd pulled on her pants, she'd likely never imagined they'd be the clothes in which she would die.

He didn't know her story. He couldn't know that she'd survived nearly as much loss as he had since the Scourge devoured so much of the world.

Sally had escaped the Scourge on a boat. Her parents had taken her and strangers off the coast to outlast the plague. It almost worked. But even after she'd found land again, her life was adrift. Not until the railroad gave her purpose was she truly anchored. It was that same anchor that dragged her off the tracks.

Marcus would never know any of that. He would never understand her sacrifice, her wounds, her insecurities, her depression, her desire to live a life in sunshine as opposed to one in shadows.

He did know she'd given up the life in the pursuit of saving his, Lou's, Dallas's, Andrea's, and the children's. That was all he needed to know to love who she was. He thanked her silently as he pulled the keys from her pocket.

Marcus got back up and gave the keys to Dallas. The truck started and Dallas shifted into gear.

"Start moving," said Marcus. "I'll get in."

Marcus moved around the front of the truck, staying low, as it lurched forward. Dallas pulled the driver's door shut. Marcus stayed behind the passenger's door, walking backward with the truck as he returned fire. His aim found three more guards and dropped them before he edged around the door, kicked the rear passenger's door shut, and dove into the front passenger's seat. He reached back behind Dallas and across the crying boys to yank the rear driver's side door shut. The stretch sent a lightning bolt of pain from his wounds that radiated to his fingers and toes.

The truck bounced, then bounced again. It had hit something.

"Oops," said Dallas. "I ran over the guy in the ugly coat. My bad."

"Did you aim for him?" asked Marcus, his eyes on the kids.

"Maybe," said Dallas. "Just had to finish what Lou started."

The pain was getting worse. His fingers were going numb. Marcus groaned but forced a clenched smile to ease the fear on the boys' faces.

"It's okay," he said to David and Javier. "We're going to be okay."

"I did my best to keep them calm," said Dallas. "I really tried. But I—"

"It's okay, Dallas," said Marcus. "You did a good job."

Each word was more difficult to utter than the one before it.

"Quiero mi madre, por favor," said Javi. *"¿Donde esta mi madre?"*

"He wants his mother," said David.

Marcus gritted his teeth through the pain and hissed through his teeth. Then he smiled. "Where'd you learn Spanish?"

"Norma."

Marcus nodded. Of course Norma taught him Spanish. She was a good woman.

"Both your moms are okay," said Marcus. His body jerked to one side as Dallas turned left. "We're going to them now."

The boys nodded their understanding. David took Javier's hand and gripped it tight.

Marcus tried to see through the truck's rear window. It was still blocked by the cargo they'd hauled with them. Holding his side, he shrank back into the passenger's seat and exhaled.

His vision was wobbly. He was losing blood. It wasn't as bad as that guard Krespan, he didn't think, but it wasn't good either.

"You're hit," said Dallas. "You got hit."

"Keep your eyes on the road," Marcus grunted.

"You okay?"

Marcus nodded, but he wasn't sure. He was light-headed now, his breathing labored. Shock? Or something worse? He couldn't feel his feet.

"I don't see the van," said Dallas.

"Head south and east," said Marcus. "Go back toward the park. You'll find it."

"What if the boat's not there? What do we do then?"

"Don't worry," Marcus replied. "Focus on the task at hand." He gave a long explanation as to why the boat would be there, told Dallas he was proud of him. He told him he loved him.

All Dallas said was, "What?"

Marcus started to repeat himself. The edges of his vision were dark now, his breathing shallow. He was sweating but cold.

"Marcus," said Dallas, "you're mumbling. I can't understand you. What are you…"

Marcus didn't hear the rest of it. The numbness spread from his fingers and toes to his arms and legs. The motion of the truck, bouncing and rocking, was like a lullaby urging him to sleep. He was tired. His body hurt, where he could feel it, and it was cold, so cold. Maybe a little sleep would help. A short rest between here and the boat.

Dallas was shouting at him now, his words urgent. They were spiked with fear.

The world went dark. And Marcus was at peace. This was what it felt like to be at peace. At long last, no pain, no sadness, only peace.

CHAPTER 30

APRIL 24, 2054, 4:00 PM
SCOURGE +21 YEARS, 7 MONTHS
BUXTON, NORTH CAROLINA

Norma stood in the sand. It covered her feet. The grains shifted and rubbed against the spaces between her toes. The cold water surged against her ankles in a rhythm brought about by the moon and tides.

She shivered. Ripples of chill and goose bumps moved up her legs, to her torso, the back of her neck, and tingled her fingers. But she didn't feel the cold. Not really. Her heart was warm. In the surf, puttering beyond the break, was a boat. It was bigger than she expected. The vessel was longer than the one that brought her here and wider than the boat that had delivered Gladys hours earlier. On its side and at its aft, its name was painted in fading red letters that looked brown. It reminded her of the way dried blood changed its color after time, how the elements deadened the vibrancy and life of the initial hue.

STELLA.

That was the boat's name. It was Latin. Translated into English it meant "star." The boat rose and sank on the waves before they rolled beyond the break and crashed into the shore.

"Took them long enough," said Rudy. "I thought they'd be here

216

last night or this morning at the latest."

"They had to stay offshore longer than expected," said Gladys. She stood between the couple.

The sea breeze fluttered across Norma's face. She inhaled the scent of seaweed and salt. It was so different from the dirt of west and central Texas, the constant dust and heat.

Overhead, clouds rolled inland, pushed by the breeze. They were white and wispy, absent the potential of rain.

As the *Stella* bobbed in the surf, a line off its bow alternating a slack and taught position like a rubber band stretched between fingers, a raft pitched and yawed its way back toward the beach.

Aboard the raft, the kind once often used with an outboard engine, were at least four people. The spray of the surf and the dance of light off the water made it difficult to distinguish the shapes.

Rudy pointed to the raft. "I think that's her. See the ball cap on her head?"

Norma covered her mouth with both hands. She pushed onto her tiptoes and leaned from side to side, trying to catch a glimpse for confirmation.

It came a minute later when the raft was close enough for her to make out the features on the faces of those aboard. She didn't recognize two of them.

Norma waded out into the surf as the raft slowed, riding the waves. Its starboard side was parallel to the shore.

"Norma!" Rudy called after her.

She waved him off and trudged through the ankle-deep water. It splashed against her thighs. She kicked her feet out, running awkwardly, as the water rose to her waist. It took her breath away when it dipped past her navel.

"Lou!" She waved. "Oh, Lou, you made it!"

Her eyes were so locked onto Lou's, Norma didn't notice the infant in her arms until she reached the side of the raft. The craft bounced against her hip and she reached up toward Lou. Then she pulled back, seeing the newborn. Her hands found her mouth again. She gasped and nearly lost her balance when the raft pushed against her a second time.

"Let's get close to the beach," said a man at the aft, oars in both hands. "I don't want to risk the babies falling into the water."

Babies? Norma backed away, confused. Had Lou had twins?

Then she saw the stranger, the other woman with an infant in her arms, and Norma's heart surged. They'd made it with two infants, not one. It was all the more miraculous.

Norma looked down at David, who was closest to her. His tiny features were bright. He smiled at Norma and she reached out to take his hand, holding his tiny fingers in hers. They weren't as tiny as she remembered.

Had he grown in the few days since she'd last seen him? Was he getting bigger?

Norma waded back to the beach, standing in ankle-deep water again. Rudy joined her, and together they helped the travelers from the raft. The group walked up the beach to waiting blankets and towels, to bottled water and pieces of warm bread.

The raft headed back to the boat, the oarsman churning against the surf.

Norma had so many questions. So many. None of them came to mind.

They sat on the blankets. Lou offered the child, bundled in a large T-shirt, to Norma. "Hold him. He's been waiting to meet you."

"A boy?" asked Norma. She took the child in her arms and pulled him to her chest. She picked back the folds of fabric to look at his face. Her eyes welled. "He's beautiful," she said. "He looks like Dallas."

Lou nudged Norma with her elbow. "You're saying my husband is beautiful?"

Norma chuckled. She was so full right now, she wondered if her heart might explode with joy.

She lifted the baby toward her face and inhaled the sweet aroma of a newborn. Babies always smelled so good. "He smells like David did. I love that smell."

David smiled proudly. He got onto his knees and leaned over his little brother. Then he took his finger and tickled the baby's nose.

The infant opened his eyes, squinting. He blinked and pursed his lips.

Norma looked at Rudy. "You want to hold him?"

Rudy begged off. "I might break him."

"His name is Rudy," said Lou.

Rudy's chin quivered, his eyes dancing back and forth between Lou and the child.

"Rudy?" he repeated. His voice squeaked.

Lou smiled.

"David was taken," said the boy.

They all laughed.

Norma's attention shifted to the raft. It had nearly reached the *Stella*. "Dallas okay?"

Lou nodded. Her eyes glossed and she blinked away tears.

Norma didn't want to ask about Marcus. She knew he was wounded. That much had been relayed to the Harbor. There was also a Pop Guard soldier who'd flipped and was helping them.

She took a deep breath of the briny air and forced a smile, turning to the stranger. "Andrea, is it?"

The woman nodded. She was trying to nurse. The baby was struggling to latch onto her.

"And your handsome young son?"

The baby managed to catch. Its cheeks sucked inward. Andrea winced and repositioned herself to better accommodate the nursing child and her own comfort. "Javier," she said. "We call him Javi."

Norma sensed the hint of accent in her voice. She spoke to her in Spanish, asking her about her travels, her health, her situation. Although hesitant at first, Andrea gradually relaxed and answered the questions Norma asked, plus some she didn't.

The raft was on its way back, its bow pitching up and down in the surf.

Lou got to her feet. She nodded at the raft as it rode across the break and entered the calmer roll of surf at the shore's edge. "I'm going to get Dallas."

Lou walked the beach toward the water. Sprays of sand kicked up from her bare heels as she moved away. The farther she got, the more she looked like the girl Norma had met so many years ago.

The raft came ashore and two men got out. Lou waded into the water to help one of them. She hugged him, merging her body with his.

Norma knew the other man wasn't Marcus, but she held out hope until his features came into focus as he climbed the beach.

He wore a Pop Guard uniform. His left arm was in a sling, his hand hanging limply from the edge of the cradle that held his arm against his body. He lumbered more than walked, resignation in his steps.

The raft headed back toward the *Stella*. Again the man worked the oars together, pulling against the surf to reach the break.

"This is Krespan," said Lou.

The guard stood with Lou and Dallas in front of the blankets. David, his mouth full of bread, jumped up and leg tackled his father. It was less than an hour since he'd seen him, but it had evidently been long enough.

Krespan waved sheepishly with his right hand and nodded a greeting. "I know I'm not the kind of person you'd expect to have here," he said, "but I think I can help you. I know a lot about how they think, how they work their patrols. I mean, I did."

"His captain is dead," said Lou. "I killed him. But not before he tried to kill Krespan for questioning orders."

Norma eyed the soldier. She held his gaze; he didn't look away. His eyes were kind. There was sadness there, one she recognized in so many people who'd survived the various incarnations of the world post-Scourge. It was a sadness absent in the eyes of those bent on doing bad things.

"Why were you in the guard?" asked Norma.

Krespan's face flushed and he looked away, his gaze falling to the sand and his feet.

Beyond him, Norma saw the raft at the *Stella*. It was almost there. Soon enough it would confirm what Norma feared was true but was afraid to ask. The longer she went without seeing Marcus's lifeless body, the longer she could pretend he was alive.

She swallowed hard and listened to Krespan offer his explanation.

"I was doing the right thing," he said. "I bought into the propaganda of it. It was a good job. In theory. But a couple of times in the field, it didn't seem right. Like the reason we were given for our jobs wasn't the real reason. I kept doing my job. I did the best I could, followed orders, but I listened. I had to pick the right moment to speak up. I guess I was a little late. I—"

"I get it," said Norma. "It's not easy to do what you did. If Lou says you belong here, you belong here."

Krespan's shoulders relaxed and his expression eased. He bowed his head. "Thank you."

"Get some water, some bread," she said. "You can sit down over there." She motioned toward an empty blanket. Krespan took her advice and found a seat on the sandy fabric, lay back, and stared at the sky.

Norma followed his gaze to the brush of white clouds moving ashore. The clouds were thicker the farther she got from the beach. Then she found the horizon and focused again on the *Stella*. A knot thickened in her throat.

Two men aboard the *Stella* were transferring something long from the boat to the raft. Was it a body? She couldn't be sure. Her chest tightened again. This time it wasn't from joy.

Norma got up from the blanket. The others talked, ate and drank, relaxed for the first time in days. She left them behind and stepped purposely toward the surf until she stood at the water's edge. The cold salt water lapped at her ankles. The raft pushed off from the *Stella*, the man at the oars working to turn the small craft in the opposite direction and head toward shore. There was no other visible movement on the raft.

However, there was movement at the *Stella*. They were weighing anchor. One man worked the line, hand over hand, pulling it in the vessel while the other aboard rolled it neatly into wide loops.

The rope became something darker and heavier. A chain. He was pulling up a chain. Then the anchor. And the *Stella* was drifting again.

Norma felt as adrift. Her heart fluttered in her tight chest.

The raft moved closer to shore. Up and down, the raft pitched in the water. Foam thickened in the surf as it roiled across Norma's legs. She tasted it on her lips and licked it in her mouth, confused as to how the seawater had found its way there. She hadn't felt it splash.

It wasn't seawater, she realized then. They were tears. She was crying. She was mourning.

The raft was close now. Close enough that she could make out the craft's cargo. It was a body. A man was strapped to a board of some kind. He wasn't moving except for the shift from the rock of the surf.

Norma took another step into the water, then another. Before she knew it, she was waist deep in the chilly water once more. Shells and rocks crunched beneath her feet, digging into her arches and poking her heels.

The raft drifted closer. Norma took another step, her feet sinking into the bed beneath the surf.

It was close enough now that she could see the face of the man on the board. She knew who he was before she saw him. Marcus Battle was strapped flat to the board. He was pale, his eyes closed, his mouth a flat line.

He looked so much older in death than he had in life. The gray at his temples and across his scalp glistened in the waves of sunlight bouncing off the surrounding water.

His wrinkles were deeper. They creased his face along the sides of his nose, at the edges of his eyes.

The clothes on his body were tattered and bloodied. His arms were folded across his chest.

Norma's vision blurred. Her legs felt heavy even in buoyant water. She wasn't sure she could do this. Her breathing came in short, stuttering gasps.

The oarsman called out to her, "Hey, I'm glad you're here. I need help getting him ashore. We can float him."

She nodded her understanding. He rowed past her a couple of feet before hopping from the aft of the raft. He splashed into the water, the raft tipping from side to side. He moved around to the port side of the raft, opposite Norma. With his chin, he motioned toward the shore. She kept her eyes on him until she shifted her weight and stared at the shoreline. She couldn't look at Marcus's body. It was too much. Norma could barely step without losing her balance. On the shore, the others were on the blankets. None of them seemed moved by the watery procession toward land. Was it because they'd already accepted what Norma didn't want to believe was true? Was it because none of them wanted to revisit what they'd experienced for the last two days? Perhaps they'd said their goodbyes, made peace in a way she wasn't sure she could.

"You okay?" asked the oarsman. "We can go slower. There's no rush."

Of course there was no rush. They were carting a dead man.

"I'm fine," she said. "We have to find a place to bury him. I was just thinking about that. I don't know where we're going to bury him."

Norma wasn't sure why she'd said that aloud. So many things were dancing around in her head, competing for space, it was that little thing that leaked out. His burial.

There wasn't a place for burials in the Harbor. Not yet. Norma's mind started to wander again, when a raspy voice surprised her.

"Bury me?"

Norma stumbled against the grit on the seabed. She gripped the side of the raft and steadied herself. Lifting herself up to her feet, she saw Marcus's eyes were open. Barely, but they were open.

Norma coughed out a laugh and then a cry. She reached for him, her fingers gripping a fistful of his shirt. "You're alive?" she managed. *"Alive?"*

"Yeah," Marcus said. "Disappointed?"

Norma shook her head. She almost climbed into the raft as the oarsmen steadied it. She threw her arms around Marcus. All she could say, amidst gasps for air, was how sorry she was.

The oarsman put his hand on her back. "Hey, let's get him to shore. We're going to tip."

Norma wiped her face. She touched a wet hand to Marcus's pale cheek.

"I should die more often," Marcus said. "People like me more when they think I'm dead."

CHAPTER 31

APRIL 25, 2054, 7:00 PM
SCOURGE +21 YEARS, 7 MONTHS
BUXTON, NORTH CAROLINA

The dinner table was drenched in the dim yellow light of simulated incandescent light. Lou sat between Dallas and David. Across from her Marcus slurped a bowl of broth. He still wasn't eating solid food.

She smiled to herself, watching the old man eat his dinner. He blew on the spoon to cool the broth. Steam swirled around his face and then evaporated.

Dallas put his hand on her leg. She squeezed his hand and smiled at him.

Norma and Rudy were at one end of the table, Gladys at the head opposite them. Andrea and Javi were next to Marcus.

It reminded Lou of the dinners they'd shared in Baird. She lifted a spoon to her mouth, blew on the broth, and took a taste. It was salty and hot with a hint of chicken or poultry of some kind.

The Harbor was a magnificent place. Built near the lighthouse on the Hatteras Seashore, it was a complex of buildings and tents. There was a greenhouse, a large rainwater cistern, and a water filtration system.

The bridges leading to the island off the North Carolina coast were long gone. Decay or deliberate vandalism had rendered them useless. The only way to access the Harbor was by boat.

There were five hundred and seventeen people living here, all of them having arrived via the underground railroad. Some had spent time in West Virginia in an alternate harbor that didn't prove as life-sustaining as what they'd constructed on the Outer Banks.

They had defense systems in place, and people tasked with security patrols. Lou had her first in the morning.

For the most part, this was as safe as any place Lou had ever lived. Somehow, without a wall or without the help of a government, life was sustaining itself in the Harbor. It was a good place with good people.

There were challenges, of course. It wasn't Utopia. And if the drought ever ended, the threat of hurricanes might return. But this was good.

Lou was happy, her children were happy. Her husband, her friends, Marcus...all of them smiled more in the last couple of days than they had in her memory.

She looked around the table, spending a moment on each person there. Without having to think about it, she knew how each person had positively impacted her life.

Her father would have loved this. As distant as her memory of him had become, as much as his face and voice were patchworks of things true and imagined, she knew deep down he would be at peace here.

And she hoped, if he were looking down on her, hand in hand with her mother, he would know she was at peace too.

It occurred to her that her child Rudy might never know the pain and violence of her world. If she were lucky, she'd never have to tell him how to hide in rafters or wield a blade.

She chuckled to herself. Who was she kidding? That kid would be slinging knives the moment he could walk.

Marcus took another loud slurp of his soup. He was improving.

His wounds, which she'd thought might kill him when they'd first dragged his limp body onto the boat, were healing. While he'd lost a lot of blood, both bullets went through and through, missing any organs.

Once he'd recovered enough to talk and before they'd given him drugs to knock him unconscious, she'd asked him if he would stay.

"I'm not much for the whole family thing," he'd hedged. "I'm not good at it."

She'd done her best to convince him otherwise. He'd listened before his eyes fluttered and he sank into a stupor.

He hadn't brought it up again. Neither had she. She was afraid to ask him, afraid to know when he'd leave her again.

Marcus Battle was a solitary man. His was a loneliness born of circumstance and, for some reason, the unending product of self-preservation.

Lou was aware Norma also tried to talk Marcus into staying. She wanted him to be a part of this new collective. It was safe; it didn't need his violence. And so, the violence that seemed to follow him wasn't needed either.

Rudy did his best. He played the guilt card, telling Marcus he couldn't be the only old man in a sea of women and babies.

Dallas also prodded gently, apologizing to Marcus for his treatment. He thanked the old man for his help, for his sacrifice. Dallas told Marcus, as did they all, that they couldn't have made it to the Harbor without him.

Gladys stayed silent on the matter. She stayed silent on a lot of matters. Lou didn't blame her. The idea of leaving Atlanta, of sheltering at the Harbor herself, would take getting used to for her.

The railroad would still function, still save women and children. But Gladys wouldn't be in as much control anymore. Lou doubted Gladys cared one way or the other about Marcus's decision to stay or leave.

Marcus finished his soup and pushed back from the table. He

thanked everyone for dinner, set his empty bowl in the sink, washed it with soapy water, and set it on a rack to dry. When he limped away, Lou called after him.

"Where are you going?"

"I'm tired," he said. "I need to sleep. And I've got a lot to dream about."

Lou understood. They all did.

CHAPTER 32

MAY 4, 2054, SUNRISE
SCOURGE +21 YEARS, 7 MONTHS
BUXTON, NORTH CAROLINA

Marcus's knees ached. He gripped the handrail and took another step up the narrow stairwell. It was damp inside the space, the pleasant odor of salt air hanging heavily in the air. He rested for a moment on the second landing and looked up. Another thirty-one steps to go and he'd be there.

"I know this was built a long time ago," he muttered aloud, "but couldn't they have put in a freaking elevator? Would it have been too much to ask?"

Step by step, he climbed. His hand glided along the rail to one side, the rough, countless layers of old paint cold under the palm of his hand and against his fingers.

Although his side ached, the wounds were healing. The skin around the sutures and scabs itched. It was red but not infected. He couldn't count how many times he'd been shot. And all these years later, he couldn't wrap his head around the idea that he'd taken more fire in his homeland than he had in Syria. Even if that idea wasn't entirely accurate, it certainly felt that way. The war at home had stretched a lot longer than the one overseas. That part was indisputable. Was it finally over? He prayed it was the case.

Marcus glanced down, glad to be alone for a few minutes. While he, surprisingly, didn't miss his solitary life, he did appreciate a few stolen moments here and there.

While mostly everyone was still asleep, there were the early risers who walked along the beach or scoured the dunes for shells and long-lost trinkets. One woman had somehow managed to resurrect an old-fashioned metal detector. Not only did she have an incredible collection of junk, she was immensely popular among the school-aged children.

He reached the top landing, exhaled, and chuckled to himself. Marcus would have thought that this morning ritual might have earned him some stamina. Perhaps it had. But stamina had nothing to do with the stiffness in his knees and lower back. He stretched, twisting from side to side until he felt the muscles lengthen, and stepped out onto the balcony.

It was a beautiful spring morning. The sun was inching above the horizon, its light painting the ocean gold, making the soft, rolling waves shimmer.

Marcus leaned on the black iron railing that curved around the circumference of the Cape Hatteras Lighthouse. He was one hundred sixty-five feet from the ground below him. Somehow, after more than two hundred years, the tallest brick lighthouse in the former United States still stood guard. A stiff breeze greeted Marcus when he moved around the balcony to face the Atlantic. The wind chilled his skin, blew across his scalp, dried his eyes. But he didn't mind it. The briny air was refreshing, rejuvenating, life-giving.

His gnarled hands gripped the curved black railing in front of him, and he let the moisture wick onto his skin. The tide was ebbing. Curls of foam stuck to the white sand as the water receded along the shoreline. The bubbles grew and popped in time for the next roll of waves to stretch toward them.

In between the gusts of wind, the sounds of those waves washed through the air. Marcus was lost in thought as his eyes drifted past the shoreline and toward the rising sun.

In his mind, he saw the treehouse he'd built for Wesson's ninth birthday. He'd painstakingly designed and constructed the fort by hand. He remembered stepping onto the front porch of their home, his boy tackling his leg.

"Is it finished?" Wes asked. He craned his neck to look up, almost vertically, into Marcus's eyes.

"Yes," Marcus told him. "You'll be able to play in the fort until you shove off to college."

Wesson had buried his head in his father's leg and squeezed. Tears had welled in Marcus's eyes then, as they did now, standing on the lighthouse balcony.

He couldn't remember Wesson's face anymore. Not the finer details, only the vague shape of his head, the mop of hair atop it, the gangly arms and legs. The same was true for Sylvia. The shape of her, the sound of her laugh, her beautiful smile were there in his memory, but he couldn't smell her anymore. He didn't remember her voice or the color of her eyes. Where were her freckles? She had freckles, didn't she?

They'd named their son after her maiden name.

He leaned forward on the railing, letting the breeze drive through him. It took his breath away and he closed his eyes. His elbows resting on the railing, his mind drifted to the small burial plot behind their home near Rising Star.

For five years he'd built his life around their graves, their ghosts, unwilling to let go or move along. He was going crazy, no doubt about that. If Lola hadn't happened onto his ranch, he might have gone completely mad. If she hadn't insisted, begged, cajoled him into finding her son, Sawyer, he'd have died alone.

In some ways their deaths were worse than Sylvia's and Wesson's. It wasn't because he loved them more. He didn't; he loved them differently. It was because the pain of their loss reignited the pain he'd never fully extinguished from the loss of his wife and son.

Marcus's vision blurred as he thought about this. He couldn't be sure if the sheen of tears on his eyes was from the wind or from his soul.

"Hey." A voice startled him. "Whatcha doin'?"

Marcus spun around, blinking back the tears. Sniffing in the salty air, he smirked. "Morning, Lou. What are you doing up?"

She moved toward him, adjusting the Astros ball cap on her head, and tightened the ponytail at the back of her head. She had the groggy look of someone who'd been startled awake. "Looking for you."

They stood next to each other, staring out at the semicircle of a blazing sun and its mirrored reflection in the water at the ocean's edge.

She leaned on her elbows. "That's not true," she admitted, bumping his side with her hip. "I knew where to find you."

"Did you? How's that?"

"You've been doing this every morning for days now," she said. "The baby wakes up before sunrise. It's like he's a rooster or something."

"Rudy the rooster?"

She laughed. "Exactly. I'm sure Norma would love to hear you call the baby that."

"Rudy would like it."

"Probably."

Another thirty seconds of silence passed between them. Another breeze gusted past them, through them. Marcus stole a glance. The feral little girl he'd nearly killed at the gas station so many years ago was a smart, confident woman now. She was still feral, and she had serious anger issues, but Marcus thought that was part of her charm.

"So you're stalking me, then?" he asked.

"Sort of. I guess I'm making sure you're not leaving."

"Leaving?" He asked the question like her suggesting it was an inconceivable possibility.

Lou shrugged. "Yeah. I don't think that's an unreasonable fear. You're known to disappear."

Marcus watched the bottom of the sun, warbling against the edge of the atmosphere, lift above the horizon. The golden water was taking on an orange hue. It was spectacular.

"I guess so," he said, "but you don't have to worry. I'm not going anywhere."

Lou's hand found his on the railing. It was warm, somehow. "Really?"

Marcus heard the break in her voice. She was looking up at him, tears rolling down her bronze cheeks. Her eyes were wide with hope.

Marcus put his hands on her shoulders and held her gaze. "I'm staying," he said. "You're my family, Lou. I never should have left. No matter what anybody else thought or reasoned, or how I thought I might do the right thing by leaving, I should have stayed."

Her face brightened despite the tears. A smile threatened to broaden across her face. "What changed your mind?"

Marcus thought of a dozen different ways he could answer her. He might have said it was because he was old and tired. He might have said it was because he loved her like a daughter, and of all the people left on Earth, she was the only one who truly understood him. He might have told her it was because he wanted to see her children grow up. Or it was because he knew, even in his old age, he could help protect her against whatever might come. He chose none of those reasons, even though each one was valid in and of itself. Instead, he offered her four words, and they were enough. They would tell her everything she needed to know, everything that would assure her he would stay until the day he died.

A breeze swirled around the two of them, sending another chill through his body. He lifted his aching fingers from her shoulders and placed them on either side of her face. Her cheeks were wet against his palms. She smiled. He smiled.

"Because, Lou, I'm home."

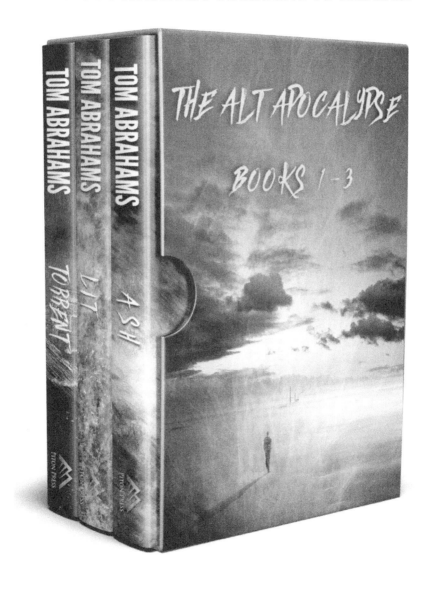

THE SPACEMAN CHRONICLES

ACKNOWLEDGMENTS

Thanks to the fans who've made this series what it is. I am forever grateful for the life you've given these stories and characters who lived (and died) within the pages of an epic tale.

To my team of wonderful experts, big props and fist bumps; Felicia Sullivan, Pauline Nolet, Patricia Wilson, Stef McDaid at Write Into Print, and Histro Kovatliev. All of you played critical roles in getting these books into the hands of voracious readers. Bless you.

To Steve Kremer for your guidance and vast knowledge of all things, I'm appreciative. To author friends, Steven Konkoly, Franklin Horton, Nicholas Sansbury Smith, R.E. McDermott, AR Shaw, Lisa Brackmann, Anthony Melchiorri, G. Michael Hopf, and Russell Blake, Murray McDonald, Rhett Bruno, and countless others—thanks for your guidance and support.

To Kevin Pierce, the voice of Marcus Battle…wow. You've brought to life the stories that bounce around in my head. And now I hear them in your dulcet tones. Thank you.

To the real Rudy and Norma-you inspire me with your grace and courage. And to both Johns—Mubarak and Carreon—I love talking Marcus Battle with you. It's the most fun I have talking about what hell I've dragged him through.

Thanks to my parents, siblings, and in-laws for their viral marketing efforts and their shouts-out to the masses. And to my Aunt Jane Daroff, always the defender of my work, you have my love and appreciation.

Finally to my family, despite being a writer I have no words for the support you offer through long days and nights of writing, editing, and plotting. Courtney, Sam, and Luke—you are my harbor and my home.

Made in the USA
Coppell, TX
29 January 2025

45149525R00146